KING OF WALL STREET

LOUISE BAY

Published by Louise Bay 2016

ISBN – 978-1-910747-37-7

BOOKS BY LOUISE BAY

The Mister Series

Mr. Mayfair

Mr. Knightsbridge

Mr. Smithfield

Mr. Park Lane

Mr. Bloomsbury

Mr. Notting Hill

The Christmas Collection

The 14 Days of Christmas

This Christmas

The Player Series

International Player

Private Player

Dr. Off Limits

Standalones

Hollywood Scandal

Love Unexpected

Hopeful

The Empire State Series

Sign up to the Louise Bay mailing list at
www.louisebay/mailinglist

Read more at www.louisebay.com

ONE

Harper

Ten. Whole. Minutes. It didn't sound like a long time, but as I sat across from Max King, the so-called King of Wall Street, while he silently read through the first draft of a report I'd produced on the textile industry in Bangladesh, it felt like a lifetime.

Resisting the urge to revert to my fourteen-year-old self and ask him what he was thinking, I glanced around, trying to find something else to fixate on.

Max's office suited him perfectly—the A/C was set to the average temperature of an igloo; the walls, ceilings, and floors were all blinding white, adding to the arctic ambience. His desk was glass and chrome, and the New York sun bled through the opaque blinds, trying without success to thaw the frost that penetrated the room. I hated it. Every time I entered the place I had the urge to flash my bra or graffiti the walls in bright red lipstick. It was the place fun came to die.

Max's sigh pulled my attention back to his long index

finger that he trailed down the page of my research. He shook his head. My stomach somersaulted. I knew impressing him would be an impossible task but that didn't mean I hadn't secretly hoped I'd nailed it. I'd worked so hard on this report, my first research for *the* Max King. I'd barely slept, working double so I didn't neglect my other duties in the office. I'd printed off and examined everything that had been written on the industry in the last decade. I'd pored over the statistics, trying to find patterns and draw conclusions. And I'd scoured the King & Associates archives trying to find any historical research that we'd produced so we could explain any inconsistencies. I'd covered every base, hadn't I? When I'd printed it out earlier that morning, long before anyone else had arrived, I'd been happy—proud even. I'd done a good job.

"You spoke to Marvin about the latest data?" he asked.

I nodded, though he didn't look up, so I said, "Yes. All the graphs are based on the latest figures." Did they look wrong? Had he expected something else?

I just wanted him to say, "Good job."

I'd been desperate to work for Max King since before I enrolled at business school. He was the power behind the throne of many of the Wall Street success stories in the last few years. King & Associates provided investment banks with critical research that helped their investment decisions. I liked the idea that there were a ton of flashy suits from investment banks shouting about how rich they were and the man who had made it happen was happy to go quietly about his business, just being amazing at what he did. Understated, determined, supremely successful—he was everything I wanted to be. When I got the offer during my final semester to be a junior researcher at King & Associates, I was thrilled, but I also felt an odd sense that the universe was simply unravelling how it should, as though it was simply the next step in my destiny.

Destiny could kiss my ass. My first six weeks in my new position had been nothing I'd expected. I'd assumed I'd be surrounded by ambitious, intelligent, well-dressed twenty and thirty somethings and I'd been right about that. And the clients we worked for—almost every investment bank in Manhattan—were phenomenal and lived up to every expectation I'd had. Max King, however, had turned out to be a huge letdown. The fact was, despite being crazy smart, respected by everyone on Wall Street, and looking as if he should have been on a poster on teenage me's bedroom wall, he was . . .

Cold.

Blunt.

Uncompromising.

A total asshole.

He was as handsome in real life as he was in his picture on the cover of Forbes or any of the other publicity shots I'd clicked through as I stalked him during my MBA at Berkeley. One morning, I'd arrived super early, seen him in his running gear—sweaty, panting, Lycra clad. Thighs so strong they looked as if they might be made of marble. Broad shoulders; a strong Roman nose; dark-brown, glossy hair— the kind wasted on a man—and a year-round tan that screamed, *I vacation four times a year.* In the office he wore custom suits. Handmade suits fell a particular way on the shoulders that I recognized from the few meetings I'd had with my father. His face and body lived up to every expectation I'd had. Working with him, not so much.

I hadn't expected him to be such a tyrant.

Each morning, as he swooped through the throng of open-plan desks to his office, he never so much as greeted any of us with a good morning. He regularly yelled into his phone so loud he could be heard from the elevator lobby. And last Tuesday? When I'd passed him in the office and smiled at him, the veins in his neck began to bulge and he looked as if he was going to reach out and choke me.

I smoothed my palms down the fabric of my Zara skirt. Perhaps I irritated him because I wasn't as sleek as the other women in the office. I didn't dress in the regulation Prada. Did I look as though I didn't care? I just couldn't afford anything better at the moment.

As the most junior member of the team, I was at the bottom of the pecking order. Which meant I knew Mr. King's sandwich order, how to untangle the photocopier, and I had every courier company on speed dial. But that was to be expected and I was just happy because I got to work with the guy I'd looked up to and admired for years.

And here he was, shaking his head and wielding a pen with the reddest ink I'd ever seen. With each circle, criss-cross, and exaggerated question mark he made, I seemed to shrink.

"Where are your references?" he asked without looking up.

References? When I looked at the other reports we produced, they never had the sources in the report. "I have them back at my desk—"

"Did you speak to Donny?"

"I'm waiting to hear back from him." He looked up and I tried not to wince. I'd put in two calls to Max's contact at the World Trade Organization, but I couldn't *make* the guy talk to me.

He shook his head and grabbed his phone and dialed. "Hey, hotshot," he said. "I need to understand the position on Everything But Arms. I heard your guys are putting pressure on the EU?" Max didn't put the phone on speaker, so I watched as he scribbled notes over my paper. "It would really help for this thing I'm doing about Bangladesh." Max grinned, looked up briefly, caught my eye, and looked away as if just the sight of me irritated him. *Great.*

Max hung up.

"I put in two calls—"

"Results, not effort, get rewarded," he said in a clipped tone.

So he gave no credit for trying? What could I have done other than turn up at the guy's place of business? I wasn't Max King. Why would someone at the WTO take a call from a barely paid researcher?

Jesus, couldn't he give a girl a break?

Before I had a chance to respond, his cell vibrated on his desk.

"Amanda?" he barked into the phone. Jesus. This was a small office, so I knew Amanda didn't work at King & Associates. I got an odd sense of satisfaction he wasn't just sharp with me. I didn't see him interact much with others, but somehow his attitude toward me felt personal. But it sounded as if Amanda got the same brusque treatment I did. "We're not having this discussion again. I said no." Girlfriend? Page Six had never had any reports of Max dating. But he had to be. A man built like that, asshole or not, wasn't going without. It sounded as though Amanda had the honor of putting up with him outside office hours.

Hanging up, he slung his phone against the desk, watching as it skidded across the glass and came to rest against his laptop. Continuing to read, he rubbed his long, tan fingers over his forehead as if Amanda had given him a headache. I didn't think my report was helping much.

"Typos are not acceptable, Ms. Jayne. There's no excuse

for being anything less than exceptional when it comes to something that *only* requires effort." He closed my report, sat back in his chair, and fixed his stare on me. "Attention to detail doesn't require ingenuity, creativity, or lateral thinking. If you can't get the basics right, why should I trust you with anything more complicated?"

Typos? I'd read through that report a thousand times.

He steepled his fingers in front of him. "Revise in accordance with my notes and don't bring it back to me until it's typo free. I'll fine you for every mistake I find."

Fine me? I wanted to fire back that if I could fine him every time he was a penis, I'd retire inside of three months. Asshole.

Slowly, I reached for my report, wondering if he had anything else to add, any words of encouragement or thanks.

But no. I took the stack of papers and headed to the door.

"Oh, and Ms. Jayne?"

This is it. He's going to leave me some morsel of dignity. I turned to him, holding my breath.

"Pastrami on rye, no pickle."

I stood glued to the spot, breathing through the sucker punch to the gut.

What. A. Douche.

"For my lunch," he added, clearly not understanding why I hadn't left already.

I nodded and opened the door. If I didn't leave right now, I might just throw myself across his desk and pull out all his perfect hair.

As I closed the door, Donna, Max's assistant, asked, "How did it go?"

I rolled my eyes. "I don't know how you do it, working

for him. He's so . . ." I started to flick through the report, looking for the typos he'd referred to.

Donna rolled her chair away from her desk and stood. "His bark is worse than his bite. Are you off to the deli?"

"Yeah. Pastrami today."

Donna pulled on her jacket. "I'll walk with you. I need a break." She grabbed her wallet and we made our way out into downtown New York. Of course, Max didn't like any of the sandwich shops near the office. Instead we had to head five blocks northeast to Joey's Café. At least it was sunny, and too early in the year for the humidity to make a trip to the deli feel like a midday hike along the streets of Calcutta.

"Hey, Donna. Hey, Harper," Joey, the owner, called as we entered through the glass door. The deli was exactly the opposite of the type of place where I'd expect Max to order his lunch. It was very clearly a family-owned place that hadn't seen a remodeling since the Beatles were together. In here there was nothing of the slick, modern, ruthless persona that made up Max King.

"How's the bossman?" Joey asked.

"Oh, you know," Donna said. "Working too hard, as usual. What was his order, Harper?"

"Pastrami on rye. Extra pickle." Nothing like passive-aggressive revenge.

Joey raised his eyebrows. "Extra pickle?" Jesus, of course Joey knew Max's preferences.

"Okay." I winced. "No pickle."

Donna elbowed me. "And I'll have a turkey salad on sourdough," she said, then turned to me. "Let's eat in and we can talk."

"Make that two," I said to Joey.

The deli had a few tables, all with mismatched chairs. Most customers took their orders to go, but today I was grateful for a few extra minutes out of the office. I followed Donna as she led us to one of the back tables.

"Extra pickle?" she asked, grinning.

"I know." I sighed. "That was childish. I'm sorry. I just wish he wasn't such a . . . "

"Tell me what happened."

I gave her the rundown on our meeting—his irritation that I hadn't spoken to his contact at the WTO, the lecture about typos, his lack of appreciation for any of my hard work.

"Tell Max the Yankees deserved all they got this weekend," Joey said as he placed our order in front of us, sliding two cans of soda onto the melamine surface, even though we'd not ordered any drinks. Did Joey talk baseball with Max? Had they even met?

"I'll tell him," Donna said, smiling, "but he might move his business elsewhere if I do. You know how touchy he is when the Mets do well."

"He's going to have to get used to it this season. And I'm not worried about losing him. He's been coming here for over a decade."

Over a decade?

"You know what he'd say to that?" Donna asked, unwrapping the waxed-paper parcel in front of her.

"Yeah, yeah, never take your customers for granted." Joey headed back behind the counter. "You know what always shuts him up?" he asked over his shoulder.

Donna laughed. "When you tell him to come back after his business has lasted three generations and is still going?"

Joey pointed at Donna. "You got it."

"So Max has been coming here a long time, huh?" I asked as Joey turned back to the counter to tend to the line of people that had built up since we'd arrived.

"Since I've been working for him. And that's nearly seven years."

"A creature of habit. I get that." There wasn't much spontaneous about Max from what I'd seen.

Donna cocked her head. "More a huge sense of loyalty. As this area built up and lunch places opened up on every corner, Joey's business took a bit of a hit. Max has never gone anywhere else. He's even brought clients here."

Donna's description jarred with the cold egomaniac I encountered in the office. I bit into my sandwich.

"He can be challenging and demanding and a pain in the ass, but that's a big part of what's made him successful."

I wanted to be successful but still a decent human being. Was I naïve to think that was possible on Wall Street?

Donna pressed the top layer of bread down onto the turkey with her fingertips, pushing the layers together. "He's not as bad as you think he is. I mean, if he'd said your report was good to go, what would you have learned?" She picked up her sandwich. "You can't expect to get it all right your first time. And the stuff about the typos—was he wrong?" She took a bite, and waited for me to answer.

"No." I bit the inside of my lip. "But you have to admit, his delivery sucks." I pulled out a piece of my turkey from under the sourdough and put it in my mouth. I'd worked so hard; I'd expected some kind of recognition for that.

"Sometimes. Until you've proved yourself. But once you have, he'll back you completely. He gave me this job knowing I was a single mother, and he's made sure I've never missed a game, event, or PTA meeting." She cracked open a can of soda. "When my daughter got chicken pox just after I started working here, I came into the office anyway. I've never seen him so mad. When he spotted me, he marched me out of the building and sent me home. I mean, my mom was looking after her, she was fine, but he insisted I stay home until she was back in school."

I swallowed. That didn't sound like the Max I knew.

"He's a really good guy. He's just focused and driven. And he takes his responsibility to his employees seriously—especially if they have potential."

"I don't see him taking his responsibility to not be a condescending asshole very seriously."

Donna chuckled. "You're there to learn, to get better. And he's going to teach you, but just saying you did a good job isn't going to help you."

I grabbed a napkin from the old-fashioned dispenser at the edge of the table and wiped the corner of my mouth. How had today helped me other than wrecking my confidence completely?

"If you had known how today's meeting would play out, what would you have done differently?" Donna asked.

I shrugged. I'd done good work, but he'd refused to acknowledge it.

"Come on. You can't tell me you'd do things exactly the same."

"Okay, no. I would have printed out the sources and brought them into the meeting."

Donna nodded. "Good. What else?" She took another bite of her sandwich.

"I would have probably tried Max's contact at the WTO a few more times—maybe emailed him. I could have tried harder to pin him down. And I could have sent the whole thing to proofreading." We had an overnight service, but because I'd worked late on it, I'd missed the deadline to send it. I should have made sure it was ready in time.

I glanced up from picking apart my sandwich. "I'm not saying I didn't learn anything. I just thought he'd be nicer. I've wanted to work with him a long time. I just didn't imagine I'd fantasize about punching him in the face quite so often."

Donna laughed. "That, Harper, is what having a boss means."

Okay, I could accept that Max was nice to Donna, and Joey, by the looks of things. But he wasn't nice to me. Which only made everything worse. What had I ever done to him? Was I being singled out for special treatment? Yes, my report could be improved, but despite what Donna said, I hadn't deserved the reaction I got. He could have thrown me a bone.

Now that my expectations of working with Max were well and truly shattered, I had to concentrate on getting what I could from the experience and moving on. I'd go through my report and make it perfect. I'd take everything I could from working for King & Associates, make a ton of contacts, and then after two years I'd be well placed to set up on my own, or go and work directly for a bank.

———

HOW I'D TALKED my best friend, Grace, into moving me into my new apartment, I had no idea. Growing up on Park Avenue, she wasn't raised for manual labor.

"What's in here, a dead body?" she asked, a sheen of sweat on her forehead catching the light in the elevator.

"Yeah, my last best friend." I tipped my head toward the old pine blanket box at our feet and the last thing in the truck. "There's room for another." I laughed.

"There'd better be wine in the refrigerator." Grace

fanned her face. "I'm not used to being this physical with my clothes on."

"You see, then you should be grateful. I'm expanding your horizons," I replied with a grin. "Showing you how us ordinary gals live."

I'd been staying with Grace since I got to New York from Berkeley almost three months ago. She'd been fantastically understanding when my mother shipped all my things to her apartment in Brooklyn, but now that I was making her help me move everything into my new place, her patience was running out. "And I'm too poor for a refrigerator. And wine." The rent on my studio was horrific. But it was in Manhattan and that was all I cared about. I wasn't about to be a New Yorker who lived in Brooklyn. I wanted to milk this experience for everything it was worth, so I'd sacrificed space for location—a small Victorian building on the corner of Rivington and Clinton in Lower Manhattan. The buildings on either side were covered with graffiti, but this place had been recently refurbished and I'd been assured it was full of young professionals, being so close to Wall Street. Professional what? Hitmen?

"It's going to be . . . cozy," Grace said. "Are you sure you don't want me to ask about the one bedroom across the hall from me?"

My apartment at Berkeley had been at least twice the size of my new place. Grace's place in Brooklyn was a palace in comparison, but I was okay with small. "I'm sure. It's all part of the New York experience, isn't it?"

"So are roaches, but you don't have to seek them out. The idea is to avoid them." Grace was the person who tried to make everyone else's lives a little bit better, and that was one of the reasons I loved her.

"Yeah, but I want to be in the center of things. Besides,

there's a gym in the basement, so I'm saving money there. And on the commute. I can walk to work from here. Hell, I can practically see the office from my bedroom window."

"I thought you hated work. Wouldn't it be better to be further away?" she asked as the elevator pinged open at my floor.

I reached for the bottom of the wooden box. "I don't hate work. I hate my boss."

"The hot one?" Grace asked.

"Can you pick up your end?" I asked. I didn't want to be reminded about my boss's score on the hot-o-meter. I stuck out my leg to try to stop the closing elevator doors. "Crap. Have you got it?" We lurched forward, turning left toward my apartment door.

"We need a man for this shit," Grace said as I struggled with my keys.

"We need men for sex and foot rubs," I replied. "We can carry our own furniture."

"In the future, *you* can carry *your* furniture. I'll find a man."

I opened the door and we slid the box into the living space. "Just leave it here until I decide whether or not it should go at the end of the bed."

"Where's that wine you promised me?" Grace pushed past me and collapsed on my small two-seater couch.

Despite my protestations, the only things my refrigerator *did* contain were two bottles of wine and a slab of parmesan cheese.

"What were you saying about your hot boss? I thought you'd changed religion to the Church of King while you were at Berkeley. What's changed?"

I handed Grace a glass of wine, sat down, and kicked off my sneakers. I didn't want to think about Max or the way he made me feel so inadequate, so out of place and uncomfortable. "I think I need to update my work wardrobe." The more I thought about what I'd worn for my meeting with Max, the more I realized I must stick out like a sore thumb against all the Max Mara and Prada of Wall Street.

"You look fine. You're always super polished. Are you trying to impress your hot boss?"

I rolled my eyes. "That would be impossible. He's the most arrogant man you'll ever meet. Nothing's ever good enough."

My conversation with Donna at lunch yesterday had temporarily dampened my fury at Max, but it was back in full swing today. He might be the best at what he did and look so hot you'd get a tan if you stood too close, but that didn't excuse his assholyness. But I wasn't about to let him beat me. I hated him. Determined to show him he had me wrong, I'd brought home the Bangladesh report to work on over the weekend. A lot of the comments he'd made indicated he knew much more about the textile industry in Bangladesh than I did, even after my research. Had this whole project just been a test? Whether it was or not, I was going to spend the rest of the weekend making my work the best thing he'd ever seen.

"Nothing's ever good enough?" Grace asked. "Sounds familiar."

"I might be a bit of a perfectionist, but I've got nothing on this guy. Believe me. I worked my heart out on a piece of work he gave me, and then he just ripped it to shreds. He had nothing good to say about it at all."

"Why are you letting it bother you? Shrug it off."

Why *wouldn't* I let it bother me? I wanted to be good at my job. I wanted Max to see I was good at my job.

"But I worked really hard on it and it was a good piece of work. He's an asshole."

"So? If he's a total wanker then why does his opinion count for anything?" Grace had lived in the US since she was five, but she still retained some key Britishisms from her family. Her use of wanker was one of my favorites. Especially as it suited Max King perfectly.

"I'm not saying it matters. Just that I'm pissed about it." Except that it did matter, however much I denied it.

"What did you expect? A man that rich and good looking is bound to have a downside." She shrugged and took a sip of wine. "You can't let it affect you so much. Your expectations of men are way too high. You're going to spend your whole life disappointed."

My cell began to ring. "Speaking of being disappointed." I showed the screen to Grace. It was my father's lawyer.

"Harper speaking," I answered.

"Ms. Jayne. It's Kenneth Bray." Why was he calling me at the weekend?

"Yes, Mr. Bray. How can I help?" I rolled my eyes at Grace.

Apparently my father had set me up a trust fund. The letters I'd received about it were stuffed into the chest that we'd just lugged up from the truck. I hadn't answered any of them. I didn't want my father's money. I started accepting his money in college. I figured he owed me that much but after a year, I took a job and stopped cashing his checks. I couldn't accept money from a stranger, even if he was genetically related to me.

"I want to arrange for you to come into the office so I can talk you through the details of the money your father has set aside for you."

"I appreciate your persistence, but I'm not interested in

my father's money." All I'd ever wanted was a guy who showed up for birthdays and school plays or for anything as far as I was concerned. Grace was wrong; my expectations of men were at rock bottom. My father's absence from my childhood had ensured that. I didn't expect anything from men except disappointment.

Mr. Bray tried to convince me to meet with him and I resisted. In the end I told him I'd read the paperwork and get back to him.

I hung up and took a deep breath.

"Are you okay?" Grace asked.

I wiped the edge of my glass with my thumb. "Yeah," I said. It was easier when I could pretend my father didn't exist. When I heard from him, or even his lawyer, I felt like Sisyphus watching my boulder tumble back down the hill. It put me back at square one, and all the thoughts of how I should have had a different father, a different life, a different family that I normally managed to bury came rushing to the surface.

My father had gotten my mother pregnant and then refused to do the right thing and marry her. He'd abandoned us both. He'd sent us money—so we were financially taken care of. But what I'd really wanted was a father. Eventually all the broken promises built up into a mountain I couldn't see over. The birthday parties where I watched the door, hoping he'd show up, took their toll. There were one too many Christmases where the only thing I asked Santa for was my dad. It was his absence from my life that had been the real problem because it felt as if there was always someone else that came first, somewhere else he'd rather be. It left me with the feeling that I wasn't worth anyone's time.

"You want to talk about it?" Grace asked.

I smiled. "Absolutely not. I wanna get a little drunk in my new apartment with my best friend. Maybe gossip and eat some ice cream."

"That *is* our speciality," Grace replied. "Can we talk about boys?"

"We can talk about boys but I'm warning you, if you try to set me up I'm kicking your ass back to Brooklyn."

"But you haven't even heard who it's with yet."

I laughed. She was so easy to read. "I'm not interested in dating. I'm focusing on my career. That way I can't be disappointed." Max King's words, *results, not effort, get rewarded*, rang in my ears. I would just have to do better, work harder. There wasn't any time for dating or setups.

"You're so cynical. Not every man is like your father."

"I didn't say they were. Don't play amateur shrink on me. I just want to get established here in New York. Dating isn't my priority. That's all." I took a sip of my wine and tucked my legs under me.

I would win Max King around if it killed me. I'd followed his career so carefully it'd felt as if I knew him. But I'd imagined myself as his protégée. I'd start working for him and he'd tell me he'd never met anyone so talented. I'd assumed within a few days we'd be able to finish each other's sentences and we'd high five each other after meetings. And I admit it, I may have had a sex dream about him. Or two.

That had all been before I'd met him. I'd been an idiot.

"Sex," I blurted. "That's what men are good for. Maybe I'll take a lover."

"That's all?" Grace asked.

I traced the rim of my glass with my finger. "What else do we need them for?"

"Friendship?"

"I have you," I replied.

"Emotional support?"

"Again, that's your job. You share it with ice cream, wine, and the occasional retail overspend."

"And it's a job the four of us take very seriously. But what about when you want babies?" Grace asked.

Kids were the last thing on my mind. My mother had changed careers from working in finance to becoming a teacher so she could spend more time with me. I was sure I wouldn't be able to make such a sacrifice. "If and when I ever get around to thinking about that stuff, I'll go to a sperm bank. Worked for my mother."

"Your mom didn't go to a sperm bank."

I took a gulp from my glass. "Might as well have." I didn't have a father as far as I was concerned.

"Hand me your iPad. I want to see this hot boss of yours again."

I groaned. "Don't." I reached for the tablet on the table beside the couch and handed it over despite myself.

"Max King, right?"

I didn't respond.

"He really is ridiculously good looking." Grace swiped and flicked at the screen. I deliberately didn't look. He didn't deserve my attention.

"Put it away. It's enough that I have to deal with him Monday through Friday. Let me enjoy my weekend without having to look at his arrogant face." I glanced at the Forbes cover image Grace had brought up. Crossed arms, stern expression, full pouty lips.

Asshole.

A crash above me caught my attention and I looked up at my ceiling. The pretty glass light swayed from side to side. "Was that a bomb that just went off?" I asked.

"Sounds like your upstairs neighbor just dropped an anvil on the roadrunner."

I placed my finger over my lips and listened intently. Grace's eyes grew wide as what had started as incoherent mumbling morphed into the unmistakable sound of a woman having sex.

Panting. Moaning. Begging.

Then another crash. What the fuck was going on up there? Were there more than two people involved?

Skin slapped against skin followed by the sound of a woman crying out. Heat crept up my neck and spread across my cheeks. Someone was having much more fun on a Saturday afternoon than we were.

An unmistakably male voice shouted "fuck" and the woman's cries tumbled out fast and desperate. The knock of a headboard against drywall thudded louder and louder. The woman's breathless moaning almost sounded panicked. My chandelier started to sway more furiously, and I swear the vibrations from whatever furniture was knocking against whatever wall travelled down from the ceiling and straight to my groin. I squeezed my thighs together just as the man yelled out to God and she gave a final, sharp scream that echoed through my box-filled apartment.

In the silence that followed, my heart thudded through my sweater. I was half exhilarated by what I'd heard; half embarrassed I'd consciously eavesdropped on something so personal.

Someone less than three yards away from me had just come for America.

"That might be a guy I have to get to know," Grace said when it was clear the sexcapades had stopped. "He certainly sounded like he knew what he was doing."

"They seemed very . . . compatible." Had I ever

sounded that desperate during sex, that hungry for my orgasm? I knew the sounds of a woman who *exaggerated* in the bedroom. The woman upstairs hadn't been faking. Like jumping at the scary bits of a horror movie, the sounds from her had been involuntary.

"They sound like they have excellent sex. Maybe you should knock on their door and suggest a threesome."

I rolled my eyes. "Yeah, along with a cup of sugar."

Footsteps clipped along the ceiling. "She kept her heels on," Grace said. "Nice."

The tapping wandered across my ceiling toward my blanket box. The upstairs front door creaked, then slammed. The sound of footsteps disappeared.

"Well, she got what she wanted and split. You're not going to need a TV in this place. You can just tune into the soap opera that is your neighbor."

"You think she was a prostitute?" I asked. A woman leaving less than five minutes after an orgasm like that wasn't normal. Surely she'd stick around for oxygen or round two? Hell, I wasn't sure I'd have made it to a vertical position, let alone in heels, within an hour of what she'd experienced.

"A prostitute? She's a lucky one if she is." Grace giggled. "But I don't think so. A guy who can make a woman sound like that doesn't need to pay for it." She leaned forward and placed her empty glass on one of the dozens of boxes littered about the apartment. "Right, I'm going to get home to my vibrator."

"That's really way too much information."

"But keep me posted on your neighbors. And if you run into them, try to get a picture."

"Yes, because if you're going to masturbate over my

neighbors, it would go better with pictures." I nodded sarcastically. "You're a pervert. You know that, right?"

Grace shrugged and stood. "It was better than porn."

She was right. I just hoped it wasn't a regular show I was going to get. If nothing else, I felt plenty inadequate at work. I didn't need to have the same feeling at home.

TWO

Max

Harper Jayne was *really* pissing me off.

She'd irritated me from the moment she'd started work almost two months ago. Up until now I'd managed to keep my distance.

She was smart. That wasn't a problem.

And she got on with her co-workers well enough. I couldn't complain.

She didn't seem to mind helping Donna with the photo-copier. There were no delusions of grandeur for me to moan about.

She was eager to learn. That had been one of the first things that grated on me. She was *too* eager. The way she looked at me with those big brown eyes as if she'd be willing to do just about anything I suggested was maddening. Every time I glanced at her, even if it was a glimpse of her in the kitchen as I came into the office, I imagined her sliding to her knees in my office, opening her red, wet mouth, and begging for my cock.

And *that* was a problem.

I always had a strict divide between my business life and my personal life, and there'd never been any exception. I was the boss, with a reputation to protect. I didn't want my personal life to ever be more interesting that my business life.

I tapped my pen against my desk. I needed to figure this out. Either fire her or forget about her. But I needed to do something.

I found myself spending more and more time in my office with the door closed in an attempt to create some distance between Harper and me. Ordinarily, I'd spend time out on the floor with people, checking in on how things were going. But the open-plan area felt like contaminated land. When I had to interact with her, I addressed her as *Ms. Jayne* as a way of keeping her at arm's length. It wasn't working. I pushed my hands into my hair. I needed a plan. I couldn't have some junior researcher changing the way I did business, because the way I did business had meant King & Associates was the best at what they did, and the whole of Wall Street knew it.

Distractions were the last thing I needed right now. My focus was split enough as it was. Living with Amanda full time was more challenging than I'd expected and it meant a lot more time out of the office as I spent more time in Connecticut. I was also trying to land a new account with an investment bank King & Associates hadn't worked for before, and I had a key meeting with an insider coming up.

"Come in," I called to the knock at the door, hoping it wasn't Harper with her revised report.

"Good morning, Max," Donna said as she entered my office, closing the door behind her.

"Thanks." I took the tall cup of coffee she offered to me, trying to read her face. "How are you?"

"I'm good. We have a lot to get through." We had a daily lunchtime briefing.

I reached for my collar. "Is it me, or is it hotter in here than normal?"

Donna shook her head. "No, and I'm not turning up the A/C, either. It's ridiculously cold in here."

I sighed. It wasn't worth arguing with Donna about. Most things weren't. That was what I'd learned from the women in my life—pick your battles.

"So," Donna said as she slipped into the seat in front of my desk. The same chair Harper had sat in on Friday. Harper had sat with her legs crossed and her arms fixed to the arms of the chair, almost as if she were bracing herself for a bumpy landing. But it had given me a perfect view of her high tight breasts and her long brown hair sitting gently on her shoulders.

"What's going on?" Donna asked.

"Huh?" I asked, glancing up to look at her.

"Are you okay? You seem distracted."

I shook my head and leaned back in my chair. I needed to focus. "I'm fine. I just have a million things going on in my head. It's going to be a busy week."

"Okay then, let's get started. You have a lunch tomorrow with Wilson at D&G Consulting. It's fixed for twelve at Tribeca Grill."

"I suppose we can't cancel?" Wilson was a competitor and such an egomaniac that canceling would be a problem. And because he couldn't help but be a braggart, I usually got some useful information from our lunches.

"Yes, it's too late. You've canceled the last three times."

"And we can't go to Joey's?"

Donna just raised her eyebrows. I sighed as I reminded myself this was another battle not worth fighting.

"And Harper wanted some time this afternoon as she's revised her report."

I started to click at my calendar. I'd seen Harper on Friday. I needed to be seeing less of her not more.

"What are you doing? I have your calendar right here." She pointed to her tablet. "You have time this afternoon at four."

"I don't think we need a meeting. She should just leave what she's done with you, and I'll look at it when I can." I stared down at my notepad, writing down *Lunch with Wilson* for no particular reason.

"You usually like a follow-up meeting."

"I'm busy and haven't got time to go through work that's probably not good enough." That was unfair. Harper's work hadn't been bad. It had some mistakes in it, but nothing I wouldn't expect of someone who'd never worked with me before—the quality I was used to from new junior researchers was far sloppier and I was demanding, I knew that. She hadn't managed to get hold of Donny, but he was a hierarchical son of a bitch. Asking her to speak to him was asking an almost impossible task.

Turns out she was good at her job—she'd even had some really creative insights—so it didn't look as though she was going to give me a reason to fire her any time soon.

That could be a problem.

"Was the report really that bad?" Donna asked.

"No, but I don't need her sitting there watching me read it through, either." I'd found it utterly distracting on Friday, having her just a couple of yards away. I could barely concentrate because I'd been trying to place her scent—a kind of musky, sexy smell. The way her hands had gripped and then loosened around the arms of the chair—I found myself getting hard at the thought of those hands sliding down my chest and around my cock.

Fuck, she was a problem.

"Especially if you're going to make me have lunch with Wilson," I added when I glanced at Donna and she was looking at me with narrowed eyes. I didn't want her asking any more questions about Harper, even if it was about the quality of her work.

She took a deep breath. "Look, I don't want to speak out of turn—"

"Then don't," I snapped. What was she going to say? Could she tell I was treating Harper differently? That I was attracted to her?

Attracted. Shit. I needed to back up. She was just a pretty face with fantastic tits and a great ass. I knew plenty of women like that. My phone had plenty of women like that on speed dial who would come over and help me get Harper out of my system tonight if I thought it would help. She was nothing special.

"You're being pretty harsh with her, and I don't think it's about her performance in the office."

Pins and needles crackled through me as if my hand had been caught in the cookie jar. I froze, not wanting to react in a way that would confirm any suspicion she had.

"Has this got anything to do with Amanda?" she asked, her head cocked to one side.

My shoulders sagged. She'd not read anything into my interactions with Harper after all.

"It must be an adjustment for both of you. How long since Pandora left?" she asked.

"About six weeks. Yes, it's an adjustment." I raised my eyebrows. Amanda's mother, Pandora, and her husband,

Jason, had flown to Zurich because Jason had a new job. "I've always been so involved in her life; I didn't realize how much would change." I'd always shared custody of my four-teen-year-old daughter, but for me that had meant week-ends and holidays. I was quickly realizing that for the past fourteen years, I'd gotten the easy bit, the fun times with Amanda. I hadn't had to concern myself with homework, hair dye, or makeup.

"We're getting used to each other. And the commute is a challenge."

I was used to staying in Connecticut for the weekends only, but Pandora and I'd agreed Amanda should stay in her current school. So now I was in Manhattan just two nights a week, when Amanda stayed with her grandparents. I worked on the train and after Amanda went to bed, but it wasn't what I was used to.

Neither was the attitude I was getting from my daugh-ter. "She wants to dye her hair. I've said no a million times, but she won't drop it." I sighed. I wasn't used to having to repeat myself. "I swear I'm going to get home one day to find she's done it anyway."

Donna laughed. "Teenage girls are a challenge. I'm happy I'm still a few years away from that. I mean, I know what used to go through my head at fourteen. It's not pretty."

I had no idea what went on in Amanda's head most of the time. "I'm not sure I want to know," I replied, scrubbing my hands over my face.

Donna grinned. "Believe me, you're better off in the dark. Try to say yes sometimes, that way everything isn't a fight. What does Pandora say?"

"That she'd cut my balls off if I let her dye her hair."

"Well at least you're on the same page."

Pandora and I agreed about most things when it came to our daughter. Because we'd both been so young when Pandora had gotten pregnant, we'd started with a fresh slate. There was no baggage between us. No ill feelings. We'd both just done the best we could. We'd briefly flirted with the idea of trying to make things work between us, but neither of us tried that hard. It'd been a pre-college fling and nothing more.

I wasn't sure whether or not it was a conscious decision, but from the moment Amanda was born, I knew my life was all about my daughter. Yes, my business was important, but it was needing to support Amanda, wanting her to have every advantage, that had driven me. I was determined that even though Pandora and I had made a mistake in getting pregnant, having a daughter never would be. She was the only important thing in my life and the reason there'd never been room for anyone else.

Support from our parents meant we'd both finished college. Pandora had met Jason in her sophomore year and they'd married shortly after graduation. I'd been an usher and Amanda had sat on my lap during the ceremony. It was a weird setup but it worked all these years. But looking back, Pandora had shouldered the day-to-day of bringing Amanda up. Now her baton had been passed to me.

"Yeah. It's more of a change than I expected, though. Before if she'd asked to dye her hair I'd have either told her to ask her mother, or said no and dropped her off at home, leaving Pandora with the fallout. Now it's all on me."

"Remember, Amanda's probably missing her mother, too."

"It was her idea for them to go without her. Jason was ready to turn down the job in Zurich."

"I know, but she's at the age when sometimes she can

see an adult's point of view, and yet sometimes still be a kid."

I nodded and my heart tugged in that way only Amanda could elicit. She was only fourteen. Christ, you couldn't pay me enough to go back to that time. Everything was just so awkward. "They Skype all the time. I think I have more to do with Pandora now than I ever did before. We literally Skyped all through dinner last night." I laughed. "It was nice actually. I think Pandora's worried she hasn't done the right thing leaving her with me."

"I'm sure it'll be fine. You just need to get used to each other."

I nodded. "Yes, I hope if she—" My FaceTime chimed. "Here she is now." I picked up my phone. "Hey, Donna's here, say hi."

"Hey, Donna," my daughter replied.

"Hi, Amanda. You look so pretty."

"But I'd look better with blond hair, right?"

Donna chuckled and stood. "I'm so not getting into that. I'll give you guys a few minutes."

"Hey, peanut. What's up?" I asked as Donna closed the door behind her.

"Was just wondering when you were coming home."

I checked the clock on my laptop. It was only noon. "Probably not until eight. Marion's there, right?"

My housekeeper had known Amanda since she was a baby so was the perfect after-school and holiday sitter. This week Amanda was on break.

"Yeah, she's here. I just thought maybe you'd be back early today."

My heart squeezed again. Ninety percent of the time she drove me nuts, but it was moments like these that I lived for. She might be fourteen, but sometimes she still needed her dad.

"How was your morning?"

"Ugh. I don't want to talk about it."

"Are you still fighting with Samantha? You know you'll feel better if you get it out. Problems are like shit—"

"Daaad."

I chuckled. She didn't like any talk that involved bowels or farting, so I teased her with it every chance I got.

"Samantha got asked to the dance already," she mumbled.

That caught my attention. "What do you mean asked? Like a boy asked her? On a date?" My throat started to constrict and I coughed. "You're in middle school, for Christ's sake—you can't be dating." Amanda's eighth grade dance was occupying an awful lot of space in my daughter's head. I'd have preferred math or geography got her focus.

"I'm fourteen, not twelve."

Was there a difference?

"But you're going with Patti and all your friends, aren't you?" I tried to keep the rising panic I felt from reflecting in my tone.

"Sure but—"

"You want a boy to ask you and he hasn't?" I desperately wanted her to say no, to deny my worst nightmare wasn't about to come true.

"No. Not yet. Thanks for reminding me. I'm going to call Mom. I'll talk to you later."

"Amanda, don't go. What—"

She hung up. Jesus, what had I done now? I wasn't getting anything right at the moment. Things were so much easier when she lived with her mother. Up until the move, I could do no wrong. All I had to do was tickle her, crack a joke, read her a bedtime story and she thought I was amazing. Now everything I did led to an eye roll or a *Daaad*.

Fuck. I needed to call to Pandora. Maybe I could send Amanda over to Zurich the weekend of the dance? That way, there would be no boys, no dating and I wouldn't have to worry about going to jail for murder. My daughter was fourteen—she wasn't ready for the reality of the male species.

"Come in," I barked at the loud rap on the door. Harper entered the room. I groaned. Being in the same room as her was the very last thing I needed.

"What?" I asked as she strode toward me.

"The revised Bangladesh report." She held up some papers.

"You could have left it with Donna."

She placed the report down on my desk with a bang. "I'm sure if I'd left it with Donna, you'd have told me I should have handed it to you directly."

Oh. Sass. I hadn't been expecting that. I had to bite down a grin. She was right; I was giving her a hard time. But it wasn't personal. Okay, it was a little bit personal. She just irritated me. I prided myself on being unemotional at work. I'd always been able to separate the different areas of my life, to shut one world down while I was in another. Harper blurred the lines. During our meetings I fixated on the curve of her neck, or the pull of her sweater across her breasts. I'd be left trying to figure out her scent or imagine how her skin would feel under my fingers. I tried to shut that part of my imagination down. Over and over.

I stared at the screen of my laptop. "Well now you're here, just leave it on my desk and I'll try to get to it later."

"I'll leave your sandwich with Donna then," she said as she turned on her heel. Was she wearing a new dress? It looked good on her, showing off her ass and the sway of her hips while being high necked and demure.

I didn't have time to answer as she headed out and slammed the door.

Jesus, I was getting attitude everywhere I turned today. Was there a full moon? I picked up my cell and dialed Amanda. No answer.

I had a pile of papers to get through, but I wanted to get to the bottom of the situation with Amanda. If she was hoping to go to her dance with a date, we had a lot to talk about. I pulled all my things together. I'd work on the train. Leaving the office would be a double bonus—I could be with my daughter and put some distance between me and Harper. But it wasn't a long-term solution. I couldn't just stop coming into the office to avoid Harper. I needed a plan to keep her away from me. A way of making sure she didn't want anything to do with me.

THE JOURNEY back to Connecticut had unwound me, and I was able to focus better with every mile put between me and Harper.

"Pancakes?" Amanda asked as she skulked into the kitchen. The French doors were open and a light breeze circled around us. Despite us being anything but a traditional family, I'd always liked that this house had a traditional family feel. It had none of the sleek lines, gloss, and glamour of my New York apartment but I liked both of them, felt at home either way.

I nodded, cracking an egg into a bowl. Since she'd transitioned to solid food, Amanda and I had shared pancakes on Sunday mornings and talked. Pancakes were our thing.

"You're home early," she said. She'd hinted that she wanted me home on the phone, but she'd never expect it. It was nice to be able to surprise her. She understood work was important but that she always came first. In so many ways she was mature, but every now and then I'd get a reminder she was still fourteen.

I nodded again.

"Like half a day early," she added.

"Thought I'd spend some time with my favorite lady. I sent Marion home, so we're having pancakes." Marion cooked for both of us on the nights I was home. Two nights a week Amanda's two sets of grandparents fought over her. Because she'd spent so much time with them when she was little, it was almost as if she had three sets of parents, and my two sisters provided the aunt input.

Amanda hopped up onto one of the barstools at the breakfast bar, watching as I whisked up the batter.

"Speak to your mom today?" I asked. I'd learned I couldn't just launch in and ask Amanda who she was hoping to ask her to the dance and on what basis. No, I had to wait for her to talk. Lucky for me, Amanda was a talker.

"Nope. Not yet."

I stayed silent, trying to encourage her to speak.

"Bobby Clapham invited Samantha to the dance."

I gripped the whisk harder but kept my mouth shut. I had to hear her out.

"And I thought that Callum Ryder would ask me, but he hasn't said anything."

Fourteen. No one told me dating was going to start this early. Could I call Pandora and agree we would lock Amanda in her room until she turned twenty-one? I could give up work and home school her for a few years, then she could do a college correspondence course. It was an option.

"Callum Ryder, he's in your class?" I'd never heard her talk about him. Or maybe I had and I'd just taken no notice. Because Amanda liked to talk, I tuned out large chunks of what she said. It was just too much to take in—all the friends, the squabbling, the concerns that would last five seconds. I couldn't keep up. The stuff I did take in passed through my brain quickly, and I retained almost nothing about her friendships at school. I was beginning to realize such an approach may have been a mistake.

"Oh my God. Don't you listen to anything I say?" she whined. "Callum moved here from San Francisco last semester. Don't you remember me telling you?"

"Oh, right." I nodded, trying to cover up the fact I had no idea what she was talking about. Why hadn't we sent her to an all-girls school? "And you want him to ask you to the dance?"

A blush crept up her face and a piercing pain shot through my chest. She was too young for all this. "Maybe," she said. "But only because he's funny, and I saw him dance once during lunch and he seemed to be able to move in time to the music."

"So everyone is going as couples?" I tried not to shudder as I spoke. My baby girl.

"What do you mean?" she asked, plucking a grape from the bowl of fruit on the counter.

"If Callum asked you to the dance, he'd pick you up and—"

"No, Samantha and I are going together. You said you'd drive us. You don't remember?" She splayed her hands in front of her as if I was possibly the stupidest man ever to have lived.

"Yeah, I remember," I lied. "But I thought you and Samantha were no longer friends?"

"Last week, Dad. Keep up."

"Okay, explain it to me because I don't know how these things work. So you'll see Callum there?"

She shrugged. "I guess."

The thudding of my pulse slowed. Maybe labelling this whole thing dating was over-dramatic. I poured the batter onto the griddle as I tried to cover my relief. "So do you have your costume yet for this dance?" I asked.

"Costume? You mean a dress? It's not a costume party."

I sighed. "Give me a break. Do you have a dress?"

She grinned. "I wondered if you wanted some company in the city this week? You know, we could go shopping maybe?"

"In Manhattan?" I wasn't sure I was qualified to take her shopping for a dance. I had no idea what would be appropriate. I didn't like Amanda in the city, and I tried to discourage her attempts to visit me when I was at the Manhattan apartment. New York was no place for a kid. There were far too many bad influences.

"Yes," she replied.

"Don't you like the shops around here?"

"I want something no one else will have." Something in my expression must have caught her eye. "Just because I'm fourteen doesn't mean finding the perfect dress isn't important, if that's what you're thinking. Perhaps if you ever dated, you'd get it."

Here we go. One crisis situation always overlapped with another. Amanda was always nagging me about getting a girlfriend. Or a wife. Women were exhausting. Work was easier. Or it was before Harper started.

"I want you to look pretty. Of course I understand that. I have plenty of women in my life." With two sisters, a daughter, and Pandora, there was no lack of estrogen in my world.

"You always think about it in such a selfish way." Amanda sighed and slipped off the stool. She began to gather plates and cutlery. Helping out in the kitchen without being asked—that was new. I was getting constant reminders about how much she was growing up, and although I was proud, it felt as if we were hurtling downhill with the brakes off. I wanted to pause for a second, enjoy the here and now for a couple of years.

"I'm being selfish by not dating?" I asked, flipping the pancakes over.

"Totally. You know how much I've always wanted a sister. Mom's been married to Jason for forever and they've completely ignored me, so it's up to you. I don't understand what you're waiting for. Don't you want to get married?"

"Hey, wait. A minute ago you were talking about you dating and now, not only do I have to date, but I have to marry a woman and get her pregnant?" She must have been talking to my sisters. They were always pestering me to date, trying to set me up with their friends. The fact was I didn't need help getting women. But neither Amanda nor my sisters had to hear about my sex life.

She laughed. "Don't you ever think about it? We're here in the big house, just the two of us, and I'll be in college soon."

"Are you trying to kill me today? You have a couple of years before you leave for college." She was right; college was really just around the corner. Of course I wanted her to go, but maybe she could still live at home. I wasn't ready to give her up entirely.

"I think it would be nice for you to have someone. And if I got a baby sister out of it? Well, then that would be even better." She placed the plates on the breakfast bar and set the cutlery on either side.

"What's brought this on? I haven't had this particular lecture from you for a while, peanut." Had this just been my sisters' influence, or did she miss Pandora? I dished up pancakes and turned off the stove. Was I not enough for her?

She shrugged. "Dunno. Samantha's mom was asking whether or not you were dating, and it just got me wondering."

Samantha's mom? Why did I think there was more behind Samantha's recently divorced mom's question than neighborly interest? Since Amanda had been living with me, a number of her friends' moms seemed to find an excuse to come by. I'd never given any one of them a reason to think I was available.

"I think it would be nice if you found someone is all. *And* I want a baby sister."

I *dated*—and by that I meant had sex, plenty of sex. But it always happened in New York. I'd never brought anyone home to Connecticut. I kept my two worlds separate. Never anything more. I had the best of both worlds—my family in Connecticut and King & Associates and my career on Wall Street. I'd never needed anything more. There were no holes in my life as far as I was concerned. Apparently Amanda disagreed.

"You wouldn't miss our father-daughter time together? Eating pancakes, watching the game?"

"Why would we have to stop doing that? The three of us could do it together, and when Chelsea was old enough, she could have pancakes, too."

"Chelsea?" I was confused.

"My baby sister. Or maybe Amy would be better. I like that our names would both begin with an A."

Of course. I chuckled as Amanda grinned at me. "You're crazy, but I love you."

"I could find you a date if you wanted."

"Stop it and eat your pancakes."

"If you agree to go on a date, I won't tell Mom you're feeding me pancakes on a Monday night. You know she'd have a cow." Wow, maybe a few of my negotiation skills had been passed through the genetic line.

"Tell me you're not trying to blackmail me." I ruffled her hair as I sat beside her at the bar. "I'll take my chances with your mother. She knows how sometimes sugar is the only solution."

"You're no fun."

"I'm your dad. I'm not supposed to be fun."

"Please just think about taking a woman to dinner. Tinder is meant to be the place to find someone."

Tinder? "Promise me you're not on Tinder, or I'm taking your phone and you're not getting it back until you hit thirty-five."

"Dad, of course I'm not on Tinder. Are you crazy? I'm fourteen." At last she was making sense. "Tinder's for old people. Like you." Amanda held the syrup high above her plate and amber stickiness trickled out.

Was Harper on Tinder? Perhaps I should try to find out. Fuck, no. Why was I thinking like that?

"Check it out, Dad. Promise me."

"I'm promising nothing," I replied, but I wasn't sure how convincing I sounded.

THREE

Harper

I'd been waiting to hear from Max about the Bangladesh report for three days. I'd worked my ass off all weekend so he could have it on Monday. I shouldn't have bothered. It was Wednesday evening and he'd canceled our follow-up meeting twice. I kicked off my shoes and slumped onto my sofa. I could hear Ben, or maybe it was Jerry, calling from the freezer.

"Knock it off, guys," I yelled. I couldn't spend the evening eating. No. I'd be productive—take advantage of the gym in the basement. That would take my mind off the asshole who was my boss. He'd strode past me in the corridor earlier in the day and totally ignored me. Okay, maybe my report could have been better, but giving me the silent treatment didn't seem like the professional thing to do. I had to keep reminding myself he wasn't the man I'd thought he would be and that still didn't mean I couldn't get a lot out of working for King & Associates.

I changed into my workout gear, grabbed a bottle of

water, and headed downstairs. A gym in the building was more than I could have hoped for when I started looking for somewhere in Manhattan, and I'd not had a chance to visit yet. Work might not be good, but home was a cocoon from anything bad. I could relax—focus on the big picture.

Thirty minutes on the elliptical would clear my head and stop me trying to think up ways to physically hurt Max King.

As I entered the gym, I noticed there were three men already there—one using the free weights, one on a bike, the other on a rower. And apart from the muted sounds of CNN coming from a TV fixed on the wall in the corner, it was quiet. I checked out the rest of the space. No mirrors, so I didn't have to look at any part of me wobbling while I moved. Perfect. It was as if I'd invented the place myself.

Moving toward an empty elliptical, I avoided the blatant stare of the guy using the weights. I dropped my water bottle into the holder on the machine just behind the man on the bike—he had an amazing ass—hopped on, and tried to find a program that wouldn't kill me. Just what I needed to stop me from thinking about the office—a hard workout and a nice view.

I found a program on the machine that I knew would be tough, but I wanted to be focused on something other than what a disappointment King & Associates was turning out to be. I needed to be able to tune out when I wasn't in the office or I'd send myself crazy. My first day on the job, my jaw ached from smiling so much. I'd finally achieved my dream, and I'd done it all on my own. It felt as though I'd arrived on the first step of a bright future—where the beginning of all my plans converged. I'd been beside myself with excitement. But the sheen had worn off pretty quickly, sometime in the first week when I was introduced to Max and he'd barely looked up from his desk to say hello.

The guy on the bike gasped and sat up, circling his shoulders, then tilting his head one way and the other as he continued to peddle. He had a nice broad back, and jet-black hair drenched in sweat. He was going to need a serious shower. If he was the guy I'd heard having sex in the penthouse, I'd be happy to keep him company.

"You live in the building?"

I jumped when the guy who'd been using the free weights draped his arm over my machine. I hadn't seen him head over. He was short, overbuilt, and so tan I wanted to ask him whether or not he'd lost a bet. He looked as if he belonged on the Jersey shore rather than downtown Manhattan. I nodded, hoping the fact I didn't speak would put him off.

"You have a nice ass, if you don't mind me saying."

Really? He held up his hands when I shot him a look to kill. "No need to be snotty. I just like a nice ass."

I fixed my stare to my machine's panel, wanting to punch the guy.

"I think you better move on," a man said from behind Jersey Shore.

"Hey," Jersey Shore replied. "I was giving the girl a compliment."

I kept my head down, not wanting to attract any more attention.

"Her loss, right?" my rescuer replied. I recognized that voice. My brain tried to work out if it was a famous person.

Jersey Shore moved away, and I glanced up with a smile. "Thank—"

It was like someone was trying to take a dump over my entire life.

Max-fucking-King stood right in front of me.

Kill. Me. Now.

The guy I'd come down here to escape was standing right in the middle of *my* gym in *my* apartment building. I glanced around. Jersey Shore had left, and the rower was still going. Max King was Nice Ass Guy. Life was just not fair.

My limbs stopped working and I half tripped, half stepped off the elliptical, stumbling into the wall behind the machines. *Really?* The hits just kept on coming.

"Are you okay?"

I peeled myself off the drywall as he moved toward me.

I nodded, unsure what I'd say if I actually managed to form words. How was this possible? My apartment was supposed to be my sanctuary from this man's assholey behavior in the office. Now I had to worry about running into him in the corridors of my apartment building while I was drunk or not wearing makeup. Not that it mattered if he saw me without makeup or in my sweats; it would just be another reason for him to think less of me.

"Okay, well. I guess you live in the building," he said, then clenched his jaw and flicked his eyes to the door as if he wanted to escape.

Fine by me.

"Yeah, I just moved in."

He looked past me and pressed his fingers to his forehead as he had when reviewing my Bangladesh report. "Right."

And that was it. Before I could think of anything else to say, he sped out the door as if his balls were on fire.

He had no more manners outside the office than in. He was still cold and rude.

Despite his nice ass.

I leaned against the wall, trying to make sense of it all. A year ago I would have thought my life had peaked at just being within a five-yard radius of Max King. Now he was not only torturing me at the office, but he'd just made my building gym a no-go area. I grabbed my water bottle and headed back to my apartment. Could my day get any worse?

AFTER MY NEAR aneurism at running into Max in the gym, I'd taken the hottest shower possible without landing in the emergency room, blow-dried my hair, and then wrapped myself in my white silk robe, which I'd bought on sale at Barney's. It always made me feel better. As if I had my shit together. I needed a BFF download, and I'd be back on track.

"Hey, Grace," I replied as she answered my call.

"You sound like you're about to put your head in the oven," she said through the sound of her chewing on something.

I wanted to ask her if I could come over and spend the night. For the rest of my lease. "Just a bad day at work." If I told her about Max being in the building, she'd have me moved back to Brooklyn before she could say the words sublet. I'd have to settle for a general gripe session, so I explained I'd still not heard back on the Bangladesh report.

"Have you ever thought about quitting your job? It really can't be worth it."

"I can't quit. This is my dream position. It's what I've worked so hard for. I just need two years on my resume, and then I'm golden." And who knew. I might have won him over with the revised Bangladesh report. I could get into the office tomorrow to find he'd turned over a new leaf.

And I might be the next Beyoncé.

"Two years is a long time to be miserable. You could always talk to your dad."

Was she serious? "Why would you even say something like that?" Grace knew I was the only one of his kids not working at JD Stanley, his investment bank. My three half brothers had all started on the graduate course the September after college. I'd thought I'd get the satisfaction of turning him down, but he never asked. Why would Grace think I would call him? I didn't want anything from him.

"You do the kind of work his firm needs, right? Don't you have like a perfect skill set for him?"

"It doesn't matter." Ben and Jerry's cries from the kitchen were growing louder. "I wouldn't work for him if he was the last man on Earth. And if you remember, he never offered me a job. I didn't have the correct reproductive equipment."

"He probably didn't think you wanted it." It didn't mean he couldn't have asked. "He doesn't know you, doesn't get how brilliant and ambitious you are. He's like a hundred years old. He's probably just old-fashioned." Was he just from a different generation who thought women should stay at home and look after the kids? If he'd ever gotten to know me, he would know I wasn't like that.

"I really can't believe we're having this conversation. I'm not about to quit my dream job, and I'm not about to ask my father for anything." I swung my legs up onto the couch and lay on my back staring at the ceiling. "It's really starting to upset me that you're defending him."

"I'm really not. I'm just trying to offer you a way out."

Grace was always trying to solve my problems. And the

problems of all the guys she dated. There just wasn't anything Grace could do to fix this situation.

Footsteps thudded across the ceiling, causing my light fixture to rock gently back and forth. Jesus, the last thing I needed was my neighbors going at it again. I didn't want to be reminded of my lack of sex life.

"Thank you, but I don't need a way out. I'm exactly where I want to be." I wasn't a quitter.

"But you're miserable."

"I'm not." I should complain less. I was just frustrated to find Max in my building. "My standards are just too high." The thudding upstairs sounded like someone pacing back and forth. "I'm going to readjust, reset, and everything's going to be just fine."

Classical music, Bach maybe, blared from upstairs. It was so loud my apartment started to vibrate. Metalheads or coked-up dance music addicts were supposed to play their music loud and annoy their neighbors, not classical music buffs.

"Do you have classical music on? Jesus, less than a week in Manhattan and we're already growing apart."

I chuckled. "No, it's not me. It's upstairs."

"The shaggers?"

"Yes. Although they're not shagging. One of them put their concrete boots on and is dancing like an elephant across my ceiling." The music hadn't drowned out the consistent pound of footsteps. "I can't tell if there are two people up there."

"Brooklyn looking a little more attractive?" Grace couldn't hide the smug tinge to her voice.

"I'm sure the music will die down in a little bit. Maybe they've had a bad day and they're trying to drown it out, like I do with—"

"Taylor Swift?"

I shrugged, unembarrassed by my Swift predilection. "I was going to say Stevie Wonder, but Taylor will do."

"You're not pissed off by the noise?"

Any other day I would be furious, but if I allowed myself to get irritated with my penthouse neighbors, I'd have nothing left. Work was so disappointing it left me hollow inside. All my excitement about the job had dissolved, and it had become just like my college bartending job—a means to an end. And now with Max in the building, the only place I felt safe was behind my front door. Surely my neighbors would stop pacing and turn down their music soon.

"Tell me about your date?" I asked. "That's why I called."

Grace had a thing for penniless musicians, artists, or really anyone who didn't have their shit together. It meant there was always drama in her life, always someone to fix.

"Ahhh," she sighed. "He's so talented. He just needs to find the right patron, catch a break, you know?" I'd forgotten what this one did. They all seemed to morph into one guy whose middle name was loser.

"You think he's got what it takes?" Grace liked the idea of finding a guy before they made it and being the one who was there from the beginning. Problem was they never made it. She just jumped from one loser to another.

"I really do. This guy is the next Damien Hirst or Jeff Koons, I swear."

Oh, right. This one was an artist. I glanced up at the ceiling as the light fixture swayed even more violently.

"He's putting together an installation in New Jersey next week. You should come. You'll love it."

I wasn't sure New Jersey was the place to showcase the

next Jeff Koons, but hey, it would get me out. "Sure. But when you say 'installation', what do you mean?"

"It's an interactive piece he's working on. He won't show me, but I'm sure it's amazing."

Grace was so sensible and practical in every way but wanted to believe the absolute best of everything. It was kinda endearing, kinda annoying.

"And he has a friend I want to introduce you to."

I groaned. "Grace."

"No, you'll like this guy. He's a suit."

Upstairs cranked up the volume. I didn't know classical music, though my mom had a thing for Johann's cello suites. Nice, but did it really have to be this loud?

"I can dress my dog in a suit. It doesn't mean I want to date him."

It wasn't wealth that attracted me; it was drive. It didn't matter if they wore a suit—although there was nothing like a man who could fill out custom-cut, navy wool as though he owned it. I might hate Max King, but Jesus, did he know how to wear a suit. And gym clothes, apparently. Seeing him in the gym hadn't changed my mind that he'd clearly been in the front of the line when they were dealing out hot.

"You don't have a dog," Grace said.

"Not really my point." I didn't want to date anyone, didn't want love to distract me. I'd seen a number of my friends doing so well in their careers and suddenly becoming less ambitious because they'd fallen for some guy, and then when they'd taken their foot off the pedal, the guy would predictably dump them. It had even happened to my mother. And I wasn't going to make the same mistake.

"This guy is successful. He does something in finance, or maybe it was architecture."

"Yeah, I can see how you'd get the two mixed up." The

very last thing I wanted was a man in finance. The industry bred men like my father and they were the worst kinds.

Grace laughed. "You know what I mean. Will you come?"

"If you promise not to set me up with anyone. I'm not interested."

"I'm not setting you up. But what can I say? He'll be there; you'll be there."

"I'm hanging up. I have to get my beauty sleep." I pressed cancel on the phone and tossed it on the table. It was just after ten, but an early night would be impossible until my Bach-loving neighbors shut the hell up.

Warm milk and a Benadryl would help me sleep, but I only had wine, and I was out of Benadryl.

I poured myself a glass of Pinot Noir, climbed into bed, and turned on the TV.

After forty-five minutes I could barely hear my TV through the music, and the thudding footsteps hadn't lessened. What, was someone training to climb Kilimanjaro up there? My limbs began to twitch with irritation. Whoever was up there didn't sound as if they were changing things up anytime soon, and I wanted to sleep. I'd been *more* than patient. Could I call the police? Wasn't there something in the lease about not making noise after a certain time? Where had I put my lease?

I threw my covers off and stomped out of bed, then flung open the blanket box Grace and I had lugged up here when I moved in. The box of denial—it was where all my life admin went. Eventually I found the papers I'd signed just over a week ago, and I started to flip through the pages, almost ripping one in half. How could anyone be so selfish? Loud sex was one thing, but music and marching practice was another. I ran my fingers down the pages as I became increasingly impatient. Yes. It said I wasn't allowed to disturb any other neighbor after ten in the evening. The people upstairs were breaching their lease. Clasping my papers, I scrambled toward the front door, grabbed my keys, and took the stairs one flight up. I glanced around. There was just one apartment door. Well at least I didn't have to worry about disturbing the wrong person.

I knocked on the metal, trying to swallow down the anger bubbling at the surface. It was all too much. First I found the perfect job for it to be ruined by the reality of Max King, then I couldn't escape him in my building. Now my noisy neighbors were stopping me from sleeping. Everything seemed so unfair.

I knocked again, louder this time. Did they not know how loud they were being?

Who was I kidding? I was pretty sure I could hear these guys from the Hamptons.

The stomping continued to go up and down, up and down. There was no one coming toward the door.

I slammed my fists against the cold metal and screamed, "Open the fucking door."

Almost immediately the footsteps stopped, then changed direction. My heart began beating out of my chest. Had I gone too far? I might be knocking on the door of a serial killer or drug dealer with penchant for Bach.

Locks began to clunk and I folded my arms, ready to give my loud neighbor a piece of my mind. I should have pulled a sweater on over my silk robe.

The door opened wide and for the second time, I came face to face with Max King where I least expected to find him.

And of course, he had to be shirtless.

"Are you kidding me?" I bellowed, flinging my arms in the air in exasperation.

His eyes were wide and trailed down my body. I followed his eye line; shit, my robe had begun to part. I grabbed the silk and pulled it together, trying to ignore the fact I was almost naked in front of my boss.

His eyebrows nearly hit the ceiling and he reached out. "Get in here," he said as he pulled me by the elbows. "You're not dressed."

I tried to stand firm, but he gripped me with such force I went crashing into him, and we stumbled backward into his apartment.

"Jesus, Harper," he growled, and he pushed me away but didn't let go of my arms. I realized it was the first time I'd heard him call me by my first name. He normally called me Ms. Jayne. He closed his eyes and with gritted teeth, he asked, "What are you doing here?"

FOUR

Max

Being close to her like this made me crazy. Because I'd done such wicked things to her in my head, I was always concerned I'd be over familiar with her in the flesh. And now I had hold of her, I didn't know what to do. I just knew I didn't want to let her go.

"What are you doing up here?" She tried to hold up some papers, but I held her arms firmly by her sides, pushing her up against the wall. "My ceiling is caving in from all the thumping."

My brain wasn't able to function. Why was she in my apartment? Why was she shouting?

Seeing that mafia boss lookalike at the gym hit on Harper had taken away the shock of realizing she was a resident of *my* building. I'd wanted to lift him up and kick him out on his ass. Then when he left I noticed her workout clothes stretched over her body so tight she might as well have been naked, and I'd bolted out of the gym, running away from the twitching across my skin that told me I had to leave before I embarrassed myself.

And now she was against my apartment wall. Enraged. And only partially dressed.

I was speechless.

She was always so cool and in control at work. It was odd to see her so . . . agitated. I clearly didn't know her well, probably because I barely gave her the time of day, too desperate to keep as much distance between us as possible. I'd hate for her to guess what was going on in my perverted little brain, for her to know all the things I imagined doing with her.

"And the music. Anyone would think you had the New York Philharmonic up here. What the hell is going on?"

My hands burned from being wrapped around her arms. I loosened my grip, but couldn't let her go entirely.

"Answer me!" she yelled. "I have to put up with you ignoring me in the office, but you don't sign my paychecks here. You're breaching your lease."

I'd had an inkling there was more under her professional exterior than I normally saw. She'd hinted a couple of times that she thought I was an asshole. It was a relief, because if she hated me it made things easier. It made the distance wider.

But nothing was easy now, not with her right here, almost naked in front of me. Her smooth skin, hot under my fingers, wasn't helping. The scent of musk and sex seeping through my body and going straight to my dick. The way her nipples poked at the silk of her robe. None of it helped. I closed my eyes, trying to claw back some kind of control over what I was feeling.

"Are you listening to me?"

I wasn't. I could hear she was upset, but I couldn't

process what she was saying. My senses were too overloaded.

She tipped her head back, exposing her long, creamy neck, and sighed, exasperated. Before I could stop myself, I released her arm and stroked my index finger across her jaw and down her neck. She gasped, but I couldn't hold back. I trailed my finger lower, into the dip at the base of her throat. She was like a drug. Every hit I took of her made me want more. I was chasing the high—her high.

"What are you doing, you asshole?"

Her words brought me up short. Asshole? I froze and looked up. Shit, I did things like that to her in my imagination, not in person.

"I . . . I'm sorry." I let her go and stepped back, pushing my hands through my hair. What was I thinking? I was a father. A businessman. Nothing else mattered.

She paused and frowned at me. "You're vile to me in the office," she said, her voice quiet and questioning.

I nodded. "I know." It was deliberate.

I fixed my stare on her full, pouty lips. All the things I'd imagined those lips doing . . . She was right. I was an asshole.

"And you think I'm stupid," she said.

"Stupid?" If that were true she wouldn't be quite so alluring. Yes, she'd still be beautiful, but there were plenty of beautiful women on this planet. "I don't think you're stupid."

"Then why do you treat me like shit?" She pointed at me; her voice got louder. "You act as if I don't exist." She jabbed her finger into my chest. It was as if she'd pressed a button with the word "cock" on it. My dick pulsed in response to every touch from her.

I grabbed her finger, forcing her to stop pressing her skin

against mine, and froze, not wanting to let go, and she didn't pull her hand away from me. Instead we just looked at each other, not knowing what happened next, needing answers from the other. Was she done yelling? Could I keep my hands to myself a second longer?

To my surprise, she dropped her papers, took a step forward, wrapped her free hand around my neck, and pressed her lips to mine. Relief rolled through my body, and instead of pushing her away, I snaked my greedy tongue into her mouth. She groaned, the sound reverberating throughout my body. She touched me as if it were practiced, as if she'd been thinking of it as much as I had.

I pulled back for a second and a look of confusion passed over her face. It was just the encouragement I needed. I pushed her against the wall and dropped my lips to her collarbone.

"I hate you," she whispered.

She wasn't acting as if she hated me, wasn't trying to get away. Had I read her wrong? I glanced up and she frowned.

"Don't stop," she said.

I grinned and bowed my head. She wanted this. "Don't stop?" I asked against her neck. She threaded her fingers into my hair with one hand and smoothed the other over my shoulder. It was my turn to groan. A single touch from her and all my worst fears were confirmed—I wanted this woman. No, it was more than that. I'd found women attractive before, but I'd never had an overwhelming desire to be close to them, all the time. Not when I barely knew anything about them. Never found myself thinking about a woman when I was meant to be concentrating on a conference call or presentation. Never wanted to make them smile, find out all their secrets. I kneed her legs apart, and she ground her hips against my leg.

This girl could end me.

I'd suspected it the moment I saw her. Known it the moment I'd seen her work.

Talented. Beautiful. Sharp. Sexy.

I wanted it all.

There were so many reasons this couldn't happen. She worked for me. I only had sex with women; I didn't do relationships. I'd recited them silently again and again.

I pulled back and she looked up at me, mouth open. I placed my hands against the wall on either side of her head.

"What?" she asked.

"I'm your boss."

"Don't worry. Whatever happens, I'll be filing my sexual harassment claim in the morning." She reached into my pants and wrapped her fingers around my hardening cock. "You might as well make this count."

I smirked. She was going to keep me on my toes.

As I pulled open the tie of her robe, the silk slipped from her shoulders. Sweeping my hands across her skin, I avoided her breasts, then trailed down her stomach to her neatly trimmed pussy. I paused.

She arched her back, pushing her body toward me, wanting more.

"But you hate me," I teased.

"Let's see what you can do to change my mind." She pressed her hand against mine, pushing my fingers into her dampness.

She had no idea what I had planned for her and how long I'd been planning it.

An almost transient afterthought, I slid my lips against hers. And despite my fantasies, I found myself sliding to *my* knees. I needed to know I could make her as crazy as she did me. I tried to pull her leg over my shoulder but she resisted, encouraging me to stand up.

"Did you forget who's the boss?" I asked.

"In the office, maybe."

Forcefully, I pushed her back against the wall and lifted her leg. I knew once she felt my tongue she'd relent. And I was right. I always was. She thrust her hips forward and slid her leg down my back as my tongue flicked over her clit, once, then twice. If she thought I wasn't the boss in the bedroom, she was sorely mistaken.

I curled a hand around one hip and with the other pressed my palm against her flat stomach as I licked from her clit down to the source of her wetness, enjoying her sweet taste. There was so much of it. As if she'd been wet for me since we first met. Her nails dug into my scalp as her pussy pulsed against me. I couldn't remember the last time I went down on a woman, and right at that moment, I couldn't remember it ever tasting this good, this warm, this wet.

Despite my holding her, she seemed to be having a hard time standing up straight.

"I can't," she cried out.

I got the feeling there was nothing Harper couldn't do if she put her mind to it, but I wasn't about to argue with her. I stood and she looked at me, half dazed, half disappointed. Before she had a chance to tell me again how much she hated me, I hoisted her over my shoulder and carried her into my bedroom.

I tipped her onto the bed, her chestnut hair splaying out around her. I grabbed her by the legs and parted her firm thighs, pushing my fingers into her while my tongue circled her clit. She cried out, lifting her hips off the bed. I grabbed her waist and pulled her toward me. She wasn't going anywhere without an orgasm to remember me by. Jesus, just a few minutes ago I'd been coming up with strategies to spend less time with her and now here she was naked on my bed, coating my hand and tongue with her juices.

She let out small whimpers and incoherent sounds about noise and neighbors and chandeliers. I couldn't follow what she was saying. All I cared about was her sweet, hot pussy around my tongue. Her breaths grew sharper and her whole body began to shudder, her movements becoming wild before she cried out, "Max!" Hearing my name on her lips while she climaxed pierced a hole in armor I didn't realize I wore, and suddenly I didn't care that I was her boss or that I had a reputation to protect, a family to focus on. I was so overwhelmingly attracted to her and right then it was the only thing that mattered. I nearly came right with her.

Her panting slowed and she reached out. I should ask her to leave, stop this before it was too late, but instead I took her hand and climbed up next to her.

I rolled to my back, needing to focus on something other than the swell of her tight breasts, the way her body sank against *my* bedsheets, on *my* bed, in *my* apartment.

She was here. Exactly where she shouldn't be.

"Oh my God." Her arm flopped onto my chest. "Forbes was right when they said you were talented."

I couldn't stop the chuckle that rose from my throat. I turned to see her rolling to her side, apparently oblivious of how bizarre this scenario was. She kissed my jaw, and I tried not to look at her, afraid I'd never be able to look away.

Her fingers wrapped around my still rock-hard cock. Jesus. So much for me telling her to leave. She dragged her hand up over the crown. There was little hope of me getting rid of her, not while she was so expertly squeezing and pulling. I gave in and glanced over to find her staring back at me, studying me as if she was trying to work out a crossword clue.

"Got a condom?"

This was a bad idea. "Yes," I said as I reached across to my night table.

She straddled me and took the latex from me. "This is Vegas, right?" she asked.

"Vegas?" I asked as she sheathed my cock, squeezing tightly as she reached the bottom.

"This room. It's Vegas. What happens here, stays here." She positioned my cock at her entrance. "You agree? Maybe if we do this, I can stop hating you. You can just be my boss."

At the moment I'd have agreed to cut off both my legs with a blunt knife, but I liked what she was saying. That after whatever it was we were doing, everything would go back to normal or better than normal—how things should be.

"Vegas," I replied and she sank onto my dick, inch by inch. I squeezed my hands into fists to stop myself from grabbing her hips and slamming her onto me. My jaw tightened as Harper threw her head back and steadied herself. Using her hands on my chest, she sank down a little more.

"So good," she whispered. "So, so deep."

Jesus, how was I supposed to just lie here and take this? It was too much. I needed to be the one who set the pace, or I'd be coming in less than ten seconds.

Her hair fell around her shoulders, and I reached up, pushing it behind her back, wanting nothing to interrupt my view of her high, tight breasts or her pink, swollen nipples jutting out, begging for attention. I pulled at them, one then the other, and she quivered before crashing down on me as far as she would go. She was perfect, far better than I'd imagined and I'd thought about her plenty, wondered what she'd look like above me, naked, legs open, eyes hazy with lust. She was so tight around me that instinct took over, and before I gave her a chance to ride me I flipped her over onto her back and pushed in farther.

"No more," I said. "I've had enough of your constant daily teasing." I didn't know if she meant to be provocative. She wasn't obvious about it in the way a lot of women were. Her clothes weren't flashy or particularly tight; she didn't flirt or even try to make conversation with me. I pulled out and started to fuck her now that I finally had her under me, naked. Each time I thought pushing in would get easier, that she wouldn't be quite so tight, so delicious, but every time I was wrong. She was exceeding each one of the fantasies I'd had about her.

Her hands wrapped around my upper arms, her fingers so tiny they were fascinating. I wanted to pause for a second to ensure they were real, but my headboard smashing against the wall pulled my focus back to wanting to make her come. She looked so perfect, so completely beautiful and if we only had tonight, I was going to have to make it count.

I wanted to go farther, deeper, faster.

I needed to mark her, own her, climb inside her.

It was as if every inappropriate image I'd buried deep in my brain had escaped and come to life.

I lifted one of her legs higher, desperate to be closer. I could tell by the way she opened her mouth slightly wider that the change in angle ratcheted up the pleasure for us both. I dipped my head down to kiss her, and she greedily took my tongue. Despite giving me no sign in the office, she touched me as though I'd lived in her fantasies just as she'd lived in mine. There was a knowingness between us, a familiarity that was unnerving but at the same time I wanted to savor it.

She reached between us and squeezed the base of my cock. I almost exploded. I had to pause.

"You're such an asshole." She grinned and wiped sweat from my brow with her fingertips.

"You seem obsessed with that concept. Perhaps we should try your asshole out next and see if it cures you."

"You wouldn't dare." She pushed her hips up to meet mine, and I raised my eyebrow.

"Wouldn't I?" I asked. "This is Vegas. Anything goes."

"Shut up and concentrate on fucking me."

I loved that mouth, the way it called me names, the way it called *my* name.

She needed to be taught a lesson.

"I'm thinking about nothing else." I pushed into her and her eyes half shut. I started thrusting deeper and deeper, nailing her to the mattress, wanting to make it good, needing to feel her around me. I sat back on my knees, pulling her up onto my thighs, taking the opportunity to watch her breasts bounce with every thrust.

"You think I hate you now?" I asked. Didn't she feel the chemistry between us and understand I had to keep my distance otherwise something like this would happen?

"I don't care. I'm too . . ."

She trailed off and squeezed me harder, creating friction between us that heated the blood in my veins. She gave me a small smile and I wanted her closer. I pulled her up, bringing us face to face, her legs around my waist, and lifted her up and down on my cock. She wrapped her arms around my neck and pressed her lips to mine. It was such an intimate gesture, so normal, so right, as if we'd been lovers for some time, as if we'd known each other for years.

Harper increased the rhythm, her hips lifting easily in my hands and slamming down on my cock.

"Careful," I warned. I wouldn't last long like that.

"I can't stop," she whispered, her fingers running across my shoulders. "I can't stop, don't want to." Her movements grew bigger, wilder, and I used my hands over her hips to keep our rhythm steady and her pussy full of me. Her fingernails dug into my shoulders as she pulled back to look at me and screamed, "Max. Yes, Max." Her pulsating muscles drew me in and in two sharp stabs of my hips I was pouring into her, watching her orgasm seep away as mine took over.

I WOKE to traffic noise and the sun pouring into my window. Was it Saturday? No, Thursday.

Fuck. Harper.

I must have blacked out.

I bolted upright, but I was alone. Had I dreamt what had happened last night? The ache in my muscles, the bedsheets crumpled at the bottom of the bed, the tug in my stomach—no, it had happened. "Harper," I called out. She'd gone. I scrubbed my face with my hands then glanced at the clock. Fuck. It was eight thirty. I was usually knee deep in paperwork at my desk by now. I bounded out of bed for the shower.

It was only a few minutes' walk to the office and I went through the sliding doors to the King & Associates office at two minutes to nine. My hair was still wet from my shower.

I had no idea how I was going to handle Harper in the office today. I had a hundred and one things to do and no spare brain space. But the gathering gloom in my head said last night had been a bad idea—the worst idea. I couldn't have casual sex with an employee. It blurred too many lines. Having sex with women I'd see outside of the bedroom had never been an option for me. There were enough women in my life. And Amanda deserved my full attention when I wasn't in the office—it was the deal I'd struck with myself as soon as she was born. Just because I was a young father didn't mean I'd be a bad one. She would always be my priority.

As much as the night with Harper had been everything I'd fantasized about, it had been a stupid idea.

I kept my head down as I strode to my office, but I couldn't resist glancing over to Harper's desk. She'd made it in on time. Her hair was up, folded somehow against her head, revealing her long neck.

"There you are," Donna called. "I've been trying your cell."

Harper turned toward me just as I looked at Donna. Harper hadn't left a note this morning. Had she stayed the night? Did she regret what had happened?

"Did you come in from Connecticut?" Donna asked as she followed me into my office.

"No, I just had some things to sort out." Like washing the smell of sex and Harper off my body. I needed to get my head on straight.

"Okay, well Amanda called. And don't forget your lunch." I nodded and Donna left.

I put my phone on speaker and dialed the house while I took off my jacket and hung it on the back of the door.

"Hey, peanut. Donna said you called. Are you not at gymnastics today?" I took a seat at my desk and turned on my laptop.

"Um, no. It got canceled."

Odd. I was pretty sure Marion would have told me. "It was?" I asked as I scanned my emails.

"Yeah, so I thought maybe I could come into the city tonight and we could go dress shopping tomorrow?" Her tone was bright and matter of fact. She knew I couldn't say no to her I'm-such-a-good-girl voice. "I thought you might help me shop?"

"Did Marion say she'd bring you on the train?" I hoped she didn't think she was coming on her own.

"Aunt Scarlett said she'd bring me, then I could come home with you tomorrow."

"Did Scarlett say she was staying over?" The last thing I wanted was my sister in my apartment meddling.

"No, she has a date."

Dating? She hadn't shared that with me. I'd thought she was still sworn off men after her divorce.

"You should take a leaf out of her book, Dad."

Harper's satisfied smile ran across my brain. Maybe dating would help get her out of my system.

"You keep me plenty busy," I replied. "What time are you planning to arrive tonight with Scarlett?"

"I can come?"

I could hear Amanda's smile, and I couldn't help but grin. I was a sucker for that smile.

"I'm not going to let my little girl go shopping for her eighth grade dance on her own, now am I?"

She shrieked and I turned down the volume on my phone, wincing. "You've got a key, so just let yourself in if I'm not there."

"Can we get takeout?"

I rolled my eyes. "Maybe."

"And watch a mob movie like we did last time?"

I chuckled. Because Amanda didn't have a lot of her

stuff in the apartment, when she visited we usually ended up hanging out, eating takeout and watching movies. I loved it.

"No promises. I want you to swear you'll do your piano practice before you leave. If you don't pass the exam, your mother will move you to Zurich."

"It's a deal." The piano began to chime in the background. "You hear that? I've started already."

I shook my head. "See you later, peanut."

"Love you, Dad."

The three best words on the planet.

"Love you, Amanda."

As I hung up, Donna walked in.

"If you're leaving early tomorrow to go shopping, let's do a quick walk-through of your schedule for today and tomorrow."

I leaned back in my chair. "I see the women in my life know what I'm doing before I do."

"Did you ever have any doubt?"

I sighed. "I guess not." It was days like this when I felt as though my life didn't belong to me. Having my own business was tough and took up almost all my energy, but usually the rewards of working for myself outweighed the disadvantages. Today the scales were tipping in the wrong direction. I just wanted to shrug off the constant demands on my time, to check out for a day—fuck around on the internet, go ride my bike, speak to Harper. Though I had no idea what I'd say. Apologize, maybe.

"Do we need to cancel anything?" I asked.

"No, but the meeting with Andrew and his contact at JD Stanley is at ten, and I'm guessing you won't want to miss that?"

She was right. I didn't want to miss it. I was hoping for a

little inside knowledge about JD Stanley, the only major investment bank King & Associates didn't work with.

"No, Amanda can hang out at the apartment until after lunch tomorrow. Do we have anything in the afternoon?"

"A meeting with Harper at three, but I can push it to next week." As Donna said her name my face heated and the blood in my veins seemed to speed up.

I ran a finger around my collar. How was I going to approach her? Should I say sorry? She'd been just as up for things as I had, but I was her boss. I didn't want her to think it could happen again. Maybe I should be upfront with her, tell her she was great, but it was a one-time deal. Or should I just pretend it hadn't happened? I had no idea.

"Yeah, that's fine." I was the last person she probably wanted to see. After all, she thought I was an asshole.

I'D BEEN GLUED to my iPhone, taking my office mobile while Amanda was in the changing room in the small Midtown boutique we were in. My fingers hovered over my emails. Should I drop Harper a note? But I had no idea what I'd say. This was why the rules of casual sex should be established before anyone got naked. But *she'd* been the one to talk about Vegas. Perhaps we didn't need to have an awkward follow-up conversation to reestablish what had already been said. I stuffed the phone back in my pocket and tried to avoid eye contact with the sales assistants.

"What do you think?" Amanda asked, stepping out of a dressing room.

"Are you fucking kidding me?" I asked, recoiling in shock. Shopping was not my favorite activity to do—Pandora usually bought Amanda's clothes—but I was going to have to be involved in every shopping trip from now to eternity if she thought she was going to wear *that*.

Amanda rolled her eyes. "Dad, don't swear."

Don't swear? She was lucky I didn't kill someone. Someone like the designer of the dress she had on. "Take that off, right now. You're fourteen not twenty-five." It showed way too much skin—there seemed to be nothing holding it up and it was about three feet too short. It was as if she was wearing a towel.

"I'm not a child."

I didn't need a reminder she was growing up far too fast. "Yes, you are. That's what fourteen is. And a child doesn't get to wear dresses that don't have arms."

"It's called strapless."

"I don't care what it's called—it barely covers your butt. You're not wearing it." It seemed like yesterday that she'd refused to wear anything but a tutu. That particular obsession had lasted three months. She used to sleep in the thing. I'd laughed when Pandora had asked me to try to coax her out of it. I'd loved it. She'd looked adorable and it made her so happy —what more could I wish for? A tutu would be good right about now. Amanda glared at me. "I mean it, go change."

"I don't work for you. You can't just order me around."

I stared right back, raising my eyebrows. There was no way I was backing down on this. "If you want to go to the dance, you'll go back in there and change." I nodded toward the curtain behind her. "I'll be out here trying to find some-thing appropriate for you to wear."

"Thanks, Coco Chanel."

I wanted to laugh, but she needed to understand that under no circumstances would she be wearing something made for a twenty-five-year-old trying to get laid. Apart from anything else, Pandora would cut off my balls. I was going to have to get proactive.

"Excuse me," I said to the shop assistant. "Can you show me some age-appropriate dresses for my fourteen-year-old daughter?" I'd left Amanda to pick her own outfit. That had been a mistake. I could have headed off this problem before she'd changed into anything.

"Certainly, sir," the tall, blonde woman said. "It's so nice to see a father taking his daughter shopping." She smiled as if she wanted me to respond, but I wasn't in the mood for chitchat. I wanted to find a dress and take Amanda to Serendipity, where we could catch up over ice-cream sundaes and forget she was growing up.

"What about this?" The assistant held up a very short, baby-blue dress.

"Something longer," I said.

"Dad," Amanda called. I turned to see her in a skin-tight dress that looked like it was made of strips of horizontal material sewn together.

I strode toward her. "Get that off. Right now."

"It has sleeves," she said, holding out her arms.

True, but it left nothing to the imagination, clinging to her teenage body and barely covering her bottom. There was no way she was going out in public in that.

"Get it off," I snapped.

She let out a grunt of frustration and stomped back into the changing room.

"This," the assistant said, holding up a pink-lace dress, "is a very popular dress this season."

It looked as though it would hit the floor when Amanda tried it on, so that was a plus. It also had long sleeves. I stepped closer. "Is that see-through?" I asked, staring at the dress. For a second, I imagined Harper in the dress. The color would suit her.

"It's sheer, but the lace covers all the important bits, so it looks more revealing than it is," the assistant said, dissolving my thoughts of Harper.

What was the matter with people? "My daughter is fourteen. She doesn't do revealing, not even fake revealing." I turned toward the dressing room. "Amanda," I shouted. "Get dressed. We're going somewhere else." Clearly this store was in the market to dress up little girls like hookers, so we wouldn't find anything here.

Amanda didn't speak as she emerged from the changing rooms, walked straight past me and out the door into the heat. I followed her as she headed east.

"Where do you want to go now?" I asked.

"Home."

"I thought you wanted a dress?"

"Not if you're going to growl at the clerks and tell me I look slutty in everything."

I sighed. "I don't growl."

She raised her eyebrows at me.

"And you could never look slutty."

She shook her head. "I'm growing up, Dad. You've got to get your head around it."

I preferred it when Amanda screamed and cried to when she was resigned and disappointed in me. All I wanted was for her to be happy. Dressed in a burka, but happy.

"You know I love you, right?" I asked. "And I just want what's best for you."

She shrugged. "It's just you totally go off the deep end. You can have a conversation with me, you know? Use logic rather than just have a meltdown."

I tuned into the thump of my footsteps compared to the light patter of hers. "Yeah, you're right. I could have approached things a different way." I'd just been so stunned, but I didn't want a relationship where we were just fighting from now until she went to college. "I just don't want you growing up too fast, that's all."

"I know, Dad. But it's happening."

She was turning into my shrink slash daughter. "Okay, well you be patient with me and I'll try not to have a meltdown. How about that for the terms of a peace treaty?"

"We can try that," she said, shrugging.

We paused at the corner of Fifty-Sixth and Park. "Serendipity?" I asked.

She nodded. At least that was one thing she hadn't grown out of. Yet.

"You going to put bricks on my head?" she asked.

I'd teased her when she was younger about stunting her growth. Back then she'd seemed to sprout a foot a month. It was like seeing time pass right in front of my eyes.

"If you had a girlfriend, this would be easier."

I chuckled, trying to ignore the flashes of Harper's smile as Amanda said the word *girlfriend*. "How do you figure?" I asked as Amanda linked her arm through mine.

"She'd tell you that those dresses looked pretty on me," she said as we crossed the street, trying to dodge the mix of office workers and tourists coming at us from the opposite direction.

"Amanda, you'd look pretty in anything. That's not the point. A girlfriend wouldn't change my mind about you wearing clothes meant for women much older than you." I liked her dressed as she was now, in jeans and a T-shirt.

"But another girl, an adult, might be able to convince you."

"Honestly, no one would be able to change my mind, and anyway, you have your aunts, and Grandma King and Granny. And your mom. They're girls."

"Mom doesn't count because she's not here. And you've never listened to anything your sisters told you."

"I listen to Violet." I couldn't exactly pinpoint the last time I'd taken her advice, but I was sure there was an example. "And I don't have time for a girlfriend." I hadn't even had a chance to speak to Harper or to think what to say when we did speak.

"Grandpa always said you can always find time to do the things you want to do."

My dad was a very wise man, but I didn't appreciate his advice in this instance. Maybe because it cut a little too close to the bone.

"You could just agree to go to dinner with Scarlett's friend."

"What friend?" I asked as my cell buzzed in my pocket.

"You know, the one Scarlett mentioned earlier?"

I'd clearly tuned out when my sister was speaking. I didn't remember her mentioning anyone. "I don't remember."

"You do. Her friend from college who used to live in LA." She tugged on my jacket. "Please, Dad?"

"Why is this so important to you?" I didn't understand why she was so set on me dating. Was she trying to distract me, hoping if I was dating I'd suddenly have a change of heart about the hair dye and appropriate clothing?

She shrugged. "It's one night out of your life."

God, she sounded like my mother.

"And I'll do piano practice for a week without you having to ask. Think of it as the bill of rights to our treaty."

Maybe having dinner with a woman would get Harper

out of my system. She wasn't the only smart, ballsy, beau-tiful woman in New York City after all. "I shouldn't have to force you to do piano."

"It's up to you." She shrugged. "Seems like a sweet deal to me."

"A month. And you have to drop the whining about the hair dye."

She grinned up at me. "Deal."

Anything to keep my daughter happy—well, anything but a short, tight, or low-cut dress for her eighth grade dance.

FIVE

Harper

Max. Fucking. King.

I thought I'd hated him before but his assholyness had reached dizzying new heights. I stomped into my bedroom, threw the lid off my laundry basket, and started pulling out things to take to wash. I needed to channel my energy into something productive.

Okay, I had to take responsibility. I'd fucked him. I'd *wanted* to fuck him. And it had been great—a release, no more than that. It had been amazing, as if he'd known what I needed before I did. And he'd had all the right equipment and he'd known how to use it. But he hadn't spoken to me since that night two days ago. Hadn't even looked at me. We'd agreed on Vegas; I'd suggested it. But he didn't have to ignore me.

Arrogant men should be illegal. Or sent to an island without any women on it to die of sexual frustration.

Coming to my rescue in the gym suggested he wasn't quite the asshole I thought he was. Then seeing him shirtless, and the way he'd growled at me, like an animal? Well, I don't know what had come over me, but any willpower I'd had just dissolved, and I'd wanted him.

But what had I been thinking? Fucking my boss was a bad idea for so many reasons. I desperately wanted him to think I was good at my job, not just know my depilatory habits. I'd worked hard for this position, and I didn't just want him to see me as a piece of ass. I certainly didn't want it getting out and people to start gossiping about how I was sleeping my way to the top or an easy lay.

Thank God it was Friday and I wouldn't have to see him for two whole days. Not that I had to worry about that —he'd canceled three meetings with me just to avoid me. Which was the behavior of a fifteen-year-old boy.

It wasn't as if I'd expected a ring, or dinner. But, hell, a "Hello, how are you, thanks for the hot sex" was surely only polite.

I grabbed my clothes, piled them into a huge Ikea bag, and dumped it by the door, ready to head down to the laundry room. I just had to find the bra I'd taken off in front of the TV earlier that week. As I entered the sitting area, the ceiling rattled with the clip of heels. Jesus, it had only been two days since Max's dick had been in me, and now he was banging some other girl. I pitied any girl dumb enough to fuck Max King. Which, apparently, included me.

I let out a yell of frustration, then covered my mouth. Had he heard that? I didn't want him to think I cared if he had another girl in the apartment.

I didn't give a shit.

But the last thing I wanted to do was sit here listening to my boss fuck someone else. Maybe it wasn't another woman. Maybe Max liked to dress up. Nothing about that man would surprise me anymore. I smiled, happy with that particular constructed reality.

Feeling under the couch cushions, I grasped a bra strap, then pulled it free and threw it over to join the rest of my laundry. I grabbed my keys from the side table, a report from work, and the detergent I'd bought on my way home from the office. I had at least three loads to do and if I stayed down there, I'd avoid the sexcapades of Max King. As I headed for the elevator, dragging the bag of clothes behind me, the clitter-clatter of heels seemed to follow me out of the door.

The elevator didn't take as long as usual, and I realized it had come straight from the penthouse. When the doors pinged open I came face to face with the knowledge it hadn't been Max wearing the high heels after all. There was only one apartment above me, so the woman Max King had just fucked would be standing before me.

I wanted the kind of superpower where I could stop time and rearrange things. Then I could hide and ensure that when the elevator stopped on my floor, the beauty in front of me would wonder why it had stopped at all. Instead, I had to step into the elevator in my sweats, forced to look up to smile when the gorgeous woman said, "Good evening."

"Hi," I replied as I discreetly studied her. I'd always wanted to be blonde. I'd tried to dye my hair once, but it just turned out a little like orange cotton candy. At least three inches taller than me, she made me feel like a hobbit standing next to her Arwen. Any moment now she'd ruffle my hair and say, "You're a dear little thing."

Max King might be an asshole, but he had great taste in women, even if I did say so myself.

It wasn't as if I'd expected anything from Max, but it

stung a little to run into his latest conquest when he hadn't even given me the time of day. Asshole.

"Another glamourous Friday night in New York City?" she asked, smiling as she gestured toward my bag of laundry.

What a bitch. She didn't know I wasn't going out later with a hot guy or a hotter girl. "Something like that," I replied. "But better that than waste my time on men who don't deserve me."

She laughed. "Yes, doing laundry is preferable to spending time with most of the men I've dated."

Okay, maybe she was being funny rather than bitchy. Did she realize what an asshole Max was? Should I warn her?

"Let's hope my date tonight raises the bar," she said. "He seems nice so far, and every now and then you have to take a chance on someone, right?"

I couldn't reply but smiled manically. She thought Max was nice? Oh yeah, a nice kind of *asshole*.

The elevator doors opened and she stepped out.

"Enjoy your evening," she said with a little wave.

Max King was notoriously guarded about his private life. He never mentioned anyone in the articles I'd read about him. It had led to some speculation he was gay. If he was, he certainly did a great impression of a straight man. And he didn't owe me anything, but just because we'd gone to Vegas, didn't mean I wanted him making the trip with someone else quite so soon.

When the elevator got to the basement I got out, dragging my laundry behind me. Maybe I should think about trying to sublet my place and move to Brooklyn after all.

I'd dumped my Ikea bag on the floor, muttering to myself, when I realized I wasn't the only one in the laundry room. A young teen sitting on the long table opposite the washers and dryers caught my eye. I looked up.

"Hi," I said.

"Hey," she replied with a smile. Papers on her lap, she looked like she was doing homework.

"Are you hiding?" I asked. I'd loved escaping from real life at her age. There was never any peace in my house growing up, and I'd longed for quiet.

She furrowed her brow as if thinking hard about my question. "Not really. I'm doing laundry and homework at the same time."

"You do your own laundry?" I flipped open the washer and began to fish out my towels from the bag.

She shrugged. "Only certain times of the month. When I'm at my dad's place there are some things . . ."

"I get it. Boys have it easy, huh?"

She rolled her eyes and I wanted to chuckle. She was a pretty girl with olive skin and long dark hair that fell around her shoulders.

"*So* easy. I mean, no periods? How did God decide that was fair?"

I shut the first washer and flipped open a second. "Well, you've got to assume God is a man, right?" I pulled out my colored items and loaded up the machine. "And I guess he understood that men are such babies they wouldn't be able to cope."

"Babies is right. They squeal when they don't get their way, just like infants."

I laughed. "You're totally right."

"And they always think they're right about *everything*. My dad went ballistic yesterday because I picked out a dress for my eighth grade dance he didn't like." She leaned forward, making circles in the air with her hands. "I told him I'm growing up and that wearing a strapless dress doesn't make me a slut."

"No, it doesn't. But I guess dads have a different view. I can't say because I didn't have a father growing up." I'd always wanted an overprotective father. Someone who would tell my boyfriends to treat me well and keep their hands to themselves. My dad hadn't known when my eighth grade dance was, let alone had an opinion regarding my dress.

"You didn't? Did he die?" she asked, seemingly unaware of how personal her question was.

I smiled. "No. He just wasn't interested in me."

The girl paused and then said, "Well my dad is entirely too interested. I thought my mom was strict."

"What does your mom say about the dress?"

She shrugged. "Dad has the final say. Before she used to be able to talk him around, but now?" She shook her head. "I keep telling him he needs a girlfriend. He needs an adult to tell him I'm right sometimes."

"You want your dad to have a girlfriend?" Didn't kids want divorced parents to get back together rather than move on?

"Sure. He's been on his own for so long and I want him to be happy. I don't ever remember him having a girlfriend, and my mom has Jason. They've been married *forever*. I don't want my dad to be on his own."

Maybe her dad was still in love with her mom? "Does your father get along with your stepdad?"

"Yeah. They used to play basketball every week."

Okay maybe her dad wasn't hung up on her mom. "Wow, that sounds like a friendly divorce," I said.

She frowned. "My mom and dad were never married."

That sounded familiar. Poor girl. Loser dad not wanting

to take responsibility—I knew how that one went. I stayed quiet, not wanting to make her feel bad.

"Dad just works too hard, and we have fun but I think he needs fun with a girlfriend. You know. Plus, I'd like to have someone to hang out with, go shopping with. And most of all, I'd like a baby sister. I've always been the only kid around, amongst a bunch of adults. I'm always the youngest and it sucks."

I laughed. "You're trying to get him to have another baby? You have to go easy on him." I began to load a third washer with my whites. "He'd probably be just the same if he were married. Sounds like he cares about you. And because he is a man, your dad knows what goes on in boys' heads." They thought about sex a *lot*. I could understand her father's concerns. She was sweet and beautiful.

"Do you have a boyfriend?" she asked.

I shook my head. "Nope. I'm concentrating on my work for now." Which was true. I wasn't interested in the distraction a man would bring to my life at the moment. Max King had been just about sex, which was exactly what I wanted. I needed to find someone to fuck who wasn't my boss and wasn't an asshole.

"That's always my dad's answer."

"I'm not good at picking guys." I wasn't sure if I wasn't good at picking them or I wasn't looking for the right thing. I knew what I didn't want. I knew someone who put family first was important to me, and most of the men I came across were driven and ambitious. I didn't want a man who didn't understand what should be a priority. I didn't want a man like my father.

"I figure I'll work hard, make my own money, have fun, and see if Prince Charming shows up unexpectedly." Seemed unlikely but I hadn't entirely given up hope. "The thing about boys is that you can think they're going to be one thing and they turn out to be entirely another." Max King was a perfect example of that. I still didn't really know who he was. Was he an asshole? Someone who cared about a downtown deli-owner's business? Or just a man who knew how to fuck? Maybe all of the above.

"Really?" she asked, her eyes wide.

"Sure. Be careful to avoid the guys who tell you how great they are. I'm looking for a man who *shows* me what a great guy he is." By ignoring me, Max had proved he was an asshole. "Judge people by their actions, not their words."

"Everyone keeps telling me that Callum Ryder likes me, but he hasn't asked me to the dance."

"Does that happen in the eighth grade? You go as boy-girl couples?"

She tucked her hair around her ear. "You don't go together. I guess it just means you'll dance with them when you're there."

That made more sense. "Right. And you want Callum Ryder to ask you?"

"Well, if he likes me, I thought he would."

"But do you like him? Don't be satisfied with a boy just because he likes you." I poured detergent into the machines.

"He's popular, and good at sports."

"Do you get butterflies in your stomach when you see him?" I asked. I might not like him, but Max was hot. And an excellent lay. And I had to admit to a couple of tiny butterflies whenever our eyes met.

"I'm not sure. I don't think so," she replied.

"If he doesn't give you butterflies, he's not worth going toe-to-toe with your dad for. He sounds protective."

I finished loading the final washer and pressed start on all three machines.

"Don't get me wrong, I love my dad. He's just not good with women."

I laughed. "None of them are. It's a good lesson to learn early in life."

"And he wants me to stay a baby. I don't want go to my eighth grade dance wearing a frilly dress that a three-year-old would wear."

"You got a picture of the strapless one?"

She pulled out her phone, scrolled through photos, then held up her handset. The dress *was* a little revealing. "It's pretty, but I think you can do better by leaving a little more to the imagination," I replied. "Can I?" I held out my hand for her phone.

I hopped up next to her and began to scroll through websites. "Have you thought about one of those dresses with a long sheer skirt over a shorter skirt? That might make him happy."

She grinned at me. "What's your name?" she asked.

"Harper. Finder of eighth-grade-dance dresses."

"I'm Amanda. Needer of an eighth-grade-dance dress."

"It's fate," I said, tapping the phone.

"Do you think I could do strapless if it's long?"

Amanda's father didn't sound like a man who wanted his daughter to show any skin. "I don't think strapless is the most flattering style. I think you can still show off some skin here," I said, sweeping my hand below my neck, "without upsetting your dad. We need to find something off the shoulder. Suits all women, young and old."

Amanda grinned at me. "That sounds like it could work."

"And then maybe something long but with a slit up the leg?" I glanced up from the phone to see Amanda fidgeting excitedly.

We spent the next hour looking at different styles, working out what would be demure enough to please her father, but pretty enough to please her.

Eventually Amanda's laundry was ready. "I better go back. He'll be home from work and wondering where I am. I left a note, but he won't read it." She rolled her eyes. Her phone started to vibrate, *Dad* flashing on the screen. "Speak of the devil."

"Hi, Dad." She rolled her eyes. "Yes, I'm coming up now."

"He has dinner ready," she said. "I better go."

Wow. A man so devoted to his daughter he didn't date, and on top of that he cooked. Sounded like a keeper. "Never say no to a man who can cook. And remember, be nice to him. That's the way to get what you want. Men get taken in so easily by a few compliments." I winked at her.

"Thank you so much." She flung her arms around my neck and I froze, her gesture taking me by surprise.

"I'm going shopping again next week," she said as I squeezed her back. "Yesterday was a total bust, but at least now I won't just try the same things again and have the same argument."

"Exactly. Men have to think they've won. Never let on that really, you've gotten your own way."

Amanda laughed. "I need boy lessons from you."

"Single girl," I said, pointing to myself. "I don't know anything."

"That's not true. I'm not going to listen to a word boys say from now on. I'm only going to watch what they do."

"You'll go far if you remember that. It was so nice to meet you, Amanda. Have fun at your dance."

She took her pile of clean, folded laundry and left me to my three washers, my report, and thoughts of my father.

Was it because Amanda's father was of a younger generation that he was so involved with her growing up? When I
was younger, every now and then my dad had tried to get
involved in my life. I even remembered him coming to a
couple of my school plays. But it had never lasted long and
then we wouldn't see him for months. He'd just disappear
as soon as I started to expect anything of him. I grew out of
any expectation eventually.

Or maybe not. I still wanted him to ask me to go work
for him, even knowing all the times he'd let me down. I
guess I still wanted him to prove with his actions that he
loved me. It would be like he'd turned up for every birthday
and school play. My mother always told me he loved me but
I never saw any evidence. So when I graduated and he
didn't offer me a job, I stopped answering his intermittent
calls. And now my only communications with him
happened through his lawyer.

"IS THAT A PENIS?" I asked Grace matter-of-factly as we
stood in front of a canvas at the exhibition in New Jersey
she'd convinced me to attend. The space wasn't a pretty,
shiny gallery in Chelsea, but a huge warehouse in the
middle of some industrial area. I was pretty sure if we
looked hard enough, we'd find a dead body.

"No, it's not a penis. Why would my boyfriend paint a
gigantic knob?"

"Men are weird. And obsessed with their penis," I
replied. I thought that was obvious. I was always surprised
when male artists *didn't* paint their junk. I was sure Van
Gogh had plenty of penis drawings hidden away in his
attic.

"Many of the great artists painted beautiful women," Grace said.

"Exactly. Because they were obsessed with their penis. Case closed."

"How're things with your asshole boss?" Grace asked as we walked over to a plinth with an empty Perspex case on it.

I hadn't told Grace I'd wound up naked with Max. How could I explain it to her when I didn't understand it myself? She'd think I'd totally lost it. "Still an asshole." Which was true, even more so now that he was ignoring me after the nakedness.

"What are you going to do?" she asked.

I shrugged and took a sip of my warm white wine. "What can I do? I'm just going to grow a thick skin and stick it out." And try not to fuck him again. Scratch that—definitively not fuck him again. I hadn't mentioned to Grace that he lived in the same building. There wasn't any reason to hide that piece of information, but for some reason I didn't feel like sharing.

"Great. So I have to listen to you moan about him for the next two years?"

"You brought it up, and anyway, I have to put up with things like this for you." I twirled my finger in the air, then peered closer at the box in front of us. It was as if someone had stolen the artwork we were meant to be looking at. "Did they forget to put something in here?" I asked.

"No, it's supposed to be some kind of commentary on reality TV and how the public will watch anything the networks commission." Grace pulled her eyebrows together. "I think that's it. Or they might have just forgotten the art."

We giggled before being interrupted by Grace's new boyfriend, Damien, and his very tall friend.

Grace's eyes gleamed as she said, "Harper, this is George."

George had one of those faces people describe as friendly. Five-foot-ten, with brown hair cut short and in a blue, button-down shirt and jeans, he was quite attractive. There was nothing about him that would immediately have me pressing my red emergency button and running for the door, which had happened more often than not when Grace had introduced me to men.

"George, this is Harper, my best friend in the world. Keep her company? Damien's taking me to look at his etchings." Grace pulled Damien's arm, leaving George and I alone and embarrassed.

The word *setup* echoed around the space.

Couldn't we all have just stayed and talked?

"Excuse Grace. She was dropped on her head a lot," I said.

"As a baby?" George asked.

I shook my head. "No, by me, every time she tries to set me up."

He chuckled. "Yeah, she's a force of nature." A half-second of uncomfortable silence followed before George said, "Are you enjoying the art?"

"Honestly, no. I don't get it." I winced as I looked him in the eye.

"Thank God I'm not the only one," he replied, smiling back at me. "Don't tell Damien I said so, but what the fuck? Have you been into the black room?" He pointed across the space to a sectioned-off part of the warehouse. "It's full of women holding their heads and screaming."

"Really?" I asked, intrigued. "Women sick of bad dates? Sorry, present company excepted, of course."

He laughed again. "Maybe. I didn't recognize anyone,

so I'm hopeful none of my exes are in there." He winked and for the first time in my life, instead of getting an urge to put a spoon through a guy's eye, I thought the gesture was cute. "Another drink?"

"The bar I like." We walked toward the biggest crowd of people who all seemed to have similar taste in art—the kind that smelled like wine. "So, tell me about yourself. Was your mother a Wham! fan?"

"No, I'm named after my grandfather, not George Michael. Although I *am* a fan, particularly of his day-glow period."

There weren't many men who made me laugh. Maybe this wouldn't turn out to be the worst setup in the world. We got fresh drinks and found a free spot, away from the crowd and the art.

"I'm an architect, I'm from Ohio, and I don't like cats. You?"

"I'm from Sacramento," I replied. "I don't like cats either and I'm a researcher at a consulting firm."

"Grace said you were new to the city. Did you move for the job?"

"Partly." My move had been totally about King & Associates. I'd have moved anywhere to work with Max King. "And to live in New York."

"And now that you're doing it, is it all you thought it would be?"

"I don't get along with my boss."

"Oh," he said, nodding. "But does anyone? I mean, isn't it like the rule that you hate your boss? Isn't he just there to stand between you and your internet surfing habit?"

I tilted my head. "I don't resent him because he interrupts my online shopping experience. I enjoy what I do. My boss is just rude." And gorgeous. "And arrogant." And great in bed. "And ungrateful." And kisses as if it was his major in college. Max King was a man who had every right to be obsessed with his penis.

George had a dimple that appeared on the left of his face when he smiled. "I have my own firm. I wonder if one of the guys working for me is standing at a party having the exact same conversation about me."

I winced. "God, I'm sorry. I'm sure that's not happening—"

"Don't sweat it. Like I said, I think it's part of the job—some people aren't ever going to like you."

"And you're okay with that?" I asked, genuinely interested.

"I'm not sure I've thought about it. Whether or not I'm okay with it, it's still going to happen, right? Not everyone likes you, do they?"

I laughed. "Hey, you've only known me a few minutes and already you think people must hate me?"

"It's not personal. And when you're signing someone's paycheck, things just get magnified. Normally, if you don't get along with people, you don't have chemistry with someone, you can just avoid them. But at work, you're forced to spend time with them, so you're just more aware that you don't like the person."

Generally, he made sense, but he hadn't met the specific asshat that was Max King. "I guess."

"How about I distract you from work one night this week, take you to dinner and prove not all bosses are evil?"

I bit the edge of my plastic cup. "This week?" I asked.

"Yeah, unless you're booked up already."

"No. Not booked up." Did I want to go to dinner with George? The memory of Max's hips pinning me to the wall of his apartment flashed through my head. I touched my neck, as if I could still feel his breath whispering against my skin. "Dinner sounds good."

I needed new memories to replace the ones of Max King.

MONDAY AT KING & Associates was busier than I'd expected. I'd gotten pulled in on a new, high profile research project on luxury goods in China. I'd been so excited I'd almost forgotten Max King was my boss. For the first time in forever, I left work with a smile on my face, despite it being past eight.

"Hi, Barry." I waved at the doorman as I passed his desk and pressed the elevator button. I wanted a warm bath, my bed, and maybe a smidgen of *Game of Thrones*.

As the doors slid open, Max stood in front of me in his workout clothes, tall, handsome, and staring at his phone.

God-damn you, Lycra.

I froze, unsure what to do. Was he coming out or going down to the basement? At that moment he glanced up and for the first time since he'd made me come a bazillion times, he looked me in the eye.

"Harper," he said, a note of surprise in his voice.

Had he thought he'd never see me again? I worked for him, lived in his building, for Christ's sake. Maybe he wasn't as smart as people said he was.

"Going up?" I asked.

"No, yes." He sounded confused. "Get in. I've been wanting to speak to you."

"Well you know where I live, and you know where I work, so I'm not sure you gave yourself the most impossible task there." I tapped my forehead. "You just had to set your mind to it."

He grabbed my elbow with his large hand and immediately warmth flooded my body. He pulled me into the elevator just as he had when I'd turned up at his apartment door to complain about the noise, and just like that I was surrounded by him, his smell, the nearness of his breath, his tongue, and his cock.

SIX

Max

"Get your hands off me," she spat, twisting her arm and forcing me to release her.

"I thought we'd have a chance to speak at work—"

"Funny thing is, when you cancel meetings with people, it means that you don't see them."

Had I canceled meetings? "Last week was difficult. And Donna controls my schedule. I didn't deliberately—"

"Save your breath."

The elevator stopped at the basement and its doors opened. I'd been heading to the gym.

"We live in the same building. You could have knocked on my door." She folded her arms.

I had to try very hard not to smile. She was so pretty, despite her mood. Maybe even because of her mood.

"Are you getting out?" she asked.

I shook my head and she started jabbing at the seventh-floor button. "I couldn't knock on your door. I know you live on the seventh floor because you complained about the stomping on your ceiling, but there are five apartments down there. Trust me." I pulled her chin up with my index finger. "I counted them on Thursday evening."

Her stare was blank. "It's Monday, Max."

It was strange, hearing my name on her lips again. Last time I heard it she'd been about to climax.

I reached out and smoothed her hair over her shoulders. "I'm sorry." It was true; I was. Since the day Amanda was born, I'd sworn I wouldn't be the guy who messed around with women. If I didn't want anyone to do it to my daughter, I couldn't very well do it to someone else's. I might only have casual relationships, but I didn't ever pretend it was anything more. "I wasn't ignoring you. Frankly, I hadn't expected you to have gone when I woke up. I thought we'd talk before work."

"Yeah, well I wanted to be at work on time." She shrugged and I'd taken a half step toward her when the doors opened. I liked her sass. The employees at King & Associates came packaged earnest and compliant. Other than Donna, everyone just nodded their heads and said yes to me. At home, the world tipped on its head, and it was a miracle if I ever got anyone to say yes to anything. Harper continued to blur the boundaries between my work and personal life.

"You made me late," I said, not ready for our conversation to be over.

"What are you doing?" Harper asked as I followed her out of the elevator. "This isn't your floor."

"I want to talk to you." I wasn't sure what I was doing. What could I say to her? "I want to apologize," I said decisively. "For the other night. I shouldn't have taken advantage in the way I did." It was just that all the fantasies that had been filling my brain since she started at King & Associates had come rushing back when she'd stood semi-naked in front of me.

She opened her front door, stepped into her apartment, and spun to face me. "Take advantage? Jesus, you're such a fucking asshole." She tried to slam the door shut but I stuck my foot in the way.

"Get the fuck out," she yelled.

"I think you're beautiful," I said and pushed the door open and stepped inside. "Beautiful, but supremely fucking irritating."

She stared at me, her mouth open as if I'd just stolen all her words. Then she turned, threw her purse down, and stomped over to her bed. I glanced around. Her apartment was tiny and full of things everywhere including piles of books stacked on the floor and shoes wherever I looked. The bed was over to one side, where the floor was slightly raised. She kicked off her shoes and started to undo her blouse. I hardened immediately. She was undressing?

"Harper," I said as I followed her.

"I'm irritating?" she asked.

I didn't know how to react. I wanted to pin her down and make her listen to me. Kiss her. Fuck her.

"I'm irritating?" She shook her head in disbelief and turned to face me. "*I'm* fucking irritating?"

How could I make her see what I meant? I grabbed one of her hands, pulled her toward me, and kissed her. She broke free and pushed at my chest, but I snaked my arms around her so she couldn't escape. Eventually, she stopped trying to move away from me, accepted she was trapped, and stilled. "Kiss me, Harper," I said. "Do as I say."

"You're an asshole," she said as she punched me in the shoulder.

I brought my hands to her face and her lips to mine. She didn't resist. I snaked my tongue into her mouth and found hers hot and ready. I groaned against her lips and slid my hand down to her ass, to pull her against me so she could feel my erection. Her fingers slid into my hair and our kisses became frantic, biting and greedy.

She ended our kiss and moved away. "Max?"

I wasn't sure what came next. Why had she pulled out of my arms? Was she going to ask me to leave? "Yes?" I replied.

"Get your clothes off and fuck me," she said.

I grinned as she began to undo the rest of the buttons on her shirt, her fingers fumbling over each one.

"Come here," I said as I knocked her hands out of the way.

"Be careful with that. This blouse is new and I can't afford to replace it."

I'd undone the buttons before she'd finished her sentence and slid the silk over her shoulders. Her skin looked so smooth that I bent to kiss the exposed, bronzed flesh, desperate to feel her under my lips. She tipped her head back and I grinned against her skin.

"Asshole, huh?" I pulled off my running top and stepped out of my shorts.

"Do you want me to change my mind?" She cocked her hip, the bra straps falling from her shoulders.

"You're not going to change your mind," I said, leaning toward her, pushing her skirt up around her waist, and thrusting my hand into her underwear.

"Don't," she said, her voice breathy. "I can't ruin this

skirt. I just bought it." My fingers pressed into her folds and though she wasn't fighting me off, I could tell she was concerned about her clothes. Why?

"Lie down," I said, guiding her to the bed, where I quickly slid off her skirt and panties.

"Max . . ."

I wanted to sink into the way she called my name.

"Yes?" I kissed up the inside of her thigh, along her soft, tight skin, reaching her pussy. I gave her one long lick over her slit but continued to work my way up over her belly and between her breasts. The pace was slower than last week. Her anger had ebbed away and just existed in the way every now and then she scored her fingernails up my arms or whispered, "You're an asshole," as I continued to kiss and lick and suck her entire body.

She reached above her head, pointing at her nightstand. "Condom," she said. She might think I was an asshole, but she didn't mind my dick. I grabbed a condom and as quickly as I could, rolled it on. As I lay on my back, Harper rose off the bed and began to straddle me.

"I don't think so," I said, pushing her to her back. "I'm fucking you. You're not fucking me." I nudged her knees wide with my legs and pushed into her. Her eyebrows pulled together as she concentrated on not making the sound of pleasure I could tell was rippling below the surface. I pulled out and thrust in, wanting to set that moan free.

"If you're going to fuck me, you'd better make it good," she said.

Highly. Fucking. Irritating.

She knew this was so fucking good. I grabbed her leg and lifted it, going deeper, showing how good it was.

She bit down on her lip, still swallowing her reactions.

"Really? You're not going to tell me how good this is?" I asked, panting, pushing into her, feeling her pulse beneath me. "You're not going to say how this is the best you've ever had?" I slammed into her, pushing her up the bed, my jaw tightening.

"Fuck you," she bit out.

"You know it is. You love my dick inside you, making you come. You can't get enough."

A deep moan ripped from her chest. *Finally.*

"There, you see? You just need to give in and realize how good I make you feel."

She tightened around me, lifting her hips to meet my thrusts. A rumble vibrated up my throat at the dizzying sensation. "So. Fucking. Good."

She scratched her nails so hard down my back it interrupted my rhythm. When I glanced at her, she grinned. I pulled her arms down and slid my palms against hers, pinning her to the mattress, and began to push into her again. "Watch your manners, Ms. Jayne. If you're not careful, I won't let you come."

She raised an eyebrow. "As if you could stop me."

She had no idea.

I stilled. "Wanna test that theory?" She squirmed underneath me, desperate for more of my cock. "Yeah, I didn't think so."

"You're an arrogant pig," she spat out and turned her head to the side.

"I think what you meant to say is 'thank you for fucking me.'" I moved on top of her, grinding into her. I might be baiting her, but really I wanted to scream at how perfect she was, how good she made me feel. All these months of denying I wanted her burst out. Harper Jayne was every bit as sexy, passionate, and greedy as I'd imagined.

Her breaths were short and needy and her sounds louder and less and less controlled.

"You're beautiful. And sexy and—" I paused a second. I had to be careful I didn't come first. "And you drive me crazy at work." I thrust again. "Because I want to bend you over my desk and drive my cock into you. Just. Like. That."

She screamed as she came, rippling around me, pulling my come from my cock, milking it, owning it. I couldn't resist her and came, roaring her name.

I collapsed on top of her and savored the feel of my hot skin covering hers.

Rolling onto my back, I reached out and slid her into my arms.

"You looking for a high five?" she asked and I chuckled.

"Stop being annoying for five seconds and come here," I said. She moved a few inches closer and settled into me. "So irritating." I kissed the top of her head.

After a few minutes she pushed herself up on her elbow. "Do you really think about fucking me over your desk?"

I groaned. "You can't question me on stuff I say while I'm fucking."

"Why?" she asked. "Is this some rule I don't know about?"

"Yes, it's a rule. The first rule of dirty talk is that after you come, you don't discuss what was said in the heat of the moment."

I expected abuse in response, but she was quiet for a few moments before saying, "Oh. I didn't know." It was such an uncharacteristic reply. I wanted to ask her what she was thinking but despite the fact that three minutes ago I'd been fucking her, it seemed like prying.

I pulled her closer.

"Did you look at my revised Bangladesh report?"

Did she really just ask me that? "No."

"No?" she asked. "You've had it nearly a week." She ran her fingertips over my chest.

"No, we're not talking about it now. Fucking hell, Harper, I just came like five seconds ago. I don't want to be reminded of the fact that fucking you is totally inappropriate."

"Inappropriate?" she yelled. Were we back to the shouting already? "Get the fuck out of my bed." She tried to push me off the mattress.

Jesus. I couldn't do anything right with this girl. Except make her come, apparently.

I gripped her wrists and she started to kick me, so I rolled her to her back and pinned her thighs to the bed to stop her thrashing. "Jesus, woman, you go from zero to sixty in a millisecond." She closed her eyes and turned her head to the side.

"Get off me."

"Not until you tell me what's wrong and why you're freaking out."

"Unbelievable."

At least she turned and looked at me.

"What?" I asked.

"You just told me fucking me is inappropriate. Like your body acted without your consent. And you expect me not to have a reaction to that? You're an—"

"Asshole," I said, finishing her sentence. "Yes, I heard you the first fifteen thousand times you said it." I released her and rolled off the bed, pissed she was giving me such a hard time every second of every minute of every day. I was her boss; of course it was inappropriate for me to fuck her. I grabbed my shorts and T-shirt and dressed quickly.

"And now you're just going to go?" she asked, propped up on her elbows, her perfectly round tits begging me to come back to bed.

"Did you forget that you ordered me out of your apartment?"

"Whatever." She leapt out of bed and barged into the bathroom, slamming the door shut behind her.

Fucking hell. She was a total pain in the ass. Beautiful. Talented. Sexy. Perfectly infuriating.

Had I been an asshole? She was irritating, but maybe I shouldn't have told her fucking her was inappropriate right after we had sex. I wasn't used to having to mind what I said with the women I was fucking.

I sat on the edge of her bed, waiting for twenty minutes for her to emerge.

"Hi," she said when she finally came out wearing a towel. Her eyes kept flickering from me to the floor.

"Hi," I replied. "I didn't mean to upset you." I never meant to upset the women in my life but it happened far too often.

"Mean it or not, you did." She shook her head. "I don't know what it is. Maybe you don't realize how you come off."

I scrubbed my hands over my face. "I'm not good with . . ." How did I say I wasn't used to having to interact with the women I was fucking outside the bedroom?

"Women?" She finished my sentence for me, arching her eyebrow.

"I don't want to piss you off, Harper." Yes it would be awkward at work, but I actually liked the girl. "I'm the person who signs your paychecks. That's all I was trying to say."

"You need to think about what you say before you say it."

I nodded. "I'll do better in the future."

She stepped toward me. "Okay. The future starts now, right?"

I pulled her onto my lap. I cupped her neck and pressed my lips against hers. Immediately I wanted her again. It wasn't as if we were in the office anyway. Here we were neighbors, not colleagues. I tugged at her towel and it fell away from her body.

"Yeah. The future starts right now."

THE NEXT MORNING I got into the office extra early. I was trying to finish going through Harper's Bangladesh report. I didn't want any other reason for Harper to think I was an asshole.

"I said no calls, Donna," I barked into my speakerphone, then hung up.

My door burst open and I slammed my hand on my desk as I looked up.

"Max, you're going to want to take this call," Donna said. I seriously doubted it. Other than something happening to Amanda—shit. "Press line one."

Instead of leaving me to take the call, she shut the door and leaned against it, a huge grin on her face. Amanda must be okay if Donna was smiling. In fact, this probably was Amanda telling me she'd been asked to her eighth grade dance.

Just as I picked up the receiver and punched line one, Donna said, "Charles Jayne."

Fuck.

Charles Jayne was the founder and senior partner of JD Stanley. His investment bank didn't use outside firms, but I wanted them to make an exception for King & Associates. I'd been hounding them for years. They didn't use outside firms, but I wanted them to make an exception for King & Associates.

"Max King," I answered, trying to keep my voice level as my foot tapped against the desk leg.

"I hear you've been making quite a nuisance of yourself with my director of global research," a man with a deep voice said on the other end of the phone.

Shit, had I pushed things too far? My contact had given me the inside track on Harold Barker. Apparently he liked tennis, so I'd suggested he join me in my box at the US Open later in the summer. I'd invited him to the Met once when I'd run into him at a cocktail reception, but he'd politely declined. I was hoping tennis would hit the spot.

"It's a pleasure to speak to you, sir. I'm not sure I'd describe myself as a nuisance. I just think that we could do a lot for JD Stanley, and I'd like an opportunity to show you what's possible."

"Yes, well, that much you've made clear," he replied. "Which is why I'm calling. Come in on the twenty-fourth and tell us a little about what you do at King & Associates."

Holy crap.

"Yes, sir. What—"

"Ten sharp. You better live up to your hype."

Before I could ask him how long we had, who would be in the room, what he wanted to know, the line went dead. I guess when you were Charles Jayne, you didn't want to waste a second.

I hung up and stared at the phone.

Donna bounded across the room. "Well? What did he want?"

"To give me the opportunity of my career." Had that really just happened? Just like that, Charles Jayne had called and invited me in for a meeting.

"He's going to hire you?"

I shrugged. "He wants me to go in for a meeting on the twenty-fourth."

"I can't believe it," Donna said. "Looks like Harper was a smart hire."

What? I stared at her, expecting her to explain.

"I'm sure your networking helped, but hiring Harper was genius."

"Why does that matter?"

"Well, she's his daughter, right?"

"Harper?" Harper *Jayne*. I'd never made the connection.

"You didn't know?" Donna asked. "That wasn't the reason you hired her?"

"Jesus, you must think I'm a real prick. I wouldn't hire someone just because they had a connection to Charles Jayne. And since when do I get involved with hiring junior researchers?"

Is that what Harper thought? But how could she? She didn't know about my obsession with JD Stanley. "Are you sure that Charles Jayne is Harper's father?" I asked. "I mean, has she acknowledged it? Have you spoken about it?"

Donna blinked. "No, I just assumed, with her name and all. I've never mentioned it."

"Could be a coincidence," I said, thinking out loud.

"Do you want me to ask her?"

Did I? I wanted to know if there was a connection. Had she arranged the meeting?

My mind was a mess. Was Harper just here to spy on things before Charles Jayne decided to invite me to pitch?

"No, I'll ask her. Can you call her in?"

I slid my palms down the front of my pants. I wasn't sure if I was on edge from speaking to Charles Jayne or because I was about to speak to Harper.

A few minutes later, Harper walked into my office, Donna trailing behind her. "Donna, can you close the door, please?" She gave me a pleading look, clearly desperate to know the answer.

Harper watched as Donna shut the door, then turned back to me, glancing at me from under her lashes. Shit, my dick began to stir. I needed to focus.

"Have a seat, Harper." I gestured toward one of the chairs opposite my desk. She took the one I wasn't indicating. Of course.

"We need to talk," I said.

She grimaced. She thought I meant about us. "Regarding a phone call I just had."

"Oh," she said, and she smiled.

I was going to have to just come out and ask her. "Are you related to Charles Jayne?"

Her eyebrows pulled together and she clasped her hands together. "I'm not sure what my last name has to do with anything."

I sat back in my chair and exhaled. I had my answer. She was Charles Jayne's daughter. Donna had been right.

"You're his daughter?" I asked.

She stood up. "I'm not here to talk about my father."

"He just called me," I said, ignoring her glare. "He

wants me to meet him and I've wanted to add him as a client for so long—"

"Is that why you hired me?"

Her voice got higher as she spoke. I was handling this all wrong.

"Is that why you fucked me?"

I winced. Christ, I could see how it might look that way. I walked around my desk and leaned against the other side, not wanting to get too close, despite her pull. I had to stop myself from reaching out and touching her.

"You haven't answered my question," she said.

"I didn't know."

She rolled her eyes.

"I'm serious. Donna told me this morning. And anyway, I don't recruit . . ." How did I say her position was too junior for me to have anything to do with? "I don't get involved with human resources stuff."

She wrapped her arms around herself. "Be honest. How long have you been wanting JD Stanley's work?"

"Harper, JD Stanley's one of the most successful investment banks on Wall Street, of course I want to work for them. And you know better than anyone that they protect their research like it's gold bullion. That's why they do almost all of it in house. Any person in my position would want to work with them." I could really do with her inside knowledge.

She stared at me as if I were toxic.

I tapped my fingers on my desk. This could be a win-win situation. "I need your help," I said. Now that she was here, I may as well use it to my advantage. "I want you to work on the pitch with me. Help me land this thing."

"Wow. You don't waste any time, do you? We fucked last night and now you think I'll help you get ahead."

That's not how it was at all. I thought she'd welcome the opportunity to work on such a high-profile account. "No, I just thought you'd want to—"

"Want to get used by a man who wanted to land a new client bad enough to sleep with someone?"

She turned and headed out of my office before I could respond. Once again I'd managed to say the wrong thing. It was becoming a habit as far as Harper was concerned.

SEVEN

Harper

I'd called Grace right after my fight with Max, and we'd met at a bar on Murray Street in Tribeca. I waved to the bartender. "Can we get more cocktails and a snack? Something with cheese as a major component." The bartender nodded and I turned back to Grace.

"Okay, I'm totally confused now. You've been banging Max King, the person you hate most in the world?"

"You're totally focusing on the wrong thing."

"Rewind and tell me what the fuck has been going on."

She was looking at me as if I'd just told her I'd decided to move to Alaska.

"I think I got hired by King & Associates because of my sperm donor." I should have changed my last name. We'd never had any sort of connection, so it didn't feel like his name to me.

"The sperm donor being your dad?" Grace asked and I nodded. "How do you know?"

"And he slept with me, like some kind of whore." I shivered. "Well, little does Max know that my father and I only communicate through lawyers these days." How could he have been so cold? I should have trusted my instincts about him.

"We'll get to the sex later. You didn't answer my question." Grace tapped me on the arm, trying to get me to focus. "Who told you that you'd been hired because of who your father is?"

"Max. In his office." I took a sip of my mojito.

She tilted her head to the side. "He said, 'I hired you because of who your father is'?"

"Of course not. He claimed he didn't know. But he was clearly lying." He'd said himself that he really wanted to work for JD Stanley.

"Okay." Grace paused, her eyebrows drawn together. "And you were sleeping with Max? How did *that* happen?" She wiggled her eyebrows. "Late night in the office?"

"He lives in my building. He's penthouse man."

Grace's eyes went wide. "The couple who fucked like bunnies? You banged *that* guy? Jesus, I'm jealous." She took out the cocktail stick from her martini glass and bit off one of the olives.

I tried hard not to smile. She *should* be jealous. Max knew what he was doing with his cock, that was for certain. He probably should have hooked up with Grace in the first place. After all, her family's connections were far more impressive than mine.

"So what are you going to do?" she asked. "Is he boyfriend material?"

"I have no idea. And of course not." I placed my elbows on the bar and pushed my hands through my hair. "What was I thinking, fucking my boss? Now I have to quit."

"He said he didn't know who your father was. Wouldn't

he have said something already if he did? Is he the liar-y type?"

"Liar-y?" I glanced at her out of the corner of my eye.

"It's in the Dictionary of Grace. Look it up."

I hadn't thought Max *was* the sort to lie; he was too direct. But it was perfectly possible I'd just been taken in by his hard body and beautiful green eyes. Had I been seduced by his genius brain and passion for what he did? "Does it matter? He knows now. My father invited him to pitch."

"And he said your father told him?"

I waved my hands. "No, he said he put two and two together, and then he asked for my help with the pitch."

"And you don't want to work for your father?"

"Not because of my last name."

Grace nodded vigorously, alcohol clearly loosening her body parts. "I get that, but you are where you are. Max is saying he didn't know. Are you going to cut your face off to spite your nose by quitting?"

"I definitely won't be cutting my face off, or even my nose, but I do think I have to quit. It's all too humiliating. Everyone's going to know who my father is and why I got the job, and I can't work with the man who fucked me to get ahead."

"You're thinking like a woman. You need to think like you have a penis." She slapped her hand on the bar and the bartender jumped before setting down a cheese plate on the counter. "However you got this job, you need to prove you deserve it because you're good at what you do, not because of your last name and not because you're banging the boss." She took a sip of her cocktail. "Men have been getting ahead using the old boy's network for years. You have to take opportunities when you can get them. So not only can't you quit, you need to go in there and tell Max that you should be working on your father's pitch *because* of your name."

She made no sense. "How would that help? That would only make everything worse."

Grace set her glass down, her drink sloshing over the sides. "This, as they say,"—she threw her hands in the air— "is a win, win, win."

I shook my head and checked the time on my phone. I should be getting home, job or no job to go to in the morning.

"Are you listening?" Grace asked.

I wasn't, because she wasn't making any sense, but I put my phone down and gave her my full attention.

"King & Associates does the kind of work you want to do, right?"

"Correct." I nodded.

"And they're good at it, right?"

Why were we recapping this?

"Correct again. Another and you'll win a set of steak knives."

"So, why would you leave a company like that?"

She interrupted me before I could speak. "You just need to shift." She grabbed my barstool and pulled it toward her. "You need to shift your focus. King & Associates is the best place for underpinning capitalism, feeding corporate greed, and all the geeky stuff you do. Am I right?"

I rolled my eyes and took another sip of my drink.

"So stay there. And demand to work on the project. Because your dad is the best at what he does, so the person who lands that account is going to get huge kudos, right?"

"You get the steak knives, yes."

"So play this smart by sticking around. And, while you're at it, prove to your dad why he should have offered you a position in his company over his children who have penises."

I set my empty glass down as I took in what she was saying. Was she on to something? "You're saying I keep working at King & Associates?" Could I bear to keep working with Max?

"Yes, because however you got the job, you're there. So make the most of your opportunity."

"And demand to work on my father's account?"

"As you'll be a star if you land it, right? And you're flipping the bird to your father at the same time. Like I said, it's all win for you." Grace indicated to the bartender that we wanted the check.

"Unless we lose the account." That would be even more humiliating.

"When have you ever lost at anything you wanted?" she asked as she slipped off her stool and handed her black American Express card to the bartender.

"You didn't need to pay," I said.

"*I* didn't. That was courtesy of *my* daddy."

"Thank you, Mr. and Mrs. Park Avenue," I called out. "You might be on to something about not quitting. This could be my opportunity to prove to my father that I can do more than stay at home and lunch for the rest of my life. I'll show him that I'm worth more, and that he should have been begging for me to work for him and his stupid investment bank."

I jumped off my chair. "Yes. That's exactly what I'm going to do." I grabbed Grace's face in my hands and gave her a smack on the lips. "You're a genius."

SOMEHOW BETWEEN LEAVING the bar and getting back to my apartment building, all my patience had disappeared and the cocktails I'd consumed over the evening had convinced me it was a great idea to tell Max I would work on the JD Stanley account immediately.

"I'll do it," I said as Max opened his front door.

"Harper, hi." He rubbed the heel of his hand over his eyes and yawned. "I wanted to speak to you earlier, but you ran off."

What was I doing? Standing at my boss's front door in the middle of the night, clearly a little drunk. Did I want to get fired? I stepped back until I hit the wall, but let my eyes trail down Max's hard, naked torso and follow a trail of hair gathering at his belly button before disappearing beneath his pajama bottoms.

"I think you'd better come in," he said, his voice gravelly and deep.

I shook my head in an exaggerated way and slipped my hands behind my back. He stepped toward me and pulled at my elbow. "I said come in."

I lost my balance and toppled toward him. Reaching out to save myself, I pressed my palms on the hot, tight skin of Max's chest. I pushed away, but he pulled me closer, spun us around, and walked us back into his apartment.

"You're drunk," he said as he pressed me up against the wall in his entry and kicked the door shut with his foot. His face was just an inch from mine. I wanted him closer.

"A little," I confessed.

"Why did you run off? You're not quitting, if that's what you think," he said as he dragged his nose against my jaw.

"Tell me when you knew," I said, placing my hands on his bare shoulders.

"Knew?" he asked as he began to kiss my neck.

"Who my father was."

He pulled back and braced himself against the wall, his hands on either side of my head. "I swear to you, I found out today. I think Donna assumed there was a connection but she didn't mention it to me until I got the phone call." He paused and his eyes flickered over my face, as if he were trying to figure out whether I believed him. "Why didn't you say anything?"

I dipped under his arms and walked across the entry. "I don't speak to my father. I don't have anything to do with him." I fiddled with my thumbnail.

"Okay. Well you don't have to work on the pitch. I just thought . . . JD Stanley is the only investment bank on Wall Street I've never done business with."

"So," I replied, and I glanced up.

"Well I can't turn down the opportunity."

"I don't want you to turn it down."

He raised his eyebrows.

"I want you to win that fucking account—and I'm going to help you."

"What changed your mind?"

My eyes hit the floor. "It doesn't matter. You got what you want."

He took a step forward. "Tell me, Harper." I knew I shouldn't say anything more, but there was something in his tone that made it impossible not to comply.

I huffed out a breath. "He has a lot of kids, right?"

His eyes drifted over my face.

"I'm the only girl . . . and the only one he didn't offer a job right out of college."

"Because you're a girl? Or because you don't speak to each other?"

I let his questions drip into my brain. Did he have good relationships with his other children?

Max held out his hand. "Come with me."

All too easily, I slipped my palm into his, his fingers holding me tightly as he led me further down the corridor, deeper into his apartment. What was I doing? I didn't like this man. I should go downstairs to my own apartment. "I'm sorry. It's late. I shouldn't be here."

"Shhh. Let's get you hydrated."

He guided me to a barstool opposite a kitchen island in a huge room I hadn't seen before. The other night I'd only caught the dusky outline of his bedroom and the entryway. I hadn't appreciated the size of the place or how glamorous it was. Max either had incredible taste or he'd hired a great interior designer.

"Drink," he said, setting a glass of water on the white marble counter in front of me.

I took a sip, suddenly much more sober than I'd been when I knocked on his door.

"More," he growled. Jesus, he was so bossy. But I complied and gulped down a couple mouthfuls of water.

He rounded the counter and stood beside me, leaning on the marble. "Tell me about your dad. You think he didn't hire you because—"

"Because I have boobs."

He raised his eyebrows. "Really?"

"He offered me a big chunk of money." I set my glass down. "It's not that he denies my existence—he periodically asks me to dinner."

"So you do speak to him?"

I really needed to leave. "Not since my youngest half brother started his job at JD Stanley the day of his twenty-second birthday. Three weeks after I graduated business school. But not really much before that either."

Max pursed his lips.

"I thought maybe he was waiting for me to finish grad school, and of course I would have said no, but . . ."

Max's fingers stroking my arm scattered my thoughts. "He gave us money, me and my mom, but what I wanted was a family."

Max withdrew his hand.

"Sorry, I should stop talking."

"I like to listen. You have a lot to say." His voice was quiet and even, as if he were being sincere, as if he wasn't talking to a drunk woman who thought he was an asshole.

I raised my eyebrows. "I've been drinking. I have more to say in the office, but you're not so interested there."

He cupped my face. "How wrong you are."

His kisses were soft at first, and I closed my eyes, savoring each one.

"We can't do this." My mouth protested, but my hands slipped up his naked back, his warm muscles bunching under my touch. "I can't—"

"I know," he said. "If I'm going to go for the JD Stanley account, I can't exactly be fucking the boss's daughter." As if his body hadn't caught up with his brain, he pulled up my skirt. "But this ass, these legs. They've got me under some kind of spell." He smoothed his hands over my hips and under my ass, slipping inside my panties, then pulled me off the stool and tight to his body.

"We're going to be working together." I wrapped my hands around his neck. "I don't need my head full . . ." . . . *of thoughts of you.* I couldn't say that. I didn't want Max to think I wouldn't be able to concentrate if we were in the office together, but frankly, it was going to be a big ask. "We should focus on the pitch."

He nodded and captured my bottom lip between his teeth. Without thinking, I twisted my hips against his growing erection.

"If my dad suspected . . . I need to show him I'm excellent at my job, not that I got to work at King & Associates because I'm fucking the boss."

"Focused," he repeated. "No boss fucking."

"I'm serious." I pushed against his chest. "Stop thinking with your dick."

"I'm serious, too, but you're encouraging me." He grinned. It was a shock because it happened so rarely. Just for a moment my heart stopped.

"Don't grin at me, you asshole." I tried to twist out of his arms, but he just held me closer.

"Just tonight. This is Vegas. We start with a fresh slate tomorrow morning. No fucking after tonight."

"Vegas? Just for tonight?" I stared into his eyes, trying to see if he was telling the truth. Wondering if I wanted him to be. Yes. Tonight would be my last with Max King. Working on this account and showing my father what he had been missing wasn't worth risking. Not even for the King of Wall Street.

He smoothed a hand over my pussy, then pushed his fingers into my folds. "Just tonight," he whispered.

I lost strength in my knees and stumbled.

"See what a single touch does to you? See the power I have over your body?" He removed his fingers and disappointment caught my breath. I didn't have to answer. "You came here to get fucked, and I'm not going to disappoint you." He bent and lifted me over his shoulder.

"I came to tell you I'd work on the account!" I yelled at his back as I kicked my legs.

"You came to get fucked."

Well, maybe he was right about that. Except sober I'd never have risked colliding with one of his other lovers.

"Vegas," he muttered again. "Just for one more night."

He tipped me onto his bed, my ass bouncing on the mattress, and he grabbed my leg and pulled me toward him. "If I only get to have you for one more night, I need a memory of that pretty mouth of yours wrapped around my cock."

I sat up, my feet dangling over the edge of the bed, and he stepped between my legs, cupping my head in his hand.

"You can't just demand a blow job."

He raised one eyebrow as if to disagree.

I shook my head and pulled down the sides of his pajamas until they hit his ankles. His cock sprang out, hard and thick.

"It seems to be working."

I wanted to have him in my mouth, could feel myself grow wet between my thighs at the thought of his cock between my lips. But I'd clearly made it too easy for him, and I couldn't have that.

I leaned back onto the mattress, opening my legs so my skirt bunched around my hips, then reached into my underwear. Wanting him in no doubt as to what I was doing, I hitched one leg up onto the bed to improve his view and pushed my hands deeper, finding my opening.

"Really?" he asked as he fisted his cock, dragging his hand upward.

"Ask me nicely."

He chuckled, shook his head, and let go of his erection. His energy shifted and he leaned over, stripping me of my clothes. First my skirt, then my panties. Next he fiddled with the buttons of my blouse. He glanced at me, and it was my time to raise my eyebrow at him. "Finding that difficult?" I asked.

Without taking his eyes off me, he ripped my shirt apart. Fuck, that was silk and I'd only worn it three times. "You asshole!"

"Whatever," he replied, reaching behind me and unhooking my bra. "If I only have tonight, I need to see these," he said, staring at my chest as he palmed my skin and pulled at my nipples. My back arched into his touch. He was so forceful, so single-minded about sex—just as he was about everything else. To have that focus concentrated on my body was almost too much to bear.

His hands left my breasts and he dragged his palm down across my stomach until his fingers found my clit. I groaned as his thumb circled and pressed, pulling out my pleasure, inch by inch. His fingers stroked at my folds, and I threw my hands over my head, needing him to send me over the edge.

"Max," I whispered, opening my legs wider, inviting more of him.

"You're desperate for me. My hand is covered in you."

I groaned at his dirty mouth. But he was right. I *was* desperate for him.

"Look at me," he growled.

I opened my eyes. He wore the same look when he was concentrating at work—as if nothing was going to stop him from getting what he wanted.

He stilled and removed his hand, standing up straight. "I want my cock in your mouth. *Please*." His voice was thick with lust.

He'd been getting me worked up to get his dick sucked? He played dirty.

"Now," he added.

I paused while I thought about my next move. Was I going to give in to him? The thing was, it wasn't giving in if it was what I wanted. And I *did* want to have him in my mouth, to make him feel even half of what he made me feel.

I moved to sit on the edge of the bed. Opening my thighs, I tapped the mattress just in front of my pussy. I cocked my head. "You trust me not to bite?"

He chuckled. "Nope. But that just adds to the fun."

I trailed my nails up his outer thigh, and he tipped his head back on a muffled gasp.

His cock was thick and stood to attention against his stomach. I flickered my gaze from his erection to his eyes, wondering how I was going to handle him. He brushed his thumb over my cheekbone, and I gave him a small smile as I leaned forward, the flat of my tongue connecting with the base of his dick. I dragged it up his shaft.

"Jesus," he called out.

I swirled my tongue around his head and took just the tip of him in my mouth. I wouldn't be able to take him deep —he was too big. I circled my hand around his base, gripping him tight. I couldn't stop myself from letting out a moan from the memory of him inside me, filling me. My nipples pebbled, and he must have been watching because he caught them between his thumbs and forefingers and squeezed and pulled, setting off sharp circuits of pleasure from my breasts to my belly button and then lower to my clit.

I took him deeper, my jaw as wide as it would go.

"Yes, like that. That's how I've imagined you."

I circled again, then took him deeper this time. He

groaned, whispering about my mouth and my tongue. His fingers threaded into my hair. Not pushing, not directing, it was as if he just wanted to touch me, to be further connected to me. I pulled back, allowing my teeth to graze his shaft just slightly.

"You're wicked," he growled and I pumped his cock with both hands while sucking on his crown. "But it's not enough." He lifted my chin and I released my hands. I was more than certain I was giving him a great blow job. What was his problem?

"Open your legs," he said. Reaching across to his night-stand, he grabbed a condom, sheathing his cock in seconds. "Wider," he barked, pushing apart my thighs. "I'm going so deep, you're going to forget what day of the week it is."

Before I had a chance to argue, he pushed into me. The sheer force of his body, his cock, stole my breath, despite being ready for him and wet with longing. I looked into his eyes, wanting him to understand it was almost too much.

"You're okay, Harper. I have you."

At just the right time, he knew how to be gentle.

"Relax and feel me." I couldn't do anything else. It was as if I'd lost the fight. My body went limp and I took a deep breath. He circled his hands around my waist and pulled me onto him as he thrust his hips forward. If this was Vegas, I wasn't sure I ever wanted to leave.

Smoothing my hands up his arms, I tugged gently at his biceps. I wanted him over me, touching me, his body pressed against mine. I didn't have to say a word. Disconnecting from me for just a second, he reached under me, pulled me farther up the bed, then braced his body over me and drove back in deep.

Ordinarily, I liked to be on top, to control the rhythm so I could ensure things were just right, but Max left no room for that. Somehow, I didn't need it. Things were more than right. I didn't have space to think; it was all feeling, all sensation. "Oh God, Max," I screamed.

"Again." He pushed in deeper still. "Scream my name again."

It was as if he had his finger on a button deep inside me and kept pressing until everything was at capacity and I exploded. "Max, Max. Oh Jesus, Max."

The bed tilted and the room lit up in pinks and blues as he pushed into me three more times, my name echoing around the room.

Vegas was my new favorite place in America.

EIGHT

Max

I pressed my thumbs hard against the wood, ensuring the tape on the back of my sign stuck to the meeting room door.

"War room?" Donna asked, standing with her arms folded in front of Harper. They were both staring at my sign. I resisted the smile that threated the corners of my mouth as I fixated on Harper's reddened lips and the blush in her cheeks. God she was such a distraction. Perhaps inviting her to work on this pitch wasn't such a good idea after all. I would just have to control myself—she would be a useful resource.

I turned back to the door. "Yes, this is war. We need to get ready."

"Okay." Donna handed me a coffee, leaving me with Harper.

"First thing we need to do is information gather," I said. Harper nodded. Last night had been Vegas. Walking away from anything personal between us was the right thing to do, but it took every drop of self-control I had not to reach out and touch her. "Jim, Marvin," I yelled. I needed to distract myself, find the off switch in my body that would turn off the desire to kiss her, touch her, own her.

Jim and Marvin dutifully left their desks and strode toward us. "Donna."

"I'm here," Donna said from behind me, almost making me jump.

"Stop creeping up on me."

She rolled her eyes and took the tray of water and fruit she was holding past me straight into the meeting room. Or war room.

The team took their seats and I shrugged off my jacket, placing it on the back of the chair.

"We have less than three weeks. You guys know how much working with JD Stanley would mean to King & Associates, and to me personally. Now that we finally have our shot, we're going to throw everything at it." I didn't want to raise expectations. I knew our chances of landing this account were slim to none. We could be being brought in just because I'd been making a nuisance of myself. We might get told to back off. Or JD Stanley could just be using it as an opportunity to gather additional information—key geopolitical insights—without giving anything away, without hiring us. And of course, there was the possibility Harper's father wanted an opportunity to play games, get his daughter's attention. Who knew?

All I cared about was we were being given an opportunity. I was going to make the most out of it. Whatever Jayne's intentions were, I was going to make it difficult if not impossible to say no to me.

"We need to divide our time carefully. First we work out what we know about JD Stanley, Jayne, and the other executives in the business. I want to know everything from what they fed their dogs for breakfast to their mistresses middle names." I shot a glance at Harper. That had been insensitive. Fuck. But this was war and we weren't in Vegas anymore. I wasn't used to having to second-guess what I said at work because I had a single focus and I had to keep that and pretend Harper was just another employee.

Her face was blank, which was a relief. "Then we look at their trading history. I want to understand what they react to, why they invest where they do, why they prefer certain products over others. Look for patterns."

Marvin stuck his hand up. "I've started some of the stuff on their investment history and product preference. Just in my spare time. I knew we'd have this moment at some point." Marvin's capacity for research and modelling was the best I'd ever seen, and it didn't surprise me he had a jump start. He was a hard worker.

"Good. Jim and Harper, you work together on the more personal stuff. Use the agency if you need to." I'd gotten Harper's okay to tell the team about her personal connection, but I wanted to make sure I told them in a way that they understood she was here for her skills. It was obviously a sensitive issue for her. But unless it came up, I wasn't going to raise it.

"I may have some useful insights about their investment decisions," Harper said. She reached down to her laptop case and brought out a thick folio, placing it on the desk in front of her. "But I've also been tracking their investments for the last five years and noticed some interesting choices. I'd be happy to share these."

Jesus, it looked as if she'd skipped business school and dedicated the last five years to researching JD Stanley.

"I'd like to work with Marvin on that, too, if that's okay?"

"Marvin, work with Harper," I said.

Marvin was practically salivating at the sight of her papers. "Sure," he said, blushing when she smiled at him. I knew the feeling. There was something unaffected in her approach in the office that was totally disarming. She didn't have the hard veneer of so many of New York's Wall Street workers. *Focus.*

"Let's meet at seven thirty each morning to update the team. I want us to start thinking propositions, looking for angles. This isn't research for research's sake. We don't want analysis paralysis here." Heads nodded around the table.

"We also need to determine our method of presentation. Do we do PowerPoint? Is it likely to be in an auditorium or boardroom? Talk to your contacts. We need more information than we have, people."

"You should request a preliminary lunch meeting," Harper said, looking directly at me. "Call his assistant personally. Tell her you want to take him to La Grenouille. It's his favorite."

The memory of the smooth skin of her breasts under my hands paralyzed my tongue for a second, and I had to look away before I could answer. "You don't think that's too pushy?"

She shook her head. "He doesn't understand the concept of too pushy. He'll be testing your mettle. He didn't give you much information about your meeting, right?"

"Nothing," I replied.

"He's trying to send you on a wild-goose chase. Don't waste time. Take control. Ask him what he wants."

I nodded. Of course, she was right. "Donna, put some time in my calendar for me to do that." Harper looked glum, but I was grateful for her insight, despite the fact I hated the restaurant she'd suggested. I'd never been because it seemed so stuffy.

"And then in terms of who's presenting, that will be me and Harper. We'll need plenty of time to rehearse."

I glanced at Harper. Her eyes were wide, as if she hadn't expected me to take her. "Do you think that's a good idea?" she asked. "Of course I want to, but—I've never pitched before."

I took a deep breath and tapped my fingers on the back of the chairs. She could be useful, like a carrot we could dangle in front of Charles Jayne. "Donna, what pitches do we have coming up?"

"We have the Asia-Pac for Goldman's," she said. "A week from Wednesday."

"Good. Harper, get read into that. You can be my second chair in that meeting. Give you some experience. I can make a final decision after that."

"Goldman Sachs?" she asked.

"Yes. They're looking for someone to help them with a project in Asia."

"Okay." The slight quiver in her voice was the only thing betraying her lack of confidence. I doubt anyone else noticed. "I'll speak to—"

"Jean," Donna interrupted. "She'll get you read in."

"Good. I'm looking for your best work everyone. We're going to nail this." I smacked my fist on the table. "See you here tomorrow morning at seven thirty."

Silently, people filed out of the room and I crossed my arms. Working with Harper would hopefully help my brain redefine her as a colleague, rather than someone I wanted to fuck—someone from whom it was my job to extract their best work. I needed those barriers between my worlds repaired and restored. Leaving Vegas Harper as part of my history with women would be the first step toward maintaining my distance.

First meeting down.

It would get easier to stop focusing on her neck, her legs, her ass, right? My dick would stop twitching at the thought of her hands spread against the glass of my office door while I fucked her from behind. Soon I'd no longer worry if her frown hid something I could ease or resolve. We were all business and that worked. It would have to.

BEGINNING the prep for the JD Stanley pitch had fired up the competitor in me, but the evening with my daughter and sister put things back into perspective.

"You can't just ban me from wearing makeup," Amanda whined as she twisted on the stool in front of the counter. Scarlett had brought Amanda to town so the three of us could spend Saturday shopping for Amanda's dress. Hopefully it would be the last shopping trip for this dance, and Scarlett would back me up on the whole age-appropriate thing.

"I'm sure he's not saying no makeup at all," Scarlett said.

I ignored them both and continued to stir the spaghetti sauce. The Manhattan apartment had been something of a sanctuary to me over the years—everything how *I* wanted it. My place in Connecticut was always overrun with my parents, Pandora's parents, my sisters, and various friends of Amanda's. I had no complaints. I loved that side of my life, but it was all the sweeter because I got to escape it every week and come to my quiet, modern New York apartment where I got to watch the game uninterrupted and fuck one of the women who seemed to drift in and out of my life.

"Are you saying that I can't wear any makeup, Dad?"

"Of course he's not." Scarlett interrupted again and I took another opportunity to stay quiet. The less I said, the less of a chance there was to have an argument.

I loved my daughter and my sister, and it wasn't as if there wasn't room for everyone here in Manhattan. But it did mean I didn't have any mental space—a beat after my working day. The edges of my separated worlds were softening, growing fuzzy.

Everything was changing.

"I'll speak to your mother," I said, grabbing the oregano from the counter.

"We're not having pasta, are we?" Scarlett asked.

"You just watched me make the sauce."

"I wasn't watching. I was talking. You know I'm not eating wheat at the moment."

I shut my eyes, took a deep breath, then looked at Scarlett. "Why would I know that you're not eating wheat?"

"Because I've been whining about it non-stop for the last month."

"Come on, Dad. You know she's not eating wheat," Amanda said.

Why did the women in my life have the ability to make me feel so hopeless? In my day job I was respected, some would even say admired. With my family, I was just some guy who forgot that my sister wasn't eating wheat.

Jesus.

"So don't eat it," I snapped. "I have some popsicles in the freezer."

Scarlett rolled her eyes in the exact same way Amanda always did. "I'm not five. I can't have popsicles for dinner."

"Good. So you'll eat spaghetti," I replied.

Scarlett hopped off her stool. "We'll go out," she announced.

"You've just watched me make spaghetti sauce."

She shrugged. "It'll freeze. Come on, Amanda. Get your shoes on. We can go to that place on the corner. I like the sea bass there."

Unbelievable.

In the office if I shouted "jump," a cacophony of voices would ask how high. At home I got an eye roll and a shrug, if anyone heard me at all.

But, as was becoming my mantra, some battles weren't worth fighting. I turned off the stove and grabbed my wallet and my keys and followed them out to the elevators.

Amanda linked her arm into mine and instantly I felt better. She was fourteen going on twenty-seven most of the time, but every now and then she was happy just to be my daughter.

We stepped into the elevator. "Tomorrow, can we go back to the store we tried last time?" Amanda asked.

"The one where I hated everything you tried on?" I wasn't going to change my mind. Surely we weren't going to have the exact same fight in front of Scarlett this time?

"I met a lady in the laundry room the other day. She gave me an idea about a dress I think you'd like, and I think I saw some that might be similar at that store," Amanda said.

"The laundry room?" I asked. Why had Amanda been in the laundry room? I had a housekeeper to do the laundry.

"Yeah. The other day."

"Why were you doing laundry?" I asked, glancing at Scarlett, who was staring at herself in the mirrored wall of the elevator and applying lip gloss.

"Sometimes girls just need to do laundry," Amanda answered as if it were obvious.

I glanced at Scarlett, then back at Amanda, expecting one of them to provide a more detailed explanation.

The elevator stopped prematurely. The doors opened and Harper appeared. I watched in slow motion as she began to grin at my daughter. Her mouth froze when her eyes lifted to mine and then behind me to Scarlett.

I should have seen this coming.

In the same way there was a time lag between the impact of a bullet and the pain being recognized by the brain, I savored the few tenths of a second before I knew things would get messy. Harper looked beautiful. Her shiny chestnut hair was swept up into a ponytail that highlighted her long neck. Seeing her dressed in her workout clothes, I found it difficult to avoid touching her.

"Harper!" Amanda said.

I couldn't comprehend what was happening. How did Amanda know—

"Dad, this is who I was telling you about." She stared up at me, then clearly registering utter confusion on my face, she said, "In the laundry room." She waved at Harper.

I glanced at Harper, who had yet to step inside the car. "There's plenty of room," Scarlett said as she pulled Amanda back, leaving more space next to me. "Hey, we met the other day," Scarlett said.

What the fuck was going on? My separated worlds were literally and figuratively crashing into each other.

"Harper, this is my dad," Amanda said. "Dad, this is Harper."

I cleared my throat, hoping it would help my words come out in a normal pitch when I replied. "Yes, I know Harper. She works for me."

Amanda's eyes widened. "She does? Well that makes sense. She's smart. I told you she had some good ideas about dresses."

The doors shut.

"You're right. She is smart," I replied, glancing at Harper, trying to catch her reaction. It wasn't as if we had a personal relationship, but given what had happened between us, the fact I'd not told her about Amanda seemed wrong all of a sudden. Harper wore the same expression she had in the war room when I'd given people tasks for the JD Stanley research—blank and cold.

"This is perfect," Amanda said. "Like Scarlett says, it's fate."

"You shouldn't listen to everything your aunt says. Use the eighty-twenty rule. I've told you about this before."

Scarlett punched me in the arm and I caught a reaction in Harper's face that I couldn't quite place. "Harper, this is my sister, Scarlett."

Harper's beautiful brown eyes softened slightly as she smiled. "Nice to see you," she said.

"You poor thing, having to work with my brother. I expect he's a total tyrant, isn't he?"

Harper shrugged and Scarlett said, "She's got you pegged, brother."

"He's not a tyrant. He lets me have anything I want," Amanda said.

"I may not be a tyrant, Amanda, but neither am I an idiot who can be easily manipulated by flattery. I do not, and will not, let you go to your eighth grade dance dressed like a twenty-five-year-old."

Amanda ignored me. "That's why this is perfect." She smiled and turned to Harper. "Are you busy tomorrow?"

Harper squinted, trying as hard as I was to keep up with my daughter's train of thought.

"You don't make her work on a Saturday, right, Dad?" She didn't wait for my response before releasing my elbow and putting her hands together in a prayer position. "Pretty please, will you come shopping with us tomorrow? We can find one of those dresses we saw online. And I haven't even begun to find shoes. Please? If I'm on my own with dad, he'll have me go in sneakers—"

What was she asking? I needed to spend *less* time with Harper, keep my worlds *more* separate.

"Amanda, you can't just impose on people like that," I interrupted. "Harper doesn't want to spend her free time schlepping around New York trying to find *you* a dress. And Scarlett's coming with us." Spending the day trying not to touch Harper was the last thing I had on my agenda for the weekend.

"I told you I can't come tomorrow, didn't I?" Scarlett asked. "I have to get the first train back because I'm taking Pablo to the vet."

"Seriously?"

Scarlett just shrugged. Why hadn't she told me she wasn't coming? In fact, why was she in Manhattan at all?

"Sorry," Scarlett said. "I thought I told you. The vet called me this morning. He hasn't had one of the injections he was meant to have."

Amanda slouched against the wall of the elevator just as the doors opened into the lobby. "There's no point in going tomorrow if Scarlett's not there and I can't ask Harper. We'll just end up fighting," she said.

"It will be fine," Scarlett said.

I ruffled Amanda's hair. "Come on. We'll find something, I promise." I stepped off the elevator after Scarlett, holding out my elbow for Amanda, glancing at Harper who was staring at my daughter, her eyebrows pulled together.

"Please, Harper? Come with us? I promise I'll take no more than an hour. Just two stores, maximum."

Harper inhaled and the elevator doors started to close with Amanda still slumped against the mirror.

"Come on, Amanda," I said as I held the doors open. "I'm sure Harper's busy." I turned to Harper. "I'm sorry."

She shook her head. "It's fine . . . I . . . want you to have a great dress and I have a couple of hours tomorrow morning."

"You do?" Amanda clasped her hands together. "You'll come?"

My palms started to get sweaty. It was the last response I'd expected. Working with her this week had been difficult enough. I'd been haunted by flashes of her bent over the conference room table, me pushing her skirt up to reveal her high, tight ass.

"Amanda," I barked. "You can't expect people to just drop everything and do whatever you want."

"Why not?" she replied. "You do."

I caught Harper trying to stifle a giggle. "I don't mind. Honestly. We'll have fun." She grinned at Amanda. "But now I have to go to the gym."

Amanda shot out of the elevator. "And you won't change your mind?"

"If she does, then—"

Harper cut me off. "I won't change my mind. I promise. Have a good night."

Harper glanced up at me as the elevator doors closed, and I had to fight the urge to peel them open, push her against the wall, and press my lips against hers.

I pinched the bridge of my nose. The thought of

spending time with Harper on a Saturday with Amanda had given me a headache. What would I say to her? I didn't want my employees to know any other side of me other than the one in the office. And although Harper and I had fucked, it wasn't as if we'd had dinner and I'd confessed all my secrets. Despite being gorgeous, sexy, ballsy with a hint of sweetness to add to her sour, she was my employee. And Vegas was behind us—we were in Manhattan full time now.

NINE

Harper

I slumped on my couch, my phone clamped to my ear. Dressed and ready to go eighth grade dress shopping with Amanda and my boss, I was just waiting for the knock on my door. "I'm cured. I've been dreaming about his penis and just like that, it's gone. Any attraction I had to him has just disappeared because I never knew him."

"Just like that?" Grace asked, her voice suspicious.

"I'm serious. I can't find someone attractive who had a daughter who wasn't important enough to tell me about, who wasn't man enough to marry the woman he knocked up. I've lived my entire life with the consequences of that kind of selfish behavior." Running into Max in the elevator last night had been a shock. When I'd seen the woman with him, I'd assumed I'd run into him and his wife and child and I'd almost exorcist vomited all over the place. Relief she was his sister had only lasted for as long as it took to register he had a kid.

He was a father and hadn't told me. What else was he hiding?

It wasn't like we were dating; he didn't owe me anything, but the fact he was so secretive about it? It seemed dishonest. He never mentioned his daughter in interviews or around the office, there weren't even any photographs on his desk. It was as if he was hiding her. Ashamed. It made me sick to my stomach. Had that been how my father had felt about me? Embarrassed or ashamed I existed? Poor Amanda.

"But Max isn't your dad. I mean, when did Charles Jayne ever take you dress shopping?"

I dropped my head back on the cushion and stared up at my ceiling. "So he has his daughter on the weekend occasionally—doesn't mean he wants his kid around. Looked like his sister was the one who was looking after her anyway." I sighed. "But this is a good thing. It wasn't as if I enjoyed being attracted to Max—I hated the fact that I'd slept with my boss. Now I'm cured."

Being a controlling asshole was one thing. Turning your back on your family was quite another. Max being a tyrant in the office seemed inextricably linked to his success on Wall Street, so maybe I'd been able to forgive him that on a professional level. Maybe I even enjoyed it. A little. But his hiding the existence of his daughter changed my view of him completely.

I checked my watch. Amanda said she'd swing by at ten. She was a sweet kid, and I couldn't begin to fathom what it would be like to try to pick out a dress with a man who resented my existence. She deserved more, so despite wanting to spend the day in bed recovering from my grueling work week, I'd agreed to go shopping.

"I still don't get why you just stopped wanting to jump

his bones because you found out he was a father. Most women would find that a turn on," Grace said.

"Yeah, well, I'm not most women. And I doubt he's winning father of the year anytime soon."

Max wasn't about to win decent human being of the year anytime soon either. He'd seemed to leave Vegas without looking back. He wasn't affected by me at all in the office. Even that first morning after I'd turned up drunk at his door. He'd set up the war room and we'd had our first meeting about JD Stanley. There'd been no compassion in his voice, just cold calculation. He'd seen an opportunity to make money from my connections and nothing more. Well, I'd make it work in my favor, too. I'd ace the Goldman presentation so he couldn't say no to me doing the JD Stanley pitch. If I could go in front of my father as an adult, a business woman—show him what I'd become without any help from him—maybe he'd just wither in my mind and I'd never think of him again. I'd be free.

"So no more sleeping with the boss?" Grace asked.

"Definitely no more sleeping with the boss. I'm not having my father find out and assume that the only reason I got the job was because I looked good on my back." That was the only thing he thought women were good for.

"I thought you said you didn't find Max attractive anymore."

"I don't."

"So if you still found him attractive, you'd still be sleeping with him?"

"Why are you giving me such a hard time, Anderson Cooper? I have more than one reason not to sleep with him."

"Does that mean you're going to call George?"

My brain had to rifle through its filing cabinet to place the name. Oh, the art gallery guy. "Maybe."

"He said you took his number." I had. I'd liked him.

So why hadn't I called him?

I jumped at the loud bang at my door.

"Harper," Amanda called from the corridor.

Shit, this was it. I took a deep breath. "Gotta go," I said into the phone and hung up. I glanced in the mirror by the door, removed a clump of mascara from the corner of my eye, and smoothed down my hair. I could handle a couple of hours with a guy who was my boss and his daughter. Especially now Vegas was over and any attraction I'd had to him had disappeared. This would be a piece of cake.

BEING in a cab with my boss and his daughter after we'd agreed to stop having sex was beyond weird. I'd let my sympathy for Amanda override my logic when I'd agreed to go shopping today. I'd underestimated how awkward spending time with Max would be. I thought it would be a simple case of saving a fourteen-year-old from her uncompromising, uncaring father. The problem was I'd forgotten the father in question was my boss and had seen me naked.

"Do you agree?" Amanda asked, looking at her dad.

We'd taken a cab uptown and Amanda had been chattering away about the kind of dress she wanted to buy. Max seemed to have little interest in her as he stared out of the window.

"I think it's going to rain," he said.

"Dad." She punched him on the leg and he caught her hand and wrapped it in his. "Do you agree about the dress?"

"I'm not committing to anything until I see it."

"Well, if we don't find something today, I'm going naked."

Max chuckled. "If you were a couple of years older, I might worry. Right now, I think your teenage angst is my insurance policy against that happening."

"I don't understand what you just said," she said.

"And so that's a double win for me, peanut." As he scooped his arm around her shoulder to pull her close, he caught my jacket sleeve. "Sorry," he said and I smiled, staring at my hands in my lap. Unclear whether I was imagining things, I wanted to stare at the two of them. They seemed comfortable with each other, happy to be in each other's company. A pang of jealousy ran through me.

"Here we are," Amanda announced as the cab pulled up.

The humidity hit me as I got out of the car.

"It's definitely going to rain," Max mumbled, staring up at the sky.

He held the door open, gesturing for me to go before him as Amanda led the way into a boutique. I hoped this would be a one-stop shop and I'd be back home by lunchtime.

As we started looking around, Max found a chair outside the dressing rooms and concentrated on his phone rather than his daughter. Typical. Why had he come at all?

"What about this?" Amanda asked, holding a long purple gown against herself as she turned toward me.

I grinned. "We should definitely try it."

We picked out six dresses in total, and Amanda managed to sneak a couple of strapless ones in that I was sure wouldn't go down well with her father.

"We can do shoes and a bag once we get the dress," I

said as Amanda stopped on the way to the dressing room, transfixed by a table of sparkly evening bags.

I hung up the dresses I was carrying, then shut the curtain on Amanda.

"Harper, will you stay there while I change so you can see it before my dad? I want to surprise him with the perfect choice."

"Of course," I replied and leaned on the wall opposite Amanda's room. "Which one are you going to try on first?"

"The purple one. Uh-oh," she said. "My dad isn't going to like this one."

The moment she opened the curtain, I knew she was right. Max would never go for the dress. And I couldn't blame him. A twenty-five-year-old would have to make an effort not to look slutty in it. The neckline dipped very low in a big swath of fabric, but it was so low her bra was showing.

"I don't think it suits you," I said, not wanting to hurt her feelings or for her to feel as if her dad's opinion was the only one that counted. "People say that you should wear the dress, the dress shouldn't wear you. Now I'm not sure what that means, but I think we're in dangerous territory. What about the shorter one?"

Next she appeared in a beautiful yellow dress with spaghetti straps, diamanté beading across the bodice, and a netted skirt that fell just above the knee.

"What do you think?" I asked, grinning.

"I think my dad would like it," she replied, but the look on her face said even though she thought her dad would approve, she wasn't in love with it. "But I think I want to look more . . . grown-up."

I nodded. The dress was beautiful on her, though it was a lot like a bigger version of something an eight-year-old might wear. And if Max would like it and she didn't, then we wouldn't even show it to him. "Try the royal blue one. I think it would look great against your black hair, and silver accessories would go beautifully with it. It's more sophisticated."

She turned and swept up her hair and I realized she was asking me to unzip her. "Would you wear it?" she asked as I helped her out of her dress.

I nodded. "Yes. It's beautiful. Not that I would have anywhere to wear a dress like that." I closed the curtain so she could dress in private.

"On a date?" she asked. "Do you have a boyfriend yet?"

My stomach flipped over as I remembered our conversation in the laundry room. Had she told Max anything I'd said? I glanced at the exit to the changing rooms. Could Max hear our interaction? "No, not at the moment."

"You're super pretty. When I'm older, I want to love my job, but I want someone to love me, too." I'd not ruled out love. It had just never found me. Maybe Grace was right and I was looking for perfection. "My dad's like you. Always busy with work. He always says that between work and me, he has more than enough for any man."

I couldn't help but smile at that. She clearly wanted her dad's approval, and I was getting the impression the two of them actually talked. Maybe they were closer than I thought. "Do you hang out a lot?" I asked, lowering my voice.

"Me and my dad? Yeah. Like all the time," she replied.

Before I got a chance to ask Amanda more questions about her and Max's relationship, she opened the curtain, grinning. "I really like this one," she said, stepping out in a long skirt of pleated crepe, which had a slit up the side.

"It's really pretty." I leaned forward to even out the

skirt. "I love it. This looks beautiful." The shoulders were a contrasting silver material that came down and crisscrossed around her bust, in a Greek-like style. There was no cleavage, but at the same time it was dramatic. "And it looks gorgeous against your hair. Let me grab some shoes. Stay there."

As I walked out of the dressing rooms, my eyes met Max's as he looked up from his phone.

"Everything all right?" he asked.

I nodded. "Just getting some shoes."

As I passed, he grabbed my wrist. I froze. Almost immediately he dropped my hand. "Sorry. I just wanted to say thank you. This means a lot to Amanda."

I nodded but didn't look at him. My brain was misfiring. One minute Max was thanking me for making his daughter happy, the next he was yelling at me if I didn't get his sandwich order right. And then there were those kisses.

And I couldn't quite work out the dynamic between Max and Amanda. He seemed quite involved in Amanda's life. More than I'd thought. But if he'd never been married to her mother, how had that worked? It had never worked with my father.

I grabbed a pair of silver sandals with a small heel and rushed back to Amanda.

"Will he like it? Can we convince him?" she asked, taking the shoes and strapping them up. "This is the one, right?"

"You know him better than I do, but I think you look beautiful in it."

"Daaad," she called out. "I'm coming out. And I really like this one. It's perfect, so you can't be mean."

Her smile was so wide, I couldn't help but smile back. I

really hoped he approved. Amanda deserved to wear this dress. It was age appropriate and really elegant.

She stepped out onto the shop floor and I peeked around the corner at Max's face. His eyebrows were halfway up his forehead as she twirled around three hundred sixty degrees for him. "What do you think?" she asked.

He gave a small shake of his head as he stood and took a deep breath. "I think you look far too grown-up." Amanda's shoulders slumped. "And completely beautiful." He pulled her into a hug. "You found your dress, peanut." He lowered his voice and spoke into her ear as they continued to hug. "You're growing up so fast; you have to forgive me for wanting to keep you mine for longer than I should."

Tears welled in my eyes. He sounded so genuine. So completely besotted with his daughter.

"I'll always be yours, Dad," she said as she smiled. He kissed her on the cheek and released her.

Max seemed to regain his composure. "Twirl for me again," he said, lifting her hand in his and pulling his daughter into a spin.

The skirt of the dress lifted as she turned faster and faster. Max grinned and Amanda giggled. My heart squeezed. It felt as if I were encroaching on what should be a private moment. I should have my own memories like this, not have to steal other people's.

"YOU KNOW WHAT THIS MEANS?" Amanda asked as we stepped out onto the sidewalk, the heat swallowing us up immediately. She carried two white boutique bags, one with the dress and one with the shoes and a bag we'd spotted on the way to the cash register.

"We let poor Harper get on with her weekend?" Max replied.

My stomach jolted. Had I overstayed my welcome? I'd just been trying to help. Max didn't need to be so ungrateful. I opened my mouth to excuse myself, but Amanda took her father's hand and tried to pull him along the street. "No silly. It means we have something to celebrate."

Max rolled his eyes. "As if you need any excuse."

"I'll leave you guys to it. Your dress is beautiful, Amanda."

Amanda's eyes narrowed. "No. You have to come," she said. "You have to celebrate with us." She beckoned to me to follow them.

"You celebrate with your dad," I replied, glancing in the other direction. Shopping hadn't really involved much interaction with Max. Most of my time had been spent with Amanda. Other than the cab ride, things hadn't been too uncomfortable. And seeing Max with Amanda suggested they had a better relationship than I'd ever had with my father. If I left now, I would be ahead. I'd survived without calling my boss an asshole and without getting naked with him. Perhaps there was middle ground. And hopefully the constant comparisons I'd been making between Max and Amanda's relationship and my father's and mine would stop.

"I want you to come," Amanda said.

I smiled but before I could think up an excuse, Max intervened. "Amanda, Harper has things to do. We have imposed on her free time enough."

He clearly wanted to be rid of me. And I got it. Just days after agreeing to keep things strictly professional, I was standing on a sidewalk with him and his daughter. And even though I wanted to leave, it hurt just a little that he was so keen for me to go.

Amanda's face fell. "I don't want to celebrate without her. If it hadn't been for Harper, I wouldn't have found my dress. Are you sure you can't come? We're going to my favorite place."

I glanced at Max, whose gaze travelled between me and his daughter. The corners of his mouth twitched, as if he was trying to suppress a smile.

"I'm sure your dad wants to switch off from work and spend time with you—"

"Daaad," Amanda said. "You want Harper to come, don't you?"

Max ruffled his daughter's hair and she quickly moved out of reach. He turned to me and gave me the biggest panty-melting smile I'd ever seen, his green eyes dancing against the New York sun, framed by almost too long lashes. "Harper, we'd love for you to come if you can spare the time. But don't feel you have to give into my daughter's whining. She's far too used to getting her own way."

Before the sensible side of me—the part enjoying this new middle ground—could run back downtown, I agreed.

"I suppose I should have asked before I said yes, but where are we celebrating?" I asked as we walked east.

"Serendipity," Amanda replied. "It's our place. We always come in on the train at the end of summer and celebrate going back to school."

"From your mom's?" I asked.

"From Connecticut. Sometimes my mom and Jason come, but sometimes we come in together. Do you remember that year Aunt Scarlett came as well?" she asked her dad. "She wanted to order one of everything because she couldn't decide."

"She *did* order one of everything," Max said. "Which is pretty typical of my sister."

"My mom and Jason moved to Europe so it's just me and Dad now." She turned back to her dad. "You love having me living with you all the time, don't you?"

Max chuckled and glanced at me. "She's driving me crazy."

They lived together?

"I didn't realize you lived in Connecticut," I said. I was fascinated at how the King of Wall Street had a secret life away from Manhattan. I felt like an investigative journalist, putting little scraps of information together.

"Yeah, near Mom and Jason's place. And Grandma and Grandpa King and Grand-Bob and Grand-Mary. And Scarlett."

"Jesus. It makes us sound like we're living in some kind of commune." Max slung his arms around his daughter's shoulder. "We just all live close. Amanda's mother, Pandora, and I were in high school together, and it made sense after college to make sure we lived near each other. That way," he said, turning to Amanda, "when your mother got sick of you, she could get a break and dump you with me."

Amanda grinned and rolled her eyes, the explanation clearly something she was used to hearing.

"So the apartment is just a pied-à-terre?" I asked.

He nodded. "Yeah. I used to stay in Manhattan all week and go back to the country on weekends, but now I'm only in town two nights a week."

Amanda came to an abrupt halt on the sidewalk. "Oh

my God. You'll have to come out, Harper. The night of the dance. Will you help me get ready?"

I didn't know what to say. I concentrated on trying not to look too shocked. I really liked Amanda and at every turn, Max kept surprising me. I wanted to encroach on their world a little longer, but I knew it was entirely inappropriate.

Max cocked his head, indicating she needed to keep walking. "Amanda. That's enough. You can't just assume people want to be monopolized by you."

We resumed walking north towards Sixtieth. "Why not? Grandma says that I get all my charm from her and that God skipped a generation with you."

I laughed and Max rolled his eyes.

Thankfully, Amanda's attention had been diverted away from me. "Oh, I meant to say that I've decided I want to enter that piano competition next semester," she said.

"I thought we checked a few months ago and you have gymnastics the night of the practice, or will the schedule change next semester?" Max asked.

He seemed to have an intricate knowledge of his daughter's schedule, which if someone had told me yesterday, I would have thought it impossible. But as the day wore on, it was clear he was more involved in his daughter's life than I'd given him credit for.

"Well, gymnastics is at six and then piano is at eight. So I think I can do both if we can get Marion to drive me."

This was such a different version of Max King—warm, open, and relaxed. So far removed from the impatient, ruthless man who'd founded King & Associates, to the demanding, sexy man who worked my body as if it belonged to him. *This* Max King was a father and a family man.

Thunder cracked above us. "I told you it was going to

rain," Max said. "Come on." He held his hand out for me and then, as if he remembered who we were to each other, withdrew it and nodded up Third Avenue as if we were nearly there instead of two blocks away.

We weren't going to make it. Generous dots of rain began to color the ground.

"Come on, Harper," Amanda called as she and Max started to run.

Amanda pointed at a flash of light above us and began to count, "One banana, two banana, three banana, four banana." Thunder ended her countdown and Amanda squealed. "Quick, it's nearly here."

I ran behind them as we wove in between tourists and underneath umbrellas. As we arrived at Serendipity, the lightning flashed again and the rain began to fall more heavily. "Let's get inside," I said, and we piled into an already crowded entrance and waited to be seated.

"Do I look like a drowned rat, Dad?" Amanda asked, beaming up at her father. She was a beautiful girl who had inherited the large green eyes, olive skin, and near-black hair from her father.

Max chuckled. "A little bit."

I wiped my under eyes, trying to remove the inevitable mascara leak. "I'm sure I look like Alice Cooper," I said.

"You look very pretty, like from a movie or something," Amanda said. "Doesn't she, Dad?"

I shook my head and a soaked strand of hair plastered itself against my cheek. To my surprise, Max reached out and tucked it around my ear. Heat coursed through me and I wanted to reach for his hand, push my fingers through his. But instead I concentrated on the waitress behind Max, worried I'd lose control if I looked at him, maybe pull him into a kiss as I did that first night we were together.

He quickly turned back to Amanda and took her face in her hands. "Not as pretty as my drowned rat," he replied.

"Gah. That's why I'm never going to get a baby sister." She twisted away from him. "You need to learn to give ladies compliments, or you'll never get married."

Married? I kept my eyes firmly on the restaurant, hoping my makeup hid the red in my cheeks. For the first time since leaving the dress store, I felt as if I shouldn't be here. Our conversation in the laundry room came back to me. She wanted her dad to find someone. Was Amanda trying to set us up? She had to know that Max and I were . . . We weren't involved like that, weren't ever going to be involved like that.

TEN

Max

The day with Harper and Amanda had been far . . . easier than I expected. After finally getting on the train back to Connecticut, Amanda couldn't stop talking about her dress and Harper and how much she liked her. And I hadn't stopped her.

"We could invite Harper to dinner," Amanda said as she set out the knives and forks on the counter in the kitchen.

"Maybe . . . at some point." Would she like it here? Would she like *me* here? I wasn't sure.

"Well it will be the dance soon anyway. Harper will come then for sure."

I wasn't sure Harper had actually accepted that invitation. But Amanda was happy and that was all I could wish for. The fact Harper had picked out a perfect dress didn't hurt. I'd wondered if she'd secretly try something trashy, just to mess with me, get her own back for me being an asshole. I wouldn't have blamed her but she hadn't. She'd been bright and beautiful and all about Amanda. And I'd found myself wanting to extend our time together, keep her for a little bit longer.

"Who's Harper," my sister, Violet, asked. I smelled an interrogation brewing, and my instinct was to press pause on this situation and escape.

"I told you, the girl that works with dad who helped me pick out the dress."

"I thought a friend of yours had gone shopping with you," Violet said to Amanda, trying to catch my eye, but I deliberately busied myself with the salad.

"She *is* a friend of mine," Amanda replied. "She lives in the same building in the city as dad."

"*And* she works with your father?" Violet asked as she reached over the counter and took a chunk of cucumber and popped it in her mouth. I glanced at Amanda, who was nodding. "That seems like a strange coincidence." She lowered her voice. "You see a pretty girl in the corridor of your building and offer her a job sharpening your pencils?"

"Don't be ridiculous," I replied and handed her the salad to put on the counter.

A bang on the door caused Amanda to squeal. "Scarlett!" My sisters were determined to overrun me tonight. Violet lived in Brooklyn, so we didn't see her as often as Scarlett, but she still made an effort to come over once a month. I liked my sisters, but the fewer there were of them in a room at any one time, the better. I grabbed a bottle of Pinot Noir from the counter and uncorked it.

"Hey, asshole," Scarlett said as she entered the family room.

"Nice to see you, too." I handed her a glass of wine and kissed her on the cheek.

"I'm serious. Why didn't you call me back?" Scarlett asked.

"When?" I asked. I didn't remember getting a message.

"I left you a voicemail telling you about my friend April," Scarlett said as she dropped her purse on the counter and took a stool. "She asked me to fix you two up, although God knows why."

"I didn't get the message." Or maybe I'd only listened halfway through and deleted it before she could get to the bit about April. "Sorry."

"So?" she asked.

"So what?" I asked, wanting her to change the subject. I turned back to the oven, taking out the lasagna the house-keeper had left. I never wanted to date my sisters' friends. I was surprised they were still trying. My life was full to the brim.

"So will you take her out?" she asked as if I were stupid. To be fair, I was being deliberately obstructive. I just didn't need my sisters interfering with my dating life. I was happy with things as they were.

"Looks like April may have competition," Violet said. Scarlett shot her a look and Violet shrugged. "We've been talking a lot about Harper this evening. She'd definitely get Amanda's seal of approval."

I'd never had to concern myself with whether Amanda would like any of the women I'd been with. She'd never met any of them and that's the way I liked it. It was simply coincidence Amanda had gotten to meet Harper.

Scarlett continued to chat on about April, which I could easily drown out. Harper was a little more difficult to bury. "April comes from a lovely family. She's blonde, which I know you like."

Did I like blondes? I wasn't sure hair color was a

deciding factor for me. Harper's hair was chestnut brown, but had looked almost black in the rain. Images of her standing in the line for Serendipity flashed into my head. She'd looked gorgeous. Her cheeks pinked from running, her eyes bright blue. At one point she'd licked raindrops from her upper lip. It had only been Amanda's presence that had stopped me from pushing her wet hair from her face, relishing her soft skin under my thumbs, and pressing my lips to hers. If it had been just the two of us, I would have dragged her back to the apartment and spent the afternoon naked and indulging myself in her instead of ice cream.

"What are you smiling about?" Violet asked me.

"I'm not smiling about anything." I needed to shake these thoughts about Harper off. A taste of Harper was supposed to cure me. That had been my justification for fucking her the first time, the second time, *and* the third time. But seeing her today, relaxed, warm, and so focused on making sure Amanda was happy, had grown this buzz in my gut I had when she was around or when I thought about her. They laughed and talked together like old friends and listening to them in the changing rooms while I'd pretended to stay focused on my emails made me smile, made me feel good.

"Can I show them my dress?" Amanda asked.

"After dinner you can try it on."

"Daddy bought me the most beautiful shoes to go with it. I'm not sure he would have, but Harper said she'd buy them if he didn't."

"I was always going to buy the shoes. Give me some credit. I know you can't wear your sneakers." Harper's face had lit up when she'd seen the shoes. I'd wanted to ask for a pair in her size as well. Maybe I'd try to find her something similar. After all, I'd ruined her blouse.

"So I want to hear more about Harper," Scarlett said. "How old is she? Is she pretty?"

Amanda took a spoonful of salad and stopped, thinking about the question.

"Come on, Amanda," I said, trying to distract them away from this question. "Don't get it all over the table."

"My age?" Violet asked.

She nodded and dropped some salad on her plate. "I guess. Like, grown-up age. And she's really pretty."

They were right about that. She was very attractive.

"I'd say about twenty-five," Scarlett said. "Gorgeous, too, and she just happens to work with Max." I avoided Scarlett's glances. But she was right, Harper was gorgeous. And smart. And great in bed.

"She's one of my *employees* who happens to live in the building. Amanda begged her to go shopping with her. I'm sure it's the last thing she wanted to do."

"She enjoyed it," Amanda said with total confidence. Because why wouldn't a twenty-something enjoy going shopping with her boss and his kid? Harper had been exceptionally good about it. It had been nice to watch them together.

"Would she go out on a date with your dad, or is she too pretty for him?"

Amanda grinned. "Oh my God, that would be so awesome. And I know she doesn't have a boyfriend."

I pretended I wasn't listening and took the salad spoons from Amanda and finished distributing the salad for everyone. Normally I'd have put an end to the conversation by now. I'd become good at deflecting around my dating life but this was slightly different. I found I liked the conversation about Harper—enjoyed Amanda's reaction to her. And I didn't mind them considering us as some kind of couple. Not that it would ever happen—we'd agreed it wouldn't. It was just I didn't mind it being a possibility in my family's mind.

MONDAY I'D GOTTEN into the office late. I'd been shopping for shoes for Harper. It had taken me too long to make the purchase, not knowing what I was doing and why. Now I was behind and grouchy and I still wasn't decided on whether or not I'd actually give her the shoes. Next on my schedule was to follow up on the lunch invitation to Charles Jayne as Harper had suggested.

"Max, I have Margaret Hooper, Charles Jayne's assistant, on the line for you," Donna squawked from my speakerphone.

"Thank you." I cleared my throat and pulled back my shoulders. Assistants had much more power than people realized, and I was sure Margaret held considerable sway with Charles Jayne.

I picked up the receiver. "Ms. Hooper, Max King of King & Associates here." I could tell from her response, which was soft and helpful, that she was pleased I'd called her and not just asked Donna to call on my behalf. Harper had made a good suggestion. So now that Margaret was on our side, I needed to convince her to let me take Charles to lunch.

"As you know, Mr. Jayne has asked me to come in to see him on the twenty-fourth. I don't want to waste his time."

"You're right, he doesn't have much time to do anything, so how can I help?" she asked.

"I want to make the presentation as focused and helpful as possible. Now of course this benefits me because I provide Mr. Jayne with what he most needs."

"Indeed, Mr. King," she replied, skepticism rising in her voice.

"Please, call me Max."

I could hear her smile across Wall Street. "Okay, Max, what is it you want?"

"I want to create a win-win situation. If I understand what it is that Mr. Jayne is looking for then our presentation won't be a waste of anyone's time. He's happy. I'm happy. If I can get lunch with Mr. Jayne—"

"The problem is he doesn't have any lunch availability between now and the twenty-fourth. His schedule books up very quickly, unfortunately." Her tone transitioned from friendly and open to clipped and concise. I wasn't sure if she was being honest, or if I was being given the brush-off.

"I'd be very happy to come to the JD Stanley offices and bring lunch to Mr. Jayne, if that would help?" I suggested. "Alternatively, I'll get a table booked at La Grenouille if that would suit him."

"I'm sorry. If it were up to me, I'd love to find space. But I'm afraid it's not." That sounded like a brush-off. Other-wise she'd have said she'd let me know and checked with Charles Jayne.

"That's such a shame." I paused a second, considering my options. Was it worth trying to press a little more or did I risk backlash?

Maybe I should mention Harper's name. I still wasn't clear what the bad blood was between Harper and her father. It couldn't just be about the fact she didn't get offered a job when she graduated. She'd indicated things went bad between them before that.

Harper knew the reason we were going to give her a slot on the presenting team was because she was Charles Jayne's daughter, right? So she understood to a certain extent she was being used. There's no way I'd ordinarily have a junior researcher second chair a meeting like that. But at the same time, I'd discussed that with her, sought her approval before making any decisions.

I had to decide my next move quickly or Margaret would hang up. Fuck it, this was war. "I'd hoped he'd enjoy seeing his daughter in a professional environment," I said. Silence at the other end of the line nudged me to continue. "I was assuming Harper Jayne would join us for lunch. But I understand that Mr. Jayne is very busy."

"Please hold the line, Mr. King," she replied and her voice was quickly replaced with Vivaldi.

Had I just been the asshole Harper accused me of being? Was using her to get a lunch with Charles Jayne any worse than taking advantage of the fact Charles Jayne's offer of a meeting was probably linked to her working here? The problem was none of us were sure whether or not I got the phone call from Charles Jayne because of Harper. Regardless, I hadn't been the one to play that card—I hadn't even known they were related. All I'd done was take advantage of a business opportunity. Fuck.

Lunch required interaction that went beyond the professional. I had no idea whether or not Harper would think lunch was no big deal, after all she'd agreed to pitch, or if she'd knee me in the balls and hand her notice in if I even suggested it.

I should have thought this whole call through more carefully in advance, maybe had Harper in the room when I spoke to Margaret. It wasn't like me. I couldn't tell if Harper had thrown me off my game or if it was the thought of landing JD Stanley as a client.

Maybe Margaret would come back and still say that Charles Jayne's schedule was full. I reached inside my collar and ran my finger around the starched material. I shouldn't have acted so rashly.

"Mr. King, I can make some time for you on Wednesday. Mr. Jayne will see you and Harper at twelve thirty at La Grenouille."

Shit. That was the answer I wanted and the one that made me feel uncomfortable.

I hoped I'd done the right thing.

After thanking Margaret, I hung up the phone.

Maybe I didn't have to tell Harper. Maybe I could just turn up to lunch on my own and say Harper had been caught up in the office or was sick.

But then Charles Jayne hadn't founded a leading investment bank without the ability to smell bullshit a mile away. No. I'd have to confess to Harper what I'd done, and if she didn't want to come to lunch, I'd have to cancel.

Jesus, why was this so fucking complicated? I'd done what I needed in order to win. If Harper and I hadn't banged, would I be second guessing myself?

"Did you get it?" Donna asked as she burst through the door.

I nodded and leaned back in my chair. "Wednesday," I said.

"Well, why don't you look happier about it? Things are coming together just as you'd planned."

I scrubbed my face with my hands. "Yeah, maybe."

"What's the matter with you? This is great news." She closed the door.

Donna was right; this was what I'd been hoping for.

What had been my ultimate goal just three weeks ago was now tarnished with the knowledge I'd gotten there by using Harper.

People said I was ruthless in business and that may be true, but I'd never been underhanded and I always tried to do the right thing. I wanted to be someone my daughter could admire and respect and emulate in some ways. I wanted her to be ambitious and driven. But my greatest wish was for her to grow up knowing what was important, that she became someone who understood integrity and hard work was the way to go. I didn't want to raise a daughter who would sell her soul for a piece of corporate pie. And I'd worked hard not to be that guy. Had I just thrown that all away?

I'd always found the ethical boundaries were drawn quite distinctly on Wall Street, but today that line had become fuzzier and I wasn't sure on which side of it I stood.

INSTEAD OF CALLING for an elevator when I got home after work, I took the stairs. Was I about to make a dick move by giving these shoes to Harper?

Quite possibly.

My shoes made clunking sounds against the metal steps, as if they were trying to call attention to my climb, which was the last thing I wanted. The white Jimmy Choo bag swung against my side. I'd spent about an hour in the Bleaker Street store before committing to the purchase that had made me late to work. I'd never a bought a woman outside of my family anything, ever. But since I'd seen the look of pure joy lighting up Harper's face when she picked out Amanda's shoes, I'd wanted to see that expression again.

She'd been excited and bright and full of enthusiasm. And as the daughter of one of the richest men in New York, it was nice to see. She should have been used to luxury, but somehow she'd managed to make Amanda feel special.

I wanted her to feel the same way again.

The assistant at the store had been very patient with me. But I'd seen the pair I wanted as soon as I walked in. They were like an adult version of the pair I'd bought Amanda. The heel was higher and thinner and straps more intricate but they were covered in that glittery finish she and Amanda had gone wild over on Saturday.

I'd torn the buttons from her blouse so I owed her, didn't I? Memories of revealing her full breasts when I'd ripped her blouse drifted into my head, and I tried to shake them off.

But I had more than one reason to buy her shoes. She'd found a dress for my daughter that reduced the chances of me going to jail for the murder of every fourteen-year-old boy who so much as looked at her. I had to thank her, and shoes were an appropriate gift.

As I reached her floor, I paused before opening the fire door. I could just leave them on her doorstep. I wanted her to have them more than I wanted to be the one to give them to her, to see that look of pleasure on her face. At least I hoped it would be pleasure. Buying an employee shoes wasn't the actions of a boss—they had a touch of Vegas about them and I wasn't sure how she'd react to that.

I needed to stop being such a pussy.

I knocked three times on her door and stretched out my hands, trying to resist the buzz in my fingers I knew would start when she appeared. It was as if I were pre-programmed to reach for her whenever I saw her.

She appeared seconds later, dressed in a Berkeley T-shirt and leggings, her hair in a high ponytail—a style I'd never seen her wear to work. She looked breathtaking.

"Hi," she said, her mouth slightly open.

"Hi." I held out the bag.

Her eyebrows knitted together. "What's that?" she asked, though she didn't take it.

"A thank you. For Saturday and . . . You know, for giving up your time last weekend."

Her eyebrows raised and a smile twinged at the corners of her mouth. "Really?" she asked. "It was fine. You don't need to buy me a gift." And then she frowned.

I hadn't expected this reaction. I'd wanted to make her smile, maybe smooth her hands through my hair and kiss me. "Okay." I should tell her about lunch, get it out of the way. "And I have something to tell you."

She opened the door and I followed her into her apartment, leaving the Jimmy Choos underneath her coat rack. She wasn't even going to look at them? The door clicked shut behind us and instantly I knew I made a mistake. Suddenly I was back in Vegas. I couldn't stop staring at her ass, wondering whether she was wearing a bra under her shirt. The buzz in my fingers grew stronger, and I had to take a deep breath to calm my rising pulse.

"You want a drink?" she asked.

"Sure, thanks." Holding a glass would occupy my hands, stop them from wandering to the hem of her T-shirt, and skirting the smooth skin underneath.

She set two glasses on the small counter as I watched. She seemed unbothered by my presence, as if I was something other than wildly attracted to her.

She handed me a glass of lemonade and leaned against the cabinet. "So," she said.

Her small, delicate fingers wrapped around her glass

and I couldn't help imagining how they'd feel, cooled by her drink, trailing down my chest.

"Max," she said and I snapped my head up to look at her. "What did you have to tell me?"

Shit. I shifted my weight from one foot to both, trying to regain control. "I took your advice and called your father's assistant."

"I'd prefer it if you didn't call him my father."

I nodded. I wanted to know why she so clearly didn't like the man. Didn't speak to him, but kept a dossier on his business investments. Didn't want anything to do with him except to show him just how worthy of his attention she was. "Should we talk about this? I don't really understand your history. And I'd like to."

"Is talking about parents something you normally do with employees?" she asked, a frown creasing her forehead. She pushed off the counter and came toward me, clearly wanting me to move out of the way so she could leave the kitchen. Our bodies were close, the heat of her breath puffing against my shirt. I didn't move. I *liked* having her close. I wanted more.

I ran my finger up her exposed neck and her lips parted, but as her eyes met mine, she pushed past me.

I turned to find her loitering by the door. "You should go," she said, her eyes on the floor.

"I should," I agreed. But I didn't want to. I wanted to stay and peel off her T-shirt, bend her over the sofa, and slide into her. I stepped toward her and rested my hand on her hip.

"What did you have to tell me?"

Oh yes, lunch. Her presence, like some kind of fog, clouded my brain *and* my judgement.

She placed her hand on my arm and it drifted up to my shoulder. I had to consciously breathe.

"Max?"

Her clipped tone brought me to attention. "I called his assistant. She found a spot in his schedule." Taking a half step closer, I smoothed my hand from her hip to the small of her back.

She raised her eyebrows as she tilted her head up to look at me. "That's good, right?"

I nodded. "Except he seemed to be busy until I told her you'd be joining us."

Dropping her hand from my shoulder, she took two steps to the side.

"And so you're here. With gifts. And wandering hands."

I took a step back, removing my hand from her warm body. "What? No." Was that what this looked like? As if I were trying to bribe her? Seduce her into agreeing to lunch?

"Jesus, I know you think I'm an asshole. But, no."

She shrugged. Didn't she believe me? Fuck. This was why lines were better when they were clearly drawn—when business was business and fucking was fucking. I shouldn't have come here.

"Don't come to lunch." I reached for the door. "The shoes weren't anything to do with work. I bought them before my call with your father." And my desire for her was nothing to do with Charles Jayne. She conjured that up all by herself.

Jesus, I should never have bought the shoes. Should never have come here. I stepped out of her apartment

"Max," she said and I didn't respond, letting the door shut behind me.

ELEVEN

Harper

I stood by Donna's desk, shoulders back, ready for war.

It was eleven fifty. We needed to leave now if we were sure to be in Midtown on time for lunch with my father, but Max wasn't in his office.

I hadn't spoken to Max since he left my apartment. I'd expected Donna to send me a meeting request or to be summoned into Max's office and told that me going to lunch with my father and Max was for the good of the team. The thing was I was happy to do it. Okay, not happy, but I was *prepared* to lunch with my father. I wanted to be seen on the winning team. Lunch could only help my goal if it meant we were more likely to be successful in our pitch.

I wore a navy dress, just above the knee with a scoop neck, and a matching, collarless jacket I'd had tailored to nip in at the waist. It was my lucky interview suit—and as close to Prada as I could afford.

"Donna, I need to leave," Max said as he swept past me

and into his office. Donna followed him and set the file she was carrying down on her desk.

Max appeared in his doorway. "Harper," he said, fiddling with the collar on his navy jacket. I wanted to step forward and smooth my fingers over the fabric. He looked good. He *always* looked good.

"Are you ready?" I asked.

He just nodded and we headed to the elevators.

"Good luck," Donna called after us.

We stood, silently waiting for the elevators, surrounded by employees of King & Associates.

I should also thank him for the shoes. He probably thought I'd been ungrateful but that wasn't it. The present had taken me off guard and brought back memories of the extravagant gifts my father used to send me as a child to try to make up for the fact he'd forgotten my birthday or hadn't turned up to visit me when he said he would.

Perhaps it was unwrapping the beautiful Jimmy Choo's that changed my mind but as I thought about it, it occurred to me perhaps Max just didn't get how his timing had sucked. The gift had been a thank you rather than a bribe. He probably hadn't realized he'd looked as if he was trying to manipulate me with gifts and come-ons. With that real-ization came an understanding of some of his odd behavior on Saturday. I realized that for whatever reason, he was a little bit awkward with me. That clearly didn't stop him trying to seduce me or fucking me as though it was his job. But outside of the seduction and the sex, he wasn't so confi-dent, so practiced.

As Max and I settled into the cab, which sped off uptown, we started to speak at the same time.

"I wanted to say sorry," I said.

"Thank you for coming," he said.

We turned toward each other and he gave a small smile.

"The shoes were beautiful," I said.

He looked away. "It was inappropriate. I shouldn't have." He dragged his hand through his hair and I gazed at his long fingers, knowing just how they felt all over my body.

"It was a really nice thing to do."

"You just seemed to like the ones Amanda got on Saturday."

I grinned. They were a higher, sparklier, sexier take on his daughter's.

"And I know I take up too much of your time already. Giving up your weekend was—"

"No big deal." I couldn't exactly admit I'd assumed he was disinterested in his daughter and had wanted to save her from his apathy. I couldn't have been more wrong. He clearly loved Amanda and she him. The King of Wall Street had a secret identity in Connecticut as a single father and family man.

We'd first touched, kissed, fucked when I'd only known him as a career driven, ruthless, arrogant egomaniac. And somehow, his life outside work made him all the more attractive. And I knew I had to fight it.

"And thank you for coming today. I assumed you weren't going to join me," he said.

I'd kind of admired the fact he hadn't asked me to come to lunch again, hadn't tried to pressure me. But he didn't need to. I wanted to be here. "I told you. I want this as much as you. Just for different reasons."

"Have you never gotten along with your father—sorry, Charles Jayne?"

I took a breath. I didn't want to talk about this. Not now. Not ever.

I shrugged, and he didn't push me to say anything more. We just sat, the windows rolled down, the hoots and hollers of New York sucking away the silence between us. It should have been awkward. I was sure if we hadn't fucked, I would have tried to make polite conversation, maybe even tried to impress the boss. Somehow all that seemed redundant now. Ridiculous even.

The restaurant was busy with chatter and I slid into the red velvet seat. We were the first to arrive at the booth, which was a relief. I had some time to compose myself. I'd not been to La Grenouille in years, not since the last time I'd seen my father. This place hadn't changed at all.

"This is very . . ." Max looked around the restaurant, his forehead crumpled and his lips tight. I was pretty sure Max was a Four Seasons guy, the type to appreciate and prefer cool and modern. The décor at La Grenouille was old-fashioned. The wallpaper was gold and cream and the crystal chandeliers gave out a yellow light that descended like a heavy blanket. The rest of New York was celebrating twenty-first century America while we were here, pretending we were in nineteenth century France.

I had to stifle a giggle. "Have you never been here before?" I asked.

"No." He frowned. "And now I know why." He shook out his napkin and put it in his lap. "Everyone is so old. And everything is so very—" Before Max could finish his thought, the host approached with my father, who had arrived right on time.

Max stood up but my father greeted me first. "Harper, how are you?" he asked as I leaned forward, accepting his kiss on my cheek. No doubt the order of greeting was more about him trying to make sure Max felt as unimportant as possible, though I couldn't imagine Max giving a shit. In fact, having seen him with his daughter, he probably thought it would be odd any other way.

"And you must be Max King," my father said, stepping back and holding out his hand, which Max took.

He'd aged since I'd last seen him. He was still handsome, but his hair had more salt mixed with the pepper, and the dark shadows beneath his eyes were new. He was still handsome though, and I wondered whether it had been his looks that had seduced my mother and all those other women, or the money, or the power?

"So, Harper," my father said, taking a menu from the waiter. "You're working at King & Associates."

I glanced across at Max, then back to my father. "Yes. For about three months now."

He nodded and set his menu down but he didn't reply. The silence felt awkward, but I didn't know what to say. I didn't want to know anything about him, so what was the point in asking a question? I was pretty sure if I said anything it would come out pointed and a little bitchy because that's how I felt.

"We're delighted to have her on board." Max filled the silence.

My father raised his eyebrows. "Why didn't you tell me?"

What, had he forgotten we didn't speak? He occasionally tried to give me money through his lawyers, and I routinely refused. That was the extent of our relationship.

"She's produced some of the best work I've ever seen from a junior researcher," Max said, leaning back. It was clearly an exaggeration, given all the red pen he'd splashed across my Bangladesh report, but I suppose he thought it would soften up my father.

My father didn't respond. I tried not to turn my head

because I didn't want it to be obvious I was looking at Max but wanted to see the expression on his face. Was he as awkward as I was?

"You've been after my work for years, Mr. King," my father said, straightening his tie. "Is that why you hired my daughter?"

Max paused before he answered. "I was lucky to recruit someone so talented. She's smart and works hard." Max grinned. "I'm just grateful you weren't successful in convincing her to work for JD Stanley," he said as if he hadn't just given him the biggest backhanded compliment in the history of backhanded compliments, and I wanted to smile at him, touch him, give him some indication I appreciated his support. "But to answer your question, I had no idea she was your daughter until after our telephone conversation. It's not something she's ever mentioned."

"Really?" he asked.

"One thing you should know about me up front," Max said as he leaned forward. "I don't lie."

"But you've wanted to work for JD Stanley for a long time," my father said.

"You're right. I have. As have the rest of my competitors."

The waiter filled our water glasses and I pulled mine toward me, fiddling with the stem.

"You seem a little more tenacious than most. A little more willing to do whatever it takes," my father commented.

"I'm glad you've noticed my tenacity," Max replied. "It's what's helped make King & Associates the most successful geopolitical research firm in America." My father looked at me and I stared into my lap. "That and the quality of work we do."

Max clearly didn't lack confidence and rightly so. He should be proud and in that moment I was proud to know him.

"Did you know Harper was working with us when you called me?" Max asked, turning the tables on my father. It was a question I was desperate for the answer to. In my experience, my father's actions were almost always selfish, and if he called Max because he knew I was working at King & Associates, I didn't know why.

"Will my answer change anything?" my father asked.

"Absolutely not. I know that when you see our work, understand what we can do for you, then the reason you called won't matter anymore."

My father put a fist to his mouth and coughed. "People do say you're the best at what you do." He paused. "Which was the reason I called. I didn't know Harper worked for you until you called Margaret."

I took a swig of my water. I was pretty sure my father was telling the truth. Why would he have known? He'd taken little to no interest in my life up until this point; why would that change now?

"Are you enjoying your work, Harper?" he asked.

I nodded. "I am. I chose to work at King & Associates because they're the best. I didn't apply anywhere else." I felt Max's gaze on me. I'd bordered on obsessed and had been completely single-minded in getting a job working with Max. I'd tailored my projects at business school to things I thought would catch King & Associates' attention on my resume, and even visited the lobby of our building when I'd flown to New York to see Grace over the Fourth of July weekend last year. I'd always known King & Associates was where I was meant to be.

"You know that you can do anything you like with your

trust fund now you're twenty-five. You don't have to do anything you don't want to do," my father said, stroking down the front of his tie.

Was he really talking about my trust fund in front of my boss? The trust fund I didn't want anything to do with? Was he deliberately trying to embarrass me? Make Max feel awkward? I'd thought we'd come here to talk about business.

"I want to work at King & Associates. I worked hard for my opportunity. And I don't need your money." Was it so difficult for him to believe I was good enough, that I would want this? This lunch should be about business and beginning to prove to my father I didn't need a trust fund. "May I ask why you're thinking about outsourcing some of your research at this point? Has something changed at your end?" I asked.

My eyes flickered to Max, who was nodding, encouraging my question and I allowed myself to relax a little bit.

My father sighed. "Well, I think it's good to keep the people who work for you on their toes, and I've been following what you do and I thought I'd like to hear a little more about it."

I kept quiet for most of the rest of lunch, concentrating on the answers my father gave to Max's questions, committing them to memory. I tried to forget the man sitting kitty-corner to me was genetically linked to me and focused on him as a client.

It was the first time I'd seen Max with a client. And it was easy to understand why he was so successful. He had an easy charm that had my father revealing things I wasn't sure he'd planned to. And Max did it all without giving anything of himself. He let my father dominate the conversation in terms of number of words spoken, but the way

Max nudged him toward certain topics meant Max was the one pulling the strings.

He was as brilliant as they said he was.

I'd known he was smart, but I hadn't expected the rest of it—the charisma, the control. It was like watching a wizard at work, casting spells over people so they'd tell him their secrets.

"And of course Harper will work on the presentation," Max said, catching my eye as I stared at him. I glanced back at my father, giving him a tight smile.

"She will?" he asked, sounding surprised. "With so little experience?"

Great. Another put-down in front of my boss. I wondered if he knew he didn't have to verbalize every thought he had.

The worst part of it all was I was pretty sure he hadn't said it to try to put me down. I think he just had so little regard for my feelings it didn't occur to him he was being hurtful.

"Yes sir. I want to put my best people on it," Max said.

"Well, if you're as good as you say you are, I should just trust your judgment," my father replied and smiled tightly.

Memories of waiting for his car to pull up on my birthday or that call at Christmas kept interrupting my concentration. The expensive gift that would sometimes follow to apologize for not making it would trick me into liking him again until the next time he disappointed me. The tight knot that sat inside my stomach when my mother apologized for his absence at dance class or school plays nudged at my belly. The humiliation I'd felt when I realized my youngest half brother had been offered a job at JD Stanley straight after graduation heated my skin.

I thought I'd feel nothing if we came to lunch after all the time that had passed, that we could be all business.

But his abandonment was too painful to forget.

I shouldn't have come today. It was like slicing open an old scar. He didn't deserve my time or attention. He didn't deserve me to bleed for him. Not anymore.

———

STANDING IN MY KITCHEN, I poured Patron into the Golden Gate Bridge shot glass I'd placed on the counter and set the bottle beside it. Tequila would make today ebb away and help me sleep.

Max had gone on to another Midtown meeting after lunch, leaving me to go back to Wall Street on my own. I'd been grateful for the space, the time to compose myself before getting back to the office. I'd been unproductive for the rest of the afternoon, going through the motions, watching the clock, willing it to speed up. I left as soon as I could so I could come home and drink.

And so tequila. Booze would lift me out of my sense of loss, of abandonment, of shame at him still having the power to wound me.

As I reached for the glass, there was a knock at my door. It could be Grace, but it was unlikely because she would have called to make sure I was in. No, it would be Max.

The thought of Max's hard body over mine, pushing into me, filling me with nothing but him, sounded better than tequila.

I opened the door wide, inviting him in. He stepped over the threshold and I let the door slam shut.

"Hi. I just wanted to check—"

"Do you want a shot?" I asked.

He squinted at me and shook his head and I turned and headed back into the kitchen.

I picked up the full glass and before I could lift it to my lips, Max grabbed it out of my hand.

I expected him to throw back the shot, but instead he slung the glass and its contents into the sink. The sound of splintering glass hitting metal echoed into the silence between us.

Pretending he hadn't just done that, I reached into the cabinet and pulled out a shot glass featuring the space needle. I filled it with tequila, then gripped the glass so Max couldn't take it from me. He plucked it from my hand as though it was nothing. As he went to throw it into the sink, I said, "Don't break that one. I like it."

"Liquor won't help," he said, pouring it into the sink and setting the glass down. He grabbed the bottle and screwed on the cap.

I folded my arms. "You're so boring." I sounded like a teenager, but he was used to that.

He put the bottle on top of my refrigerator and stepped toward me. "I know." He lifted my chin and looked at me. "How much have you had to drink?"

I shrugged, unwilling to tell him he'd put a stop to my fun before it started.

"Tell me, Harper." He dragged his thumb along my jaw, rough and intimate. My body relaxed as if *he* were tequila, and I closed my eyes in a long blink.

I uncrossed my arms. "Nothing,"

He nodded and pulled me into a hug, wrapping his long arms around me, enveloping me in the scent I now associated with sex and comfort and peace. I let him hold me, pressing my face against his chest and tightening my arms around his waist.

"I'm not psychic, but I think that maybe today brought some issues to the surface for you." He squeezed me a little bit tighter when I didn't answer. "You want to talk about it rather than drink them away?"

"Definitely not," I replied. Him just being here, holding me, made everything feel so much better. "And I'm sorry about the shoes. They're beautiful and I love them. Sometimes I don't accept gifts well."

He chuckled. "Can I ask why?"

I shrugged and he didn't ask me anything else.

We stood in my kitchen for what seemed like hours, just holding each other until I managed to say, "I'm okay." His chest muffled my words.

He sighed, his ribcage rising and lowering against my breasts. "I should go," he said, but didn't release me.

"Don't," I whispered.

"I don't want to." He sounded tired. As if by hugging him, I'd sapped him of his energy. "And that's why I should. We said no more trips to Vegas."

We had, and it had been the right thing to do. The problem was the more time I spent with him, the more I wanted.

"Then let's go somewhere else," I said, smoothing my hands up his back, shifting my hips just a fraction.

"Harper," he whispered.

"Aruba," I suggested. "Or Paris."

He dipped his head and kissed my neck. My knees weakened in relief. It was what I'd been waiting for since he arrived, since lunch, since the last time he'd touched me.

"Or just here," I said, trailing my fingers up his sides and around his neck. "Kiss me," I whispered. "Just be here with me."

He grabbed my ass and brushed my lips with his, first

left then right. I wanted more. I wanted him. I didn't know if he was trying to torment me or still weighing the advantages and disadvantages of being with me again.

I slid my hands down his chest and he caught my wrists before I could convince him to stay.

"You want me, huh?" he asked, placing my hands on the counter behind me.

I wanted to drown out the day. "Kiss me."

"You think this is about making you feel better about today. But it's not," he said, his eyes not leaving my face. "It's about this." His hands swept up my arms and cupped my face. "About the way you feel when I touch you." He bent and placed a kiss on the corner of my lips, teasing me, making me wait. "About how you need me to fuck you more than you need your next breath." He knocked my legs apart with his knee.

I couldn't argue with him. Nothing he was saying was untrue.

I wanted him. Every second. Since before I'd met him.

Even when I thought he was an asshole, I wanted him.

But I wasn't about to admit it.

I squirmed when he reached into the waistband of my leggings, his insistent hand pushing into my panties. "You see?" he asked. "You're wet for me."

He ran two fingers up and down from my clit to my entrance, giving neither relief. I twisted my hips in an effort to feel him deeper, harder.

"Admit it," he said. "Admit how much you want me."

I shifted my hands from the counter where he'd placed them and grabbed his shirt, fumbling with the buttons.

"No," he said, removing his hands from my underwear and batting my hands away.

I groaned in frustration.

"Admit it," he said.

"I want to get fucked." It was true.

"You are the most infuriating woman I know. And that's a mighty high bar given the women in my life." He pulled up my T-shirt, making me shiver as he grazed my skin with his palms. "Fuck," he said when he realized I wasn't wearing a bra. "Tell me. Tell me now."

"You want to feel special?" I asked, taunting him. "You need to know that women desire you over anyone else?"

He shook his head slowly. "Just you. I need to hear it from *you*."

"Why?" I asked as he bent and took a nipple in his mouth, his tongue circling and sucking, his fingers tugging at the other.

"Because it's the truth," he said and he kissed me again on the lips. "Because it's what I feel whenever I think of you, whenever you're near."

Heat ran into my limbs and I put my arms around his neck, gazing into his eyes. He stared back and lifted me onto the kitchen counter.

I nodded. "It's true. I want you." The words sounded soft as they came out. Did he notice?

"I know," he said, his gaze flickering to my mouth just before he pressed his lips to mine. I sighed with relief. A layer of calm engulfed us as if our mutual admissions bound us together. My tongue found his and instead of being urgent and possessive, I allowed myself to go at his pace. I encouraged his seduction of me.

He leaned back and placed a kiss on my nose. "If you're still wearing clothes, I'm not doing something correctly," he said as he pulled at my waistband.

What had I just admitted to him? Had I said I wanted more? I wasn't sure, but all I could focus on were his fingers pulling down my leggings, the glazed look in his eyes as he examined every inch of my skin as if he couldn't quite believe what he was seeing. Nothing else seemed to matter.

As my clothes hit the floor, he scooped me off the counter and walked me out of the kitchen and over to my bed. When we'd been together before, we'd both acted as if we were against the clock. Tugging at each other, desperate to make each other feel good as soon as possible in case someone rang the bell and told us our time was up. This was different. Our kisses were lazy, our movements languid. He ran his palms down my body and brought his hand to my inner thigh as he lay next to me.

"You're wearing a tie," I whispered.

"Like I said, one of the brightest junior researchers I've ever worked with."

I smiled and reached out, pulled the silk material clear of his neck, opened the top couple of buttons of his shirt, and slipped my hand against the skin just below his neck. I sighed. He would make today go away.

Quickly, he stood, stripping completely naked in seconds, throwing his three-thousand-dollar suit on the back of my couch. Then without asking, he opened the drawer to my nightstand and took out a condom.

"Are you dating?" he asked as he joined me on the bed. "No. Don't answer that."

I stroked his cheek and he looked up at me. "Are you dating?" I asked.

"No," he responded. "I'm—"

I stroked my thumb over his lips. He didn't need to explain himself. I didn't really care, because whatever else was going on in his world, or my world, I wanted this to happen. I didn't want to think about tomorrow, to consider consequences. I wanted to drink in the way his eyes, tongue, and hands all seemed to worship me.

He leaned forward and kissed me, taking my bottom lip between his teeth before biting down until it stung, then pushed his tongue against mine. I could kiss him forever. If his penis fell off, I could be happy for the rest of my life with just his tongue. Without stopping kissing me, he put on a condom.

"I love your kisses," I said before I had time to think maybe that wasn't something I should say.

He groaned against my mouth. "And what else?" he asked, his fingers skimming the juncture of my inner thigh.

"Your fingers, your face, your cock." The words tripped out of my mouth, and before I had time to take any of them back, he was over me, pushing into me, slowly but so deep. I brought my knees up as far as they would go, opening myself as wide as I could for him.

"Like that?" he asked as he paused deep inside me.

I nodded, my fingers digging into his shoulders.

"Relax," he said. "It's just you and me."

I exhaled. It was just him and me. Nothing else mattered.

His eyes opened wider, as if he were asking me if I was ready, and I slid my hands over his ass in response. He pulled out almost as slowly as he'd filled me up and I whimpered, overcome with sensation.

"Harper," he whispered. "Look at me."

I watched as his erection entered me. I glanced up and he slammed in while I clung to him. "You love my cock. You said it, baby, and now you're going to get it. I'm going to give you everything you need."

He plunged into me, this time giving me no time to

recover before pulling out and then pushing back in. He groaned through a clenched jaw.

I do that to you, was all I could think.

This man, who looked like Gucci made suits just because he existed, groaned because of *me*.

This man, whose beautiful green eyes told everyone who met him he was the boss, was fucking *me*.

This man, who ruled Wall Street, the power behind the performance of leading investment banks in Manhattan, was having to concentrate so he didn't come too quickly because of *me*.

I brought the King of Wall Street to his knees.

"Jesus, Harper."

I pushed against his chest and shifted so he stopped. We were both going to come within seconds if we stayed like that. I moved under him.

"What? That was perfect," he said.

"Too perfect," I replied and flipped over onto my stomach. Seeing him so undone would push me over the edge too soon.

He slid his hands under my thighs and pulled me toward him and straight onto his dick. My back arched as pleasure shot through my legs and ricocheted left and right then up my body. I pushed myself up onto my hands, trying to participate in some way, but I couldn't.

I clenched as he ran the heel of his hand up my spine then clasped my shoulder. "So tight. So good," he groaned.

In seconds I was right on the edge, the change of position having done nothing to dampen my desire for him, to ward off my orgasm. His touch made sure everything was just as intense.

"Max," I cried out.

He thrust in, harder this time. "Again," he choked out.

"Max. Please. God. Max." I couldn't hold it off any longer.

As I spiraled down from my climax, Max bellowed out my name and collapsed on top of me, his front to my back, then rolled to the side, pulling me with him.

TWELVE

Max

I came out of the bathroom to find Harper hadn't moved a muscle. I couldn't blame her; we'd spent most of the night fucking and I was exhausted.

"From what I saw today, your father still has quite the hold on you."

Harper pulled the sheet up over her face. "Really? You're standing there with your dick out looking at me while I still have your come between my legs, and we're going to talk about my father?"

"You don't have my come between your legs. I just threw out the condom."

She popped out from under the sheet to scowl at me. "I meant it figuratively."

She was so completely breathtaking when she was mad with me, and I quickly forgot what we were talking about. "You look beautiful." I crawled onto the mattress. I wanted to pull her into me, but she swiped me on the arm and headed to the bathroom.

"You don't take any money from him, do you?" I called after her. Her apartment, her clothes. She wasn't taking any handouts from what I could see. I liked that about her. She was independent. Unable to be bought.

"Why do you ask?" She appeared in the bathroom doorway, one hand on the frame, totally unconcerned by her nakedness. I *really* liked that about her. I liked the way her hips flared, emphasizing her small waist. Liked the way her tits jutted out as if they wanted to join in the conversation. My dick hardened.

"Max?" she prompted, and I pulled my gaze back up to meet hers. "You're a pervert."

"You're naked. What am I going to do other than look at you?"

"I don't know, answer me?"

Even her sarcasm got me hard.

She pulled her hair back as if she were going to tie it up, which lifted up her breasts and lengthened her stomach. "Get the fuck over here before I start jerking myself off."

She released her hair and stepped toward the bed. I grabbed her, pulling her down and against me, wrapping my legs around hers, clasping her to my chest. I couldn't get close enough to quench my thirst for her.

"You're right. I don't take money from him. I started to take some money when I went to college. I figured he owed me that. But it didn't feel right. I didn't know that man."

I pulled her closer. They seemed like strangers at lunch; he was asking her the most basic questions any father should already have known the answer to. There was no affection on Harper's side. He was the man I'd never wanted to be for Amanda.

"Did he and your mother divorce?" I asked.

"No." She exhaled sharply. "He didn't have the decency to marry her in the first place."

Oh. "Pandora and I didn't marry," I replied.

"Yeah, you said. Did you not want to marry her?" she asked. After seeing her with her father today, I wondered if she'd wanted to ask me that question for a while.

I tucked one arm behind my head. "Neither of us wanted to get married."

"But you wanted Amanda. I mean you stayed in contact with her."

My thumb skirted over her hip. "Sure. Pandora and I talked about getting married, and I can't say I know why we didn't go through with it. We were both about to go off to college and maybe we knew we'd be compounding one mistake with another." It had been the right decision. "Not that Amanda was a mistake. Just the pregnancy wasn't planned. Clearly." Harper glanced up at me and I smiled at her. "Pandora and I were good friends, and just before graduation one thing led to another . . . It was never meant to be anything more than a good-bye." I sighed. "It bound us together forever."

Harper pressed her lips against my chest. "She never wanted to get married, not even after Amanda was born?"

I kissed the top of her forehead. "I don't think so. She met Jason when Amanda was about a year old."

"Did that bother you?" she asked.

"No, not at all." It genuinely never had. I liked Jason. He was good to Pandora and my daughter. "I think her parents were worried, but I always wanted Pandora to be happy. We'd been friends a long time. And it didn't stop me from wanting to be the best dad I could be."

Harper didn't respond but I could tell she had more to say. I was content to stay wrapped around her in silence.

Eventually she sighed and said, "I agreed to come shopping because I assumed Amanda would be miserable going shopping with you. I assumed you took as much interest in Amanda as my father did in me."

I pulled back slightly to look at her. "Really?" I said. "She loves shopping. Doesn't mind who she's with but I like to take her. I think since Pandora left, she misses. . ." I almost said *her mother* but I didn't want Harper to misunderstand what I was saying. "You know, the girl thing. And Scarlett is dating like a dozen men and Violet is—"

"Violet?" she asked.

"My other sister," I explained. "And both grandmas want Amanda to stay a little girl for as long as possible. So, we have mutual aims and objectives there." I pulled her close and she pressed her cheek against my chest. "She loved having you there. Didn't stop going on about you when we got home—it certainly raised some eyebrows."

"It did?" she asked. "What kind of eyebrows?"

"The busybody kind. I guess because we work together and live in the same building. I think my sisters believed . . ." What had they thought? That we were dating?

"Is Violet younger than you?" she asked and I was grateful she had gone in a different direction.

"Yes, and a complete pain in the ass. Always interfering in everyone's business. She's a meddler." I chuckled as I realized it might be a genetic thing. "She's a lot like Amanda in that way." Amanda dressed her constant whining about wanting a baby sister as self-interest but I was pretty sure she wanted me happy. "They have a lot in common."

"Sounds like you have your hands full. Even without King & Associates."

I sighed. "They occupy two different spaces in my brain."

"Maybe," she said. She wiggled her body against mine, and I rolled us over until she was on her back and I was looking down at her.

"You're the exception," I said. "You seem to have taken up residence in both spaces." I brushed my nose against hers and pulled back to look at her. "I realized it in the cab today. I liked that we could just be together, near each other. No talking, no touching."

She nodded very slightly.

"This is new to me," I said. I wasn't sure what *this* was. If I was just having a personal relationship with someone I worked with, or having sex with someone I knew more about than just their last name. Or was it the fact that whenever I saw her, whenever I thought about her, whenever I touched her, I wanted more. It was all new.

I dipped my head to kiss her nose as she wrapped her legs around me, pulling me close until my cock pushed against her.

I'd fucked a lot of attractive women with nice, firm asses; long, lean legs; and huge tits. Harper was attractive, gorgeous even, but with her, the stuff that made me hard, that had me moaning, was more than just the physical. I liked the way the silences were comfortable, the way she could make me laugh, the way she seemed to open up as I drove into her.

"You want some of this?" I asked, rocking against her. She grinned and I shook my head. "Insatiable," I said as I lowered myself onto my forearms and licked along her collarbone. She threaded her hands through the back of my hair, setting goosebumps off across my skin. I took her breasts in my hands, grazed her nipples with my tongue and then again with my teeth. She arched against me as my nips became careless and harder. My dick throbbed at her reaction, but it wouldn't find relief any time soon. Winding up her lust got me hard, her desire towing me along.

"I want to see you in those shoes I bought you," I said, my voice hoarse. Her naked in those shoes had been an image front and center of my thoughts since I made the purchase.

She grinned up at me and ducked under my arm, heading across to her closet. I shifted to my back, waiting for her. She stepped out into the door frame, her hands above her, bracing on either side of the wood, one high shoe stroking up the side of long, tan leg. I couldn't stop the groan that ripped out of my chest. I reached for her but instead she turned around, swaying her hips one way and then another. "How do they look from the back?" she asked. I didn't know where to focus—her thick, soft hair sweeping down her back, down to her small waist, or her high, tight ass as it jutted out to get my attention, or between her thighs where I knew it was so soft and wet. The shoes magnified every inch of her perfect body.

"Get over here and let me show you what I think about you in those shoes."

She took small steps toward the bed, her perfectly neat pussy mesmerizing me as she got closer. Fuck, I couldn't get enough.

She grasped her breasts, kneading them together as she approached the bed. I rose onto my knees to meet her, wanting the space between us to disappear. Reaching between her thighs with one hand, I grabbed her ass and pulled her onto my fingers. "You are perfect," I whispered. She gave me a small smile and her head tipped back as my fingers drove deeper.

Blood rushed to my dick and I wanted it in my fist, in her pussy, but I didn't want to let go of her. She stumbled slightly, which made it worse, she was so affected by just my fingers she couldn't stand. "I want you on your back, your feet in the air," I said and pulled her onto the bed.

I kissed my way down to her belly button. She shifted, getting more and more restless, twisting and squirming beneath me. I moved farther down and gripped her thighs, pushing them open, her heels high in the air either side of me.

She cried out when I blew across her sex. Her sounds urged me on. I spread the lips of her sex, exposing her clitoris. She tensed. I wasn't sure if it was in anticipation or embarrassment. I leaned forward and circled the bundle of nerves with my tongue. Her breaths came louder and deeper as I suckled before licking down to her entrance.

Like nothing I'd ever tasted before. Like springtime— warm, fresh, and inviting. I couldn't get enough as I delved into her, lapping up the wetness that hadn't already coated my chin.

I could stay like this, my face buried in her, for the rest of my days. I reached for my rock-hard cock, which was desperate to taste the sweetness coating my tongue. I dragged my fist up and forced myself to let go; I wasn't ready to come yet. As soon as I pushed into her I'd be lost— my body would crash through every urge I had to please her in an effort to get to my orgasm.

I elbowed her thighs open wider still, my tongue connecting with her clitoris as my thumbs delved into her, pulling at her entrance, twisting then circling back. Her body began to shudder and I heard the whisper of my name on her lips. I wanted it louder. I increased the pressure of my tongue and her hands flew into my hair as she called, "Max, my God, Max."

Her orgasm spread through her like an electricity bolt,

her pussy contracting, pushing against my thumbs. I removed my hands and slid my tongue back to soothe her, feeling her pulse just below the surface of her skin.

I glanced up at her, her arms overhead as her back began to lower back into the mattress. It was the first time I'd ever had the urge to film a woman before. I'd never need to date again if I had a recording of Harper coming on my tongue like that.

God, she was perfect when she was undone.

I moved to her side as she opened her eyes and smiled at me. "You're good at that," she said.

"What am I supposed to say?" I chuckled.

"Learn how to accept a compliment," she replied as she pushed herself up then straddled me. "Just say 'thank you'."

I shook my head, my hands going to her hips. Her wetness coated my cock as she shifted back and forward.

I groaned, her heat seeping into my veins. I wasn't going to last long. Desperate, I reached for the nightstand. I fumbled with the drawer, had to stretch to reach inside. The wood dug into my wrist and I scrambled for a condom.

Grinning, she took the square packet before I had a chance to argue and rolled the condom on, tantalizingly slowly, both of us staring at my jutting cock in her hands.

"It's not been long, but do you remember how good it feels?" she asked as she squeezed the base of me. "How tight I am?"

I groaned, needing her to remind me.

She lifted herself up and positioned the tip at her opening. "How you slide in so deep?"

"Fuck, Harper. Are you trying to kill me?"

She scooped up her hair, then let it tumble back down, smoothing her hands over her breasts as she twisted her hips and took me a little deeper. "You remember how you fit so good? You're almost too big." She took me in a little more. "*Almost.*" A little more. "I always think it's going to be painful, but no." She placed her hands on my torso, steadying herself, which squeezed her tits together, pushing them nearer me. Her head snapped back and I almost came right there. "It feels too good to be painful," she continued, twisting her hips, teasing me, knowing I wanted to be in deep. "Do you remember how good it feels?"

I gripped her hips, trying to do anything I could to prevent myself from jabbing my cock so deep she'd never walk again.

She let herself sink all the way down, her eyes widening with every movement, then stilled. "I never remember," she whispered. "I always forget just how good it feels."

Patience deserting me, I growled and sat up, spinning her onto her back and pushing back into her. "I'm going to make sure you never forget again."

I wanted to fuck her forever.

———

AFTER SPENDING the night with Harper, I had taken longer than usual to get through everything I needed to do, so I got a later train.

"I'm home," I shouted. I could hear the television from the family room. Usually I came back to Connecticut in the week to find Marion clearing up the kitchen, but her car wasn't in the drive. Was she here alone? "Amanda," I shouted. I supposed she didn't need to be babysat anymore but I didn't like the idea of her being alone, waiting for me to come back.

"In here," she yelled over the noise of music and shouting. I took off my jacket and put it on the back of one of the barstools and dropped my cell on the counter. A nice glass of Pinot Noir was what I needed. It had been a tough week. I placed a glass on the counter and pulled out a bottle from the wine fridge.

"Can I have one of those?" Scarlett asked from behind me.

"Hey." I grabbed another glass. "What are you doing here?"

She slid onto the middle barstool. "I didn't want to be on my own tonight. Can I stay over?"

I nodded. She clearly wanted to talk. I poured the wine into her glass as she held the stem.

"I'm thinking of moving into the city," she said, tilting her head as she watched her glass fill up. "Sometimes it feels like Connecticut is where I should be in ten years rather than now. Does that make sense?" she asked.

"It's good to change things up, I guess. You've never lived in Manhattan. What would you do about work?" She worked at an investment bank just outside Westhaven.

She shrugged.

Fuck, I hoped she wasn't going to ask me for a job.

"I thought I'd apply for a transfer. There's a treasury position in Manhattan at the moment. It's a level up, but I have the experience."

I nodded, relieved we weren't about to have a difficult conversation. My phone vibrated on the counter with a message, Harper's name flashing up on the screen. I watched as Scarlett saw the message, then met my gaze.

She didn't say anything, so I grabbed my phone and opened the message. *Manhattan's no fun when the King's not in residence.*

I grinned and glanced up at Scarlett, whose eyebrows

were so high they nearly disappeared into her hairline. "Anything you care to share?"

I swallowed my smile and picked up my glass. "Just work." I took a sip.

"Yeah, that looked like work."

Thoughts of trying to keep my feelings for Harper professional had long since disappeared. Harper had been clear she didn't want to be seen as the girl fucking the boss, and I didn't want to muddy waters between professional and personal any more than I already had. In the office we'd agreed to just avoid each other. Easily done as the morning meetings about JD Stanley were the only times we really saw each other. Some distance in the office was a good thing.

But all the distance disappeared as soon as we were back in her apartment—for some reason she refused to come up to my place, even though it was bigger.

"Hey, Dad," Amanda said, interrupting the silence.

"Hey, beautiful," I replied, bending to kiss my daughter hello. I wondered how soon she'd no longer want to kiss me. Parents kept warning me about the teenage years, assuring me our disagreement over her dress was only the tip of a very large iceberg.

"You going to text Harper back?" Scarlett asked, grinning at me. If the Pinot Noir hadn't been so good, I'd have tipped the rest of the bottle over her head. My daughter wouldn't miss the reference and Scarlett knew it.

"Harper texted?" Amanda asked predictably. "Can you ask her if she'll come help me get ready for the dance? I want her to do my eyeliner just like hers."

I put my phone back on the counter. "No, I'm not asking Harper to come out to Connecticut to help you get ready. She's not your personal stylist."

"She's too busy attending to someone else's needs in this family, isn't she?" Scarlett joked and I shot her a dirty look.

"What?" Amanda asked.

"Let's talk about your dating life, shall we, Scarlett?" I asked.

She tilted her head. "Oh, so you admit Harper's part of your dating life then?"

Shit. I was usually better at avoiding Scarlett's interrogations. I turned toward the refrigerator. "Have you eaten?" I asked Amanda, trying to ignore my sister.

"Tell me more about Harper, Amanda."

Inwardly I groaned.

"I want to be just like her when I'm older. You've seen her, right?" Amanda babbled on about how great Harper was, how wise she was about boys and what a great fashion sense she had. It sounded like Amanda'd known her for years rather than only spent time with her twice.

"So, dinner?" I asked, hoping to get them to change the subject.

"Can I have the cold lasagna in there?" Amanda asked, gesturing to the fridge.

Sounded like a great idea. Marion had even left a salad, too.

"Harper's great, isn't she?" Amanda asked.

I glanced at my sister, who held my gaze and asked Amanda, "Do you think she likes your dad?"

"Scarlett," I warned.

"Does she have a boyfriend?" Scarlett asked, which was a question I had a little more interest in. Had Harper talked to Amanda about anyone?

"No, she says she's too focused on work," Amanda replied. "When I talked to her, she pretty much agreed boys were douchebags who should be avoided at all costs."

I couldn't hold back a chuckle, which won me a suspicious glance from my sister. "She's a very sensible woman."

I put the salad on the counter. "Can you get plates?" I asked Amanda. She hopped off her stool and began to set things out as I dished up the lasagna.

"You know we just want you to be happy," my sister said, lowering her voice. "And from what I can remember, Harper is beautiful." She clinked her glass against mine before taking another sip. "Amanda clearly likes her."

I handed her a plate of food, pretending I wasn't listening.

"Have you thought about asking her out?"

Ignoring Scarlett, I spooned pasta onto mine and Amanda's plates, then placed the dish back in the refrigerator. My sister bugged me about getting a girlfriend almost as much as Amanda did, but why were they fixating on Harper? That was my job. When I turned back to the counter, Amanda and Scarlett were both staring at me as if waiting for me to say something.

"What?" I asked, grabbing the seat next to them and taking a forkful of food.

"Have you thought about asking Harper out on a date, Dad?" Amanda asked, as if I were the most ludicrous person she'd ever had to deal with.

I swallowed and put some salad on my plate. "What is with you two? I've told you, Harper works for me. What is your obsession with her?"

"I like her." Amanda shrugged.

Scarlett grinned. "And that should be reason enough. Why don't you take her to dinner? What could one evening hurt?"

Little did they know trying to keep time spent with Harper limited to just one evening would be impossible.

Whatever boundaries I set with her got torn down and over-run. We'd never really been in Vegas. Well, I hadn't managed it anyway. Even here, with my sister and daughter, a situation that had only ever been completely consuming, I was wondering what Harper was doing, who she was spending time with. Did she feel the same? And if she did, then what? Would she come out here to Connecticut? Meet my family?

Did I want her to?

"You think I should date, huh?" I asked. Scarlett was right; it was good that Amanda seemed to like Harper. If my daughter was open to it, maybe I should ask Harper out. Officially.

Amanda tapped on my head with her fist. "Come on, Dad, duh. I've only been saying this my whole life."

"Okay," I said.

"What does okay mean?" Amanda said.

"It means please don't speak with your mouth full," I said, glaring at my daughter.

She giggled and swallowed. "Sorry. But what does 'okay' mean?"

"It means, okay, I'll think about asking her out." The situation with Harper felt like a jigsaw puzzle with too many pieces. Harper working for me complicated things, and her father was the founder of JD Stanley. We also lived in the same building. I'd never really dated before—I was bound to fuck things up. There were a lot of downsides. One of Scarlett's friends would probably be less compli-cated to date. There would be fewer aftershocks if it didn't work out.

But she wouldn't be Harper.

"You will?" Amanda squealed. "Does that mean she can

come help me get ready for the dance? Can I call her now to ask?"

"I said I'd think about asking her to dinner, not employ her to do your makeup. Jeez."

Amanda paused, which meant she was thinking, which could only be bad. "You could make her dinner, here. After I leave for the dance."

I could. It would be nice to see Harper in Connecticut. It wasn't the worst idea Amanda had ever had.

"I'll think about it," I said and Amanda squealed again.

I glanced across at Scarlett, who beamed at me. "What?" I asked her.

She shrugged. "Nothing."

Amanda abandoned her plate of food and headed toward the den, no doubt to find her phone. "Can I call her now? Check if she's free? This is going to be so much fun. It will be like, the best night ever!"

"You need to lower your expectations," I told my daughter. "And prepare yourself for the fact that she might say no."

She paused and spun around to face me. "So what if she does? You've always told me that you don't take no for an answer."

I couldn't argue with that. I was used to getting what I wanted. And right now, I wanted Harper.

THIRTEEN

Harper

I couldn't ever remember being so nervous. I'd rehearsed and prepared for the Goldman's pitch and thirty minutes ago I was feeling pretty confident. But as the appointment grew closer, my heartrate had started to speed as if I were sprinting across hot coals.

"So, you'll handle any questions about the process?" Max asked.

I nodded, picking at the hem of my skirt as we sat in the back of the cab to Midtown. I wished I'd brought some water. My throat was dry and tight. They'd have water when we arrived, wouldn't they?

It was the questions I was most worried about. I'd been practicing my ass off for this presentation. It might be a warm-up to the JD Stanley pitch, but it was still important. There was six figures in profit to be lost if I fucked this up. That might be a drop in Wall Street's ocean, but it seemed like a lot of money to me.

My parts of the presentation? Those I'd own. Unlike

Max, who appeared to speak off the cuff, I'd written myself a script and memorized it. I'd practiced out loud at home over and over. I knew exactly when to pause, when to ask people to turn the pages in their slide deck, and when to draw emphasis. As long as I hadn't forgotten the printouts, I'd be fine. I scrambled at my feet, reaching into my business carryall to make sure the papers were all there. They were. Just like the last thirty-six times I'd checked.

"Don't be nervous," Max said, smoothing down his tie. "It will be fine. The rehearsal was good."

How would he know if this was going to be fine? Sure, he'd seen the rehearsal, but when the pressure was on, no one knew how things would turn out. I overcame nerves and pressure by being over-prepared—but I couldn't prepare for questions, at least not all of them.

"Easy for you to say," I replied.

"I mean it," he said, placing his hand on my knee.

I pushed it off. The last thing I needed was to be thinking about him naked. "Sorry, I need to . . ." I wasn't sure what I needed.

He glanced out the window. "Okay, I get it. What if I was to ask you a favor? Would that help take your mind off things?" he asked.

I didn't respond, unsure of everything other than my script.

"Amanda wants you to help her get ready for the dance. I said I'd ask."

That wasn't what I'd expected at all. "In Connecticut?" I asked.

He nodded. "You don't have to come, but I know Amanda would like you to. She suggested you and I have dinner together when she left."

"Is she trying to set us up?" I laughed.

"I think so. She's a big fan of yours." Max smiled. "Runs in the family, apparently."

I grinned. Max and I hadn't talked about how we felt about each other, so his comment was unexpected. I wanted to reach for him, kiss him, but I didn't. I needed to keep my head in the game.

"I'd like you to come," he said.

I liked Amanda, but I didn't know how I felt about her setting me and Max up on a date. "Is that weird, having your daughter set you up?"

Max tilted his head. "It should be, I guess. But she goes on and on about me getting marrie—dating. I'm used to it."

"Have you told her that we're . . ."

"Fucking like bunnies? Funnily enough, no," he said, chuckling.

Was that what we were doing? Just fucking? I wasn't sure. I liked the guy, really liked him, but he was my boss and he had a daughter and this whole secret life in Connecticut I'd never seen.

"I think maybe she's picked up on the fact that I like you," he said. Butterflies in my stomach took my mind off my quickening pulse. "I know my sister has."

Liked me? Did that mean it wasn't just fucking for him? I wasn't sure it was for me anymore either.

"Scarlett?" I asked.

"Yeah, she's made a few comments when your name's come up." He slung his arm across the back of the seat. "Look, don't feel any pressure, but I'd like it if you came up, even if it isn't for the dance—it's only three weeks away. You might have plans."

"I don't."

He raised an eyebrow at me. "You don't have plans?" he asked. I shook my head.

"So? Does that mean you'll come?"

"Sure." I grinned and the corner of his mouth turned up. I could tell we both wanted to touch each other, lean in for a kiss, but there was some kind of imaginary force field that existed when we were in work clothes.

The cab pulled to a halt on Fifth Avenue. Shit, we were here.

"Max King for Peter Jones," he said when we reached the receptionist.

As we made our way up in the elevators, he said, "I've done this a million times, Harper. I'll step in if it gets too much."

He meant to be reassuring, but I didn't want him to step in. I wanted to nail this so the presentation to JD Stanley would be easy. Or easier. I really wanted my father to see what I'd been able to do despite him. Maybe then he'd wonder if he'd missed out, realize just throwing money at a situation didn't mean you knew a person, influenced or inspired them.

"I'm good," I said with an open, professional smile. "Everything's fine."

As we entered the conference room, three men stood from their chairs across the oval mahogany table to greet us. All white, all balding, all slightly overweight. In fact, I could have interchanged any parts of them and I was pretty sure no one would notice.

After the introductions, we took our seats across the table.

"Gentlemen, we have some slides we'd like to pass around," Max said as I slid three copies of our presentation across the table.

Not one of them made a move to take the papers.

The man in a gray suit steepled his fingers in front of

him. "Why don't you just talk to us about the experience you have in Asia. Most of your competitors have local offices, and I'd like to understand a little more about how you'll be able to provide any real value from your desks here in Manhattan.

Shit. Shit. Shit. Shit. Shit.

This wasn't going as planned. The presentation was where I felt safe.

I glanced across at Max, who looked as relaxed as if he'd just been asked his mother's maiden name. He sat back in his chair and nodded. "Sure. I'm very happy to talk about our strategic choices in terms of international reach."

He went on to explain how his low overheads meant he could spend money employing experts on the ground, which could be different project to project, where his competitors had to use the people they'd employed in their local office regardless of whether or not they were qualified. "You see someone at their desk in Kuala Lumpur is still at their desk—they're not out meeting people, finding out what's happening on the ground. My network of contacts are the people living the day-to-day reality of the geopolitical situations across many industries." Max sat forward as he spoke, looking at his audience as if they were the most important people in the world and he had precious information to share with them. They seemed to find him as compelling as I did.

Max batted away each of the questions as if he were Nadal returning serve, and as the meeting progressed, the suits visibly relaxed, even chuckling at a few of Max's wry comments.

"Do you think the actual process produces anything we've not seen before?" The middle man tapped his fingers against the arm of his chair. "You clearly see it as part of your competitive advantage."

Max turned to me. This was the part of the presentation I'd prepared. "Harper, did you want to add anything here?"

I lifted the corner of my mouth, trying to fake a smile, wanting to cover the fact my mind had gone blank. Completely blank.

"Yes, well." I flicked through my copy of the presentation that had gone unopened. "As you said, we see this is as a key competitive advantage over others in the marketplace . . ." I glanced up and scanned the three sets of eyes all staring at me. I reached for my glass of water and took a sip. My mind was blank. I'd been over this hundreds of times, but I needed a prompt. "We like to conclude things," I blurted. That was one of my key points, wasn't it? I didn't know what I was saying. I started flicking through my presentation manically. "I . . . If I could just . . ."

Max placed his hand on my forearm. "Harper's quite right. One of the key things that differentiates us from others in the marketplace is the conclusions we are able to draw." Several times Max paused and turned to me, which would have allowed me to step in and say something if only I could have thought of a single thing to say.

Eventually I tuned out and slumped back in my seat.

I'd been given this huge opportunity and I'd totally bombed. What the hell was the matter with me? I'd been well prepared for today. I couldn't have done more. Did I subconsciously not think I deserved to be here? Had my father's comments at lunch last week burrowed deeper than I realized? I was trying so hard to prove to my father I was worthy of this job, but I wasn't sure I really believed it.

I TRIED to wash away the awful meeting at Goldman Sachs but my bath wasn't helping. Nor was the Jo Malone bath oil or the so-called soothing music filtering through from my bedroom. I was trying to relax, calm down. Nothing was working. All I could do was replay the disastrous meeting earlier in the day over and over again.

I slid under the water, submerging my entire head in the vain hope it would cleanse away the embarrassment.

I came up for air. Nope, I still wanted to die.

Max must think I'm an idiot.

My breath caught at the sharp knock at the door. Perfect timing. Here he was to tell me so. Well, I didn't have to answer the door. I ignored him.

"Harper, I know you're in there. Answer the door."

I shouldn't have put that music on. I stood up and wrapped a towel around me.

Max started pounding on the door.

"I'm coming," I shouted. I threw it open, then immediately turned around and headed back to the bathroom.

"Nice to see you, too," he mumbled. I dropped my towel and slid back into the bath.

I expected him to follow me, but instead I heard cabinet doors opening in the kitchen. What was he doing?

He appeared, barefoot, his jacket and tie gone, holding two glasses of wine. Right then he might just have been the perfect man.

"You have a nice, tight ass," I said. He grinned. "And I'm really sorry I fucked up."

He handed me a glass, which I took gratefully. He'd definitely brought the bottle with him—I didn't own anything this good. It tasted like it cost a month's salary.

He sighed, closed the bathroom door, and began unbuttoning his shirt. When he undid the last one, he took a swig of his wine and placed it on the side of the bath and stripped off the rest of his clothes.

"What are you doing?" I asked as he stepped into the bath.

He didn't respond, just sat down at the opposite end, pulling my legs over his.

"You choked today," he said, taking a sip of his wine.

"Yeah, thanks, Captain Obvious. If you're here to make me feel worse, you can leave right now."

He acted as if he hadn't heard me, stroking up the leg I had resting on his thigh. "You know Michael Jordan?"

Now he's going to talk about sports? Great. Just what I needed.

I nodded.

"Greatest basketball player of all time, right? A consummate winner."

"Er . . . yes." Where the hell was he going with this?

"Well something he said was the best business advice I've ever received. It went like this, 'I've missed more than nine-thousand shots in my career and I've lost almost three-hundred games.'" He smoothed his hands up and down my legs "'Twenty-six times I've been trusted to take the game-winning shot and missed. 'I've failed over and over and over again in my life. And that is why I succeed.'"

He paused and we stared at each other.

"We all fuck up, Harper. We all choke. It's how we get better."

I sighed and skimmed the top of the water with my palms. "Yeah, well, I'm not a basketball player," I muttered.

"Of course you are. We all are. You didn't come out of the womb ready. How many times did you fall over before you learned to walk? You can't give up when you fail the first time." He took my foot, pressing his thumbs into my sole. "The problem is there comes a point in life when you haven't fucked up in a while. You get good at passing exams, you graduate, you get a job. Everything is great. But it's a false sense of security because if you're going to learn and grow, fucking up is inevitable."

"So if you're saying my choking was always going to happen, why did you take me to the presentation?" I tried to pull my leg away but he held on tight.

"I might be good but I'm not a fucking psychic. No one knows *when* they're going to fail, just that they will at some point."

The pressure in my chest started to lift. He was right. Of course he was. "But I hate it."

"I'm sure Michael Jordan hated missing game-winning shots."

I didn't say anything. I was new and inexperienced and I'd let it show.

"Harper, it's why I wanted you to present to Goldman's. I didn't want you to choke in front of your father."

Had he really been trying to protect me? Warmth for him spread through my body. I wasn't used to someone having my back in such an obvious way. Not a man anyway. And I liked it. More than liked it.

I pulled my foot from his hands and moved to straddle him. "You always say exactly the right thing."

He chuckled. "I think my daughter would disagree."

I wrapped my arms around his neck and kissed him briefly on his jaw. "You look sexy wet," I said.

"You look sexy all the time," he replied.

"Exactly the right thing," I whispered and I pressed my lips to his. His tongue reached for mine.

He shifted, pushing me away. "Come on. Let's get out. I want to fuck you without being interrupted by neighbors complaining about water coming through their ceiling."

Well, I couldn't argue with that logic, either.

He held me tight as he walked me out of the bathroom and pushed me onto the bed, collapsing beside me. He opened my towel as if inspecting me for clues, his eyes raking over my naked body. "You're beautiful," he said, squinting as he said it, as if he couldn't quite believe it.

A rush of panic hit me in the chest as I pushed my fingers through his hair. I couldn't imagine not having this, not having him, to talk to, to kiss, to fuck. What would I do when this was all over?

"I can't wait for you to come to Connecticut," he said. "I want to have you in my bed for a change." He dipped his head and circled one of my nipples with his tongue.

The pulling sensation in my stomach chased away the panic and I shifted my hips sideways, tangling my legs with his. His towel had fallen open and I reached for his hard, heavy cock. I shivered as I began to pump my fist up and down. He hissed through his teeth, throwing his head back.

"I've been thinking about having your hands wrapped around my dick all day," he said. "You're so utterly distracting."

"And infuriating, remember?"

He reached for my pussy, and I flicked my hips up to meet his fingers, always eager for his touch. "That's part of the distraction, part of the attraction." His fingers dipped inside me, his thumb pressing against my clitoris, the frustration and embarrassment of the day dissolving under his touch.

"Do you think about me?" he asked, slowly thrusting into my hands. "You think about this?" He grazed my shoulder with his teeth, then bit down, causing me to moan.

"All the time." It was true. The only way I survived in the office was by avoiding him, but that was like trying to avoid gravity. My pull toward him was inevitable.

I released his dick and he began to slide it over my sex, teasing, promising. I reached behind me for the nightstand, but he took over my search for a condom.

"I've got to be inside you right now," he whispered. "I've been wanting you all day." He paused in his rhythm and I whimpered. "I know, Harper, I need it, too."

I'd never been so sexually vulnerable with a man, never offered up so much of myself. But with him it wasn't a choice; it was mandatory. There was no other way I could be.

He slipped his palms under my ass and pulled me toward him as he sat back onto his knees, the warmth of his eyes replacing his body heat.

His gaze bore into me as he thrust. He didn't take his time, but he didn't rush, either, just moved into me with a strong, confident force that nearly had me climaxing—the feeling of being totally consumed by him mentally and physically pushing me to the brink, threatening to tip me over the edge.

"Max," I called out.

"I'm here. I'm fucking you, needing you, owning you."

He was right. He *did* own me.

I lifted my knees and he growled, "I'm going to fuck you over my desk one day while you look out over Manhattan, your skirt around your waist, your ass in the air." He thrust again. "I want you in my bed in Connecticut, on the stairs, against the lobby wall of this apartment. I want you in every cab we ever share together. I've never wanted anyone like this."

His words drifted over me like sunshine, heating my skin, ridding my brain of shadows.

I wanted him so badly it was almost terrifying. Before fear could take hold, pleasure pushed out from my belly and down my limbs. "Max," I whispered, my fingernails digging into his skin.

"I know. I know. I know." He knew me, understood *everything*.

In that moment we were joined; we were connected; we were inseparable.

FOURTEEN

Max

"Good morning," I said as I passed Donna's desk. She looked at me suspiciously, probably because I was grinning.

"You okay?" she asked from the doorway as I shrugged off my jacket.

I looked up at her, still smiling. "I'm excellent, how are you?" Last night with Harper had been great. Sex had always been an important part of my routine, of my life, but with Harper there was a level of connection I'd never had with anyone else. Perhaps it was the reason my family continually bugged me about finding a girlfriend. Maybe they realized relationships could be this good, this easy with someone. Harper made me laugh, got me hot, and drove me crazy all within a ten-second window. I couldn't get enough of her.

"I'm okay, thanks. A little concerned the body snatchers have taken over my boss, but hey, we're in Manhattan, so it's to be expected."

"You're too young to be so cynical, Donna," I replied.

"Okay, now you're really starting to freak me out. Can I get you a coffee? Maybe that will kick you back into a normal gear," she said as her phone rang. "Be right back," she said, then closed the door.

I sat down and spun my chair around, facing out into the city. I was about to land JD Stanley, my personal Everest. Amanda was happy and healthy. I was fucking the most beautiful girl I'd ever laid eyes on. No, we were doing more than fucking. Were we dating? I turned back to my desk. Maybe when she came up to Connecticut we should have a conversation about what we were doing. I wanted her to meet Scarlett and Violet properly—they could come over for drinks that evening, but I wanted her to myself when Amanda left for the dance. Maybe brunch the next morning would be better. I hoped Harper planned to stay over. Once I had her in my house, I knew I'd find it hard to let her leave.

I pressed the speaker button when Donna buzzed my phone. "Charles Jayne on line one."

Puzzled, I picked up the receiver. Lunch had gone well. I had everything I needed and we were on track to nail our pitch next week. I hoped he wasn't going to try to cancel on me.

"Max King. How can I help?"

"I want to talk to you about the presentation next week."

Shit, he was going to cancel. I sat back in my chair. I wouldn't let him hear I was rattled. "Yes, sir, we're looking forward to it. Harper's been doing some excellent work. I'm sure you'll be impressed."

"It's Harper's involvement that I want to talk to you about."

I gripped the phone tighter. "I'm listening," I replied, my tone a little more terse than before.

"I like to keep my work life and my personal life separate," Charles began. That had been my policy before Harper smudged the lines between the two. I still believed it was a good policy. Harper was just someone I couldn't resist. But Charles had employed his sons in the business, so what he was saying didn't make much sense.

"Okay," I replied.

"I don't think it's a good idea for Harper to work on the JD Stanley account. You understand?"

I pushed my chair away from my desk. "I'm not sure I do," I replied.

"I don't want anyone to think that a decision I make on King & Associates has anything to do with Harper. Business is business."

"But I want to give you our best people and—"

"It's entirely up to you," he said. "I'm not forcing you to do anything. But if you're going to pitch next week, I don't want Harper on the team."

Shit. I mean, I got it. And I thought I'd feel the same way. I wasn't sure Harper would be so understanding. But he was a potential client, one I was desperate to land. "Of course, sir, it's entirely up to you what team you want to work with."

"I'm pleased you understand. I'm looking forward to what you have to say."

I hung up and slumped back in my chair. Should I have said no? How would I tell Harper? I guess I could pull out? But this was the opportunity I'd been waiting for and Harper knew that. She'd understand, wouldn't she? This wasn't personal. It was business.

Crap. I stood and grabbed my jacket. I needed some fresh air and common sense. "I'm going to Joey's for a coffee," I told Donna as I headed toward the elevators.

"Everything okay?" she called after me. I couldn't reply.

Harper would understand. In fact, she might be relieved. She could take some time, build up her confidence after the way she'd choked at Goldman's.

But something told me she wasn't going to think like that. This might be business to me, but it was very personal to Harper.

It was as if Charles Jayne had thrown a grenade, and I was left bracing myself for the explosion but hoping it was a dud.

Three . . . two . . . one.

"CAN YOU GET HARPER?" I asked Donna through the speakerphone, wiping the screen with my thumb.

"Sure thing."

I stood, took off my jacket, and rolled up my sleeves. Coffee and a conversation with Joey about baseball had helped me make up my mind to tell Harper she was dropped from the JD Stanley team and to do it as soon as possible. As it was a work-related matter, I should tell her at the office. Part of me wanted to take a bottle of wine over to her apartment, run a bath, and tell her when we were both a glass down. That way I could hold her if she got upset. But Harper had been clear she wanted no special treatment at work.

"Hi," Harper said as she appeared in my doorway.

"Hi," I croaked, then cleared my throat. "Close the door and take a seat."

She frowned and did as I asked.

I took a deep breath. "I want to talk to you about the JD Stanley account." Her hands curled around the arm of the chair. "I'm going to make a change and get Marvin to be my second chair on the JD Stanley pitch."

I waited for the explosion.

Her gaze fell to her lap, then came back up to meet mine. "Is this because I choked at the Goldman meeting?" she asked.

Of course that was what she'd think. This was my out. I could tell her we needed a more experienced speaker. I didn't have to tell her what her father had said. I didn't have to hurt her.

"How am I supposed to learn from my mistakes if you don't give me another shot?" She leaned forward a little. "I'm ready this time. I really know the material—even your sections."

She *was* ready. I could tell by the way she spoke in our morning meetings that instead of the failure at Goldman's sapping her confidence, it had fed it.

I brought my hands together on my desk. Should I lie to her? Could I?

I liked to get what I wanted. And I *wanted* to do the JD Stanley pitch without Harper *and* have Harper okay about it. But I couldn't be dishonest to make that happen. It wasn't the man I was.

"I know you're ready. It's not that."

"I mean it, Max. I can show you. Seriously. I can give the presentation to the whole company, bring people in off the street even. I can do this."

Fuck, this was going to be harder than I expected. She was so committed to this pitch. Even if her reasons weren't all business, her attitude was. I nodded. "I know there isn't a better person for the job."

"Then why?" she asked, slamming her hands on the arms of her chair.

"Your father called me this morning." She shifted forward in her seat and I took a deep breath. "He said he didn't want you at the presentation."

She flopped back in her chair, staring at my desk, her eyes glazed. I'd never experienced anything like this. In the office everything was so clear to me. It was at home that everything was gray and I always questioned my decisions. Telling Harper this brought out a different side of me. I wanted to go over to her and comfort her.

"Did he say why?" she asked.

"Just that he didn't want to mix personal and professional. Which I can understand."

She rose to her feet. "He employs his three male children. That's not mixing business and personal?"

I scrubbed my hands over my face. How could I make this okay? "I understand this is frustrating."

"Frustrating?" she yelled. "Are you kidding me? The guy's an asshole. He's trying to ruin my career."

I hadn't gotten the impression he was doing anything but being selfish. "Maybe he felt a little uncomfortable because the two of you are estranged." I thought I'd feel the same. "I'm sure he wasn't trying to make you look bad."

Harper laid her hands on my desk, and leaned toward me. "And so what, you just said, 'yes, sir, thank you, sir? Who cares if I fuck over the girl I've been screwing the last few weeks. Who gives a shit about her feelings? As long as I'm still in line for your business, I'll do anything you say.' Is that how it went?"

There was real venom in her tone and she was out of line. I'd acted in the best interests of King & Associates and if she was being rational she'd see it. "No, I said that I thought that you were the best person for the job." Had she expected me to argue with him? Ultimately he was the client. He got to choose his team.

She shook her head. "But you still told him you'd swap me out?"

"Harper, he's the client. He can choose who he wants working for him."

She shifted, putting her hand on her hip. "Guess what, asshole? *You* can choose who you work for, too. Don't you see? He was testing you. Seeing if he asked you to jump, if you'd ask how high. He's a piece of shit who's determined to make me miserable." She covered her face with her hands and my heart squeezed. Fuck, I hated that she did that to me. I hadn't done anything wrong. The last thing I wanted to do was upset her. I desperately wanted to go to comfort her, but this was business.

She smoothed down her skirt and pulled back her shoulders. "He asked you to choose between him and me," she said, her voice quiet. "And you made your decision. So good luck." She turned and headed to the exit.

I wanted to run after her, make her understand, but she was out of my door before I'd stood up. The last thing I wanted to do was make a scene, escalate the situation. I'd leave early, but instead of going back to Connecticut tonight, I'd go to her place and we could talk.

FIFTEEN

Harper

I arrived at Grace's apartment straight from work, tearstained. On the subway ride over, I'd tried to figure out why I was upset, who I was most upset with—my father or Max. I hadn't come to any conclusions.

"Do you think he knew?" Grace asked.

I sat on her gray five-thousand-dollar couch in Brooklyn, stroking the velvet arm, which was providing me with some small comfort. Grace handed me a huge glass of red wine and sat.

"What? That my father was testing him?" I asked. Was that what it was? A test? Or a show of power?

I'd left Max's office, gone straight back to my desk, printed out my resignation, put it into an envelope, and given it to Donna to deliver to Max. I didn't have a lot of personal items in the office and I'd managed to get them all into my work carryall.

I'd cried all the way to Brooklyn.

"No, do you think your father knew Max King was fucking his daughter?"

I lifted my head. "How could he? And anyway, why would he care?"

She shrugged. "I don't know. Fathers are protective over their daughters."

I snorted. "Yeah well, sperm donors aren't." I was pretty sure Charles Jayne hadn't had a parental instinct in his life.

"I just think it's a little strange that he accepted the lunch invitation and then didn't want you working on the account."

A lot of what Charles Jayne did didn't add up. He must have known JD Stanley was a big account and if he requested I was dropped from the team it would look bad on me. "He just doesn't want me anywhere near him." I dug my fingernail into the pile of the velvet.

Grace took a sip of her wine. "Maybe."

"Maybe?" I asked.

"It just feels like we're not seeing the whole picture."

Jesus, since when did Grace give my father the benefit of the doubt? She knew what an asshole he'd been over the years. "Are you taking his side?"

She twisted the stem of her glass between her fingers. "No, not at all. There is no side for me except yours. I'm just saying things don't add up."

I glugged down some wine, desperate for the liquid relaxation to do its magic.

"Okay, so your father's an asshole. Let's just take that as read. And, for whatever reason, he didn't want you working on his account." She rolled her lips together as if she was trying to stop herself from saying what came next. "I'm worried about how bothered you are by it. And that you resigned from a job you worked so hard for. Aren't you just letting your father control you?"

When the JD Stanley pitch had come up, I thought it would be an opportunity for me to finally be free of my father. "I just thought I had the upper hand this time. I was going to get my chance to press his nose up against the glass and show him what he'd been missing." I should have known better. I never had the upper hand as far as my father was concerned.

"I'm guessing he knew that and didn't want to see. Most assholes don't want to be reminded of their assholishness. They either reinvent reality so they're not assholes, or they avoid any situation where they could be reminded." Grace was talking from experience and suddenly I felt bad for being here and dumping all this on her. Her father had cheated on her mother more than once, and she always said afterward it was as if he'd used an imaginary chisel and gone through people's memories, re-carving history. "Your father's a powerful man and powerful men don't like to be wrong."

"But he was okay to go to lunch." I wiped a nonexistent drop of wine from the outside of my glass. Why had he agreed to lunch knowing I would be there and then had a problem with me working on the account?

Grace nodded. "He was probably curious, wanted to see if you'd forgiven him."

Lunch had been fine. Polite and professional. Had he really expected anything else?

"And he probably didn't give any thought to how you'd feel about it," Grace continued. "I'm sure he's like most men —too focused on themselves to worry about anyone else."

Selfish was exactly what my father was. When I was little and he didn't turn up when he said he would, I would pretend to my mom it was no big deal. I remember under-standing he made her cry, a lot, and that she'd cry more if I was disappointed. So I learned early to mask my hurt and upset. But it was soon replaced by anger and frustration I wasn't so good at covering up.

I looked up from my glass to find Grace poised with a top up. "I'd be surprised if he was trying to sabotage your career," she said as the wine glugged into my glass. "I'm sure he could have stopped you from getting a job on Wall Street very easily if that's what he'd wanted to do. Did he tell Max to fire you?"

I shook my head. "I don't think so. Just said he didn't want me working on the account because he wanted to keep the personal and professional separate."

Maybe Grace was right and it had been less about my father trying to ruin me and more about him protecting himself. Tears welled in my eyes. I covered my face with my free hand in some kind of futile effort to stop them from falling.

If I wasn't so embarrassed by the fact my father hadn't wanted me working on the account just like he hadn't wanted me when I was born, things might be different. A regular client requesting a team change would have been bruising but I'd have gotten over it. My father requesting I didn't work on his account if we were on good terms may have been bearable, but it was the Max element that made it so humiliating. Somehow, having told him about my father, having confided in him, I found his decision to accept my father's wishes without question rusted the knife, made the cut deeper.

I'd wanted to work for Max King for as long as I could remember and I'd ruined it by sleeping with him.

"It's such a betrayal," I managed to choke out.

The cushions beside me dipped and I moved my hand as Grace took my wine from me. She grinned. "I'm sorry. I can't have you spill red wine over this beautiful couch. Let it out, have a good cry, but don't hold red wine while you're doing it."

I laughed, her concern over her couch breaking me out of my misery. "You're right. This couch is too good to spoil for a man. You pretend you don't like the finer things in life, my friend, but you can't help generations of breeding."

She took a sip of the wine she'd just taken from me. "I know. However hard I try, I can't help reverting back to type. I have such good taste."

I laughed. "You do. However much you fight it, you're always going to be a Park Avenue princess."

"There, you see? At least I can make you laugh with my ridiculous life choices." Grace shifted, sitting cross-legged on the couch facing me, giving me her full attention. "Speaking of ridiculous choices, tell me about the resigning thing."

"Max had a decision to make. He knew how I felt about my father and he didn't hesitate to pick him over me." I shook my head. "If he'd just been my boss, if I hadn't told him how my father had abandoned me, I might have been able to swallow getting kicked off the JD Stanley account. But the way he so easily chose business over me was just too much." It was as if he'd drawn a line in the sand and said my feelings would never be more important than his job.

"I didn't realize it was that serious between you two," she said.

"It's not serious." Perhaps it had become more serious than I'd realized.

"But serious enough that you want him to pick you over

his job," Grace said. I didn't reply. I didn't know what to say. "What did he give as an excuse?" Grace asked.

"He just said that the client can pick the team."

Grace winced.

"Don't you dare say he's right." He wasn't right, was he? "It would be different if Max and I weren't fucking, but we are. Were. I'm not just his employee." I wasn't sure what we were to each other and I supposed it didn't matter anymore. But he'd owed me something. Some kind of loyalty. Hadn't he?

"I'm not sure you'd be quite this upset—so upset you handed in your notice—if it were just 'fucking'. You say it's not serious but it sounds like it is from your perspective. Do you have feelings for him?"

I scraped my hair back from my face as if it would help me see more clearly. Did I have feelings for him? "I feel like I want to punch him in the face; does that count?" I asked as Grace rubbed my back.

But I didn't want to punch Max, not really. I wasn't angry. I felt broken, as if I'd taken a right hook to my stomach. Somewhere along the road, I'd let him in, enjoyed being with him—I'd been happy, and not just when we had sex. I couldn't remember a time when that had been true of any of my other relationships. My father had ensured I grew up heartbroken, the scars of our relationship creating a barrier between me and other men. No one had ever broken through. No one except Max. It had just been sex—amazing sex—and then somewhere along the line, as he'd revealed himself to me, I'd been forced to do the same. He'd opened me up and I'd let myself care.

"I think maybe you feel more for him than you're admitting to yourself," Grace said.

Of course I had feelings for him.

Max was the only experience I'd had of being with a man where I'd not worked out how or when we would end before anything started. I knew I would leave my college boyfriend when we graduated. I knew the guy I saw occasionally at Berkeley would never leave Northern California and I'd never stay. I always saw the end before anything began. And that suited me. It meant I didn't get attached, didn't have any false expectations. With Max, I'd never seen the end and so I felt cheated of all the time we could have had together in the future. My expectations of him, of us, had been too high because they hadn't had limits.

I wanted so desperately for Max to have told my father if he didn't want me working on the account, Max didn't want his business. Finally, I wanted a man to put me first. Ahead of money, ahead of business. I wanted Max to stand up and claim me as my father never had.

I understood now my heart was closed to any happy futures. Shut down. Every man who came after this would always have limits.

I STOOD in Grace's closet, surrounded by her designer wardrobe I'd been pilfering since I arrived a little over a week ago. She might not wear them often, but she sure had a lot of beautiful clothes. I couldn't avoid going back to Manhattan any longer. I figured there was no running into Max if I went back on a Saturday. I needed to go back to my apartment.

"This is Gucci," I yelled from her bedroom, pulling out a black pencil skirt.

"Jesus, your voice carries three blocks. I think I prefer you mute."

I hadn't had much to say for the first few days of my stay at Grace's. It was as if the pain of walking away from my life had stolen my words. But after my third day in bed Grace had literally pulled me into the sitting room and forced me to watch TV and join in commentary on episode after episode of Real Housewives. Things got a little better after that and I was able to contain my gloom. But it was still there, lurking, waiting for me to be on my own so it could take over.

"Yeah, that skirt looks great with the YSL gray silk cami."

"I can't wear Gucci anything when I'm just packing up a few things and dragging a suitcase around on the subway." I wasn't sure how I was going to pay my rent, but something had stopped me giving notice on my apartment. I'd waited a long time to live in Manhattan and work at King & Associates—I just wasn't ready to let it all go yet. Reluctantly, I put the skirt back in the closet.

Grace appeared at the door to her closet and rested against the door frame. "You love me, right?"

I snapped my head around at her. When Grace started a sentence with that preface, I knew the follow-up wasn't something I wanted to hear.

I turned back to the racks of clothes. "I don't know, it depends what you're going to say next," I replied.

"Well, I was thinking that while you're in Manhattan, maybe you'd want to call your father."

I turned to look at her, completely confused. "And why would I want to do that?"

"To get some answers. Hear what he has to say."

"Why would I give him any of my time or energy?" Just because Grace seemed to be reconsidering her relationship with her parents and their money, didn't mean I had to.

"Honestly?" she asked. "Because I think you spend far too much of your time and energy on him. Everything you do seems to be a reaction to your father."

I looked up from the stack of T-shirts I was examining. "How can you say that? I haven't taken anything from him since college."

"You think ending up at King & Associates, working for the only place in town that didn't work for your father, had nothing to do with him? You walked out of a job you supposedly loved because of him."

"That wasn't about him, it was about Max," I replied. "You've got this all wrong."

She pushed off the door frame and stood in front of me, placing her hands on my shoulders. "It was about a business decision Max made regarding JD Stanley—your father's business. Despite your desire to avoid him, he's everywhere in your life, pushing you down one path or another, whether it's to avoid him or show him his mistakes." She released her hands and splayed out her fingers. "Aren't you exhausted with it?"

I was stunned. Was that what she thought? I sank to my knees, cross-legged. "You think I have some kind of warped obsession with my dad?"

Grace followed me to the floor. "Look, you're not Kathy Bates Misery obsessed, but yes, I think you let him consume too much of your life, your energy . . ." Grace paused. "Your happiness."

I looked up at her. I wanted to see doubt in her eyes but there was none. And I knew she did love me and I knew she wanted the best for me. "But he abandoned me and my mother. Fucked every woman in the tristate area. And all his sons work—"

"Look, I'm not saying you're wrong. I'm saying get some

kind of closure so you can let it go. Don't let it rule your life. You're an adult."

"Just like that, let it go?" He was always going to be my father, and he was always going to be an asshole. I didn't see that changing.

"Well, clearly it's not that easy—we're not in a Disney musical—but maybe have a conversation with him. Tell him how you feel. I don't see how you've got anything to lose. This is ruining your life."

I snorted. "That's a little dramatic, isn't it?"

She shrugged. "Maybe I've got it wrong, but you're talking to me from the floor of my closet." She put her hands on her hips. "You're convinced your father is trying to ruin you. Well, you're letting him."

I lay back on the floor, needing to think. Was I letting my father run my life? By not taking his money I thought I was doing the opposite. And I'd done well in my career without him. I'd resigned because Max had put business before me. My father wasn't the issue there . . . Except it was JD Stanley's business we were talking about.

"I'm not saying your father isn't an asshole. He's not going to win father of the year anytime soon. And I understand that when you were little he let you down again and again." He had let me down. "And I'm not saying you have to have some kind of idyllic relationship. Just accept the reality of the situation and get on with your own life. I think a conversation with him might help."

She was right. Since I'd moved to New York, my thoughts of my father had gathered like waves heading for shore. Turns out they'd just hit the beach.

My obsession with King & Associates had genuinely been all about Max King. It had nothing to with my father or the fact Max didn't work with JD Stanley. But part of me had always known going to business school had been about proving to him he was missing out on knowing me, and I was just as good as my half brothers. And Grace was right, part of the reason I'd resigned had been about my father not wanting me—the bruises he'd formed being pressed by someone else this time.

My disappointment at my father wasn't going anywhere. It floated around me like a bad smell, influencing me so subtly I didn't realize his hold over me. Grace was right; he had far too much power over my here and now.

"You have to deal with the root of the issue," Grace said. "My grandma always said, 'If you just chop the heads off of weeds, they come back.' So far, she's never been wrong."

Maybe if I just got it all out—raged at him—it would be like expelling poison and I'd be free. I had nothing to lose by confronting him, telling him how I was feeling—how he'd made me feel.

I jumped to my feet and scanned her racks of clothing. "Which one is the YSL vest?"

———

EVEN THOUGH I had no money, no job, and the fare would be something approaching the amount of a small car, I'd taken Grace's suggestion and grabbed a cab into Manhattan. I stepped onto the sidewalk, the heat almost unbearable, next to my father's Upper East Side brownstone.

I had no idea whether my father was in. Even if he was, he might have company or be busy. I probably should have called first, but I couldn't bear the idea he'd tell me no, and I was sure to chicken out if he suggested another time.

I walked up the stoop and rang the bell. Immediately footsteps scuffled behind the door.

"Hello?" My father's housekeeper squinted at me.

"Hi, Miriam, is my father home?"

"Harper? Good God, child, I've not seen you in years." She bundled me into the hallway. "You're looking too thin. Can I get you something to eat? The soup I'm making won't be ready for a few hours, but I roasted a chicken yesterday. I could make you a sandwich."

"Thank you, but I'm fine." I hadn't expected the warmth, the welcome, to be treated as if I were family. "It's nice to see you looking so well."

"Old, dear, that's how I look, but that's what I am." She began to make her way down the hall, beckoning me with her. "Let me call upstairs to his study."

I couldn't hear my father's reaction to my arrival, but the conversation was short and didn't seem to involve any cajoling to see me.

"You can go up, lovely. It's the second floor, first door on your right."

I smiled and took a deep breath. I was really doing this.

Climbing the stairs, I looked toward the top. My father stood there, looking down.

"Harper. How lovely to see you."

He acted as if it wasn't completely ridiculous for me to be here. I'd been to this house three, maybe four times in my entire life, and not once in the last five years. "Thanks for seeing me," I replied. I didn't quite know how to handle the welcome.

"Of course. I'm delighted." As I reached the top of the stairs he grasped me by my upper arms and kissed my cheek. "Did Miriam offer you something to eat or drink?"

I chuckled despite myself. "An entire roast dinner if I'd wanted, I think."

"Good, good. Come in."

We went into his office, a room in all pale blues and whites that reminded me of the ocean. It had been given a makeover since I'd been here last. I took a seat in the chair opposite his desk. He sat, then stood again. "Sorry, we shouldn't be across a desk like this. We can go downstairs. Or out in the garden. I didn't think."

He was nervous. I wasn't. I rarely saw him ruffled—he always acted as if everything was playing out exactly as he'd planned.

"I'm fine," I said, shaking my head. "Here's good."

He sat back down. "If you're sure. Miriam sent you up here because I'm not as good with the stairs since I injured my knee playing tennis last summer."

I couldn't ever remember my father being so open, sharing anything so personal with me before. "Are you okay?" I asked.

"Yes, yes, but I'm getting older and my body doesn't bounce back in the way it used to." He leaned back in his chair. "Anyway, it's very nice to see you." He nodded as if he were trying to convince himself. "We didn't really get to speak as much as I'd hoped at lunch. How are you? Are you enjoying being in New York?"

I felt as if I'd gone to the theater and during the inter-mission come back to my seat to find I was watching a completely different play. My father was talking to me as if I'd been away for the summer rather than absent from his life.

"Everything's good." I twisted my hands in my lap. "I imagine you're wondering why I'm here—"

"I don't blame you for King & Associates canceling our meeting, if that's what you think. I should never have asked for you to be replaced. I just thought it would be easier if . . ."

"What?" Easier? Easier for him maybe.

"But all's well that ends well. You're here."

The conversation wasn't going as I'd planned. I'd expected to ask him questions, for him to answer in half-truths and lies and I would call him on it. I had no idea what was going on. "I'm not following you. King & Associates canceled their meeting with you?"

"Yes, which is fine. We have excellent in-house resources."

Why would Max do that? JD Stanley could have made him considerably richer than he already was.

"Yesterday." His eyebrows pinched together. "You didn't know?"

Thoughts of Max canceling the pitch created a swirl of guilt in my stomach. Wasn't that what I'd wanted? I shook my head. I needed to focus on the here and now, not get distracted by thoughts of Max. "Can I ask you a question?"

My father looked a little uncomfortable but nodded.

"Why didn't you offer me a job at JD Stanley?"

There. It was out. And even if I didn't get an answer, I still felt a sense of relief from finally asking the question.

My father's mouth opened, but he didn't speak. He sighed and his head fell back on the chair. For a few awkward seconds we sat in silence before he finally said, "Look, I know I haven't been a very good father."

I'd never expected to hear those words. My stomach swooped and instinctively I glanced around for a trashcan, looking for something to throw up in. I'd opened a door and there was no closing it now—I'd lost control of this situation and felt as if I were tumbling down a rabbit hole.

"I never got it right with my kids when they were young. I didn't have much of a relationship with any of your mothers, and I always felt like a fraud whenever I spent time with any of you. It was easier to throw money at a situation and go about my day."

"A fraud?" I asked. Wasn't that really him simply saying he felt uncomfortable and so took the easy way out?

He raised an eyebrow. "No one could ever describe me as a family man, and your mother was a good person."

"I know." I didn't want him talking about my mother. "She did the best she could."

"Which was pretty damn good given the way you turned out. You're a beautiful, bright, accomplished woman. And I can take none of the credit."

We could both agree on that, but it was uncomfortable to hear it. I'd expected an argument, for him to justify what he'd done. Instead I was getting a mea culpa. I didn't know what to do with that.

Was he just telling me what I wanted to hear?

"It's a shitty excuse, but I guess I didn't feel I could do anything but make the situation worse. The best way I knew how to contribute was through money."

Did he know he'd also contributed to my insecurity, my pain, my lack of trust? He focused on what he gave rather than what he'd taken away.

"And I was young and I was working twenty hours a day and . . ." His eyes went wide. "You know. I liked the women. So I guess I felt like a hypocrite then, trying to play the family man."

"I guess the first time you got a girl pregnant that would make sense." My mother had been the first woman he got pregnant, but he should have learned his lesson.

He nodded. "You're right. I haven't just made mistakes in my life, I've repeated them. But I have to answer to my other children about their situation. I'm describing my reasons for acting the way I did with you."

"You haven't answered my question."

He sighed. "Why would I offer you a job when you so clearly held me in contempt? It was different with your brothers—they allowed me to make amends."

I laughed. "Right. So this is my fault." Typical. I'd expected him to shift the blame so I shouldn't be surprised.

"I'm not blaming you, but somehow I built a relationship with your brothers."

Jealousy tugged at me. Why had they ended up with a father?

"I'd hoped we would do the same, but while you were at college, you cut off all contact."

"And you threw money at the situation by setting up the trust?" I asked.

"I guess. I thought that at least if you were okay financially for the rest of your life then I didn't have that guilt to live with."

"So it wasn't because I'm a girl? Woman."

"What?" He chuckled, a look of surprise on his face. "Of course not. You made it clear you didn't want a relationship, and if I'm going to be completely honest, I didn't want a constant reminder of how I'd failed with you. It's hard knowing your kid hates you, sees you as some kind of monster. Even harder to know it's in some ways justified."

I couldn't speak. Had I let the lack of job offer fuel my resentment? Or had those feelings been there all along? "Is that why you told Max to drop me from the team?"

He took a deep breath. "Partly. But also because I couldn't engage a company for a large amount of money when my daughter was involved in the account." He held up his hand, indicating he hadn't finished. "I know I employ my sons, but I don't manage them, and their salaries are considerably less than what I would have spent with King &

Associates." He swept his hand through his hair. "I should have mentioned something at lunch, or called you afterward. It was just that things were civil between us and I didn't want to ruin that."

He laughed and put his head in his hands. "It's like I lose all sense of judgment when it comes to you. I get things wrong however hard I try."

Everything he said made sense, but instead of feeling relieved or happy, I felt cheated. As if someone had stolen my justification for hating him. He'd fucked up, gotten it wrong. But the way he explained it, his actions no longer sounded malicious. He was either the best liar I'd ever come across, or he was just a flawed human being. Maybe there was a bit of both there. It was as if I'd been suffering a chronic pain for years and, now it had just disappeared, I'd forgotten who I was without it. My hatred had become such a part of me that without it, I didn't quite know what to do. Still, Grace was right; I felt lighter from talking to him.

"I never wanted to hurt you, but I just didn't know how to avoid it," he said.

I squinted, trying to rid my eyes of the forming tears. He had hurt me. Over and over. But I didn't think he was lying when he said it hadn't been intentional. I nodded. "I believe you."

He pinched the bridge of his nose. "I can't tell you—" He paused and just nodded. "I'd like a chance to do better, if that's something you'd be interested in? Maybe we could spend some time together, have dinner or something."

He was asking for a chance to make amends. Even now when I'd not spoken to him for years. He didn't blame me, didn't express any resentment—he was just sad and regretful and it neutralized my anger toward him.

I took a deep breath and stood. "I need a chance to digest this."

He stood, stuffed his hands in his pockets, and walked around his desk toward me, his gaze trailing the floor. "I understand." He thought I was giving him the brush-off, when really I was fighting against years of rejecting him before he could reject me.

"Maybe I can stay for a drink and a sandwich next time." My words pushed out of my dry throat but I was determined to speak them. I couldn't say it but I was sorry. I'd held on to the feelings I'd had as a child and given them adult importance and justification. And although those feelings hadn't just disappeared, I saw them for what they were —pointless and unhelpful. He'd been right when he said I'd seen him as a monster. I was old enough now to know that fear of monsters was as much about imagination as reality.

He lifted his head. "I would love that. You just decide when."

I turned and we headed out of his office.

"Maybe next weekend," I said.

"I would like that very much," he said, his voice cracking at the end.

As we got to the top of the stairs, I turned to him and smiled. "Save your knee—I'll see you on Saturday."

"OH, YES AND ONE FINAL THING," I said as I gave Grace a rundown on the conversation with my father. Good friend that she was, she'd handed me a glass of wine within ninety seconds of me walking through the door. "He said Max canceled his appointment."

Had Max done that for me? I tried to think of other

possible motivations. I knew how much he wanted JD Stanley as a client.

"Wow." Grace's eyebrows disappeared into her bangs. "So now you can make up with Max."

I almost choked on my wine. "What are you talking about? Max is history," I said when I recovered. "I need to move on." The truth was, Max was never far from my mind. I wondered constantly about who he was with, what he was working on. I felt like an open wound, constantly being doused in vinegar. I did my best to not let it show. We hadn't known each other that long, and I felt stupid for taking it so hard.

Grace sighed. "I've known you a long time, Harper. You can't fool me."

"I don't know what you mean."

"If Max was history, you wouldn't have moved out of your apartment."

"I'm avoiding him because it's over." Part of the reason I hadn't turned on my phone was because I didn't want to find Max *hadn't* called or texted.

"No, you're avoiding him because you don't want it to be. First, you quit your job because he didn't choose you over a business deal," she said, holding up a finger. "Then you were practically catatonic for the first few days after you split and although you're moving around now, your neutral gear is still set to mope." She held up a second finger. "You won't turn your phone on because you're avoiding his messages." She held up a third finger. "My point is, he's the more handsome version of the best-looking man on the planet, and you are in love with him."

"In love with him?" I snorted. "Don't be ridiculous." This wasn't what love felt like. This was hurt, betrayal, anger. Wasn't it?

"And the fact that he pulled out of the JD Stanley pitch, well that's—"

"That's what? He should have done that to start with."

"Are you crazy? Max was right; the client gets to choose their team. If you two were just banging, he would have told you to suck it up. He clearly cares about you."

Had I expected too much from him? I'd felt so strongly for him; I'd just wanted him to feel the same.

"You were waiting for him to fail, to live down to who you thought your father was," Grace said.

I'd started off thinking Max King was an asshole but discovered someone very different was just below the surface, someone caring and generous and special. My heart squeezed as if it were stretching after a nap.

I missed him.

"He's not my father." But had I expected him to fail? Even looked for it?

"So turn on your phone. Actually, no, I'll do it." Grace scrambled to the kitchen. I'd left my phone on top of the refrigerator. I knew if I had it in my room at night, I'd be tempted to switch it on.

Grace wouldn't dare turn it on without my say so, would she?

Of course she would, and I didn't have the energy to argue. I was sick of missing him. I longed for Max's arms around me, his wise words telling me everything was going to be okay, for the way he didn't have to do anything but hold me to make me feel better. My stomach churned.

She tossed my beeping phone at me. "I guarantee you'll have a hundred messages and voicemails from him. Not many men can break through that invisible force field you have around your heart, my beautiful friend. Don't take it for granted. Make it right before it's too late."

SIXTEEN

Max

"You seem off," Scarlett said as she popped an olive into her mouth. She was supposed to be helping me prepare dinner, while Amanda and Violet hung out in the living room. Instead, Scarlett sat at the breakfast bar, drinking and watching me cook. "What's the matter with you?"

"You always think I'm off," I replied, but she was right. I hadn't slept well since Harper walked out of King & Associates ten days ago. She'd just disappeared. Our doorman hadn't seen her; she wasn't answering her phone. She could be in a ditch, or just ignoring me.

"True, but this is different. Tell your sister all about it. Is it work?" She gasped. "Have you become addicted to gambling? Lost all your money? Did you find out you have a horrible disease of the penis?"

I sighed. "Stop it. I'm just busy at the office." I started to slice the tomatoes, ignoring Scarlett. I was usually so good at hiding what I was feeling. Was my worry for Harper beginning to show?

"That's bullshit. I know busy-at-work off."

I glanced up. "It's nothing. A girl at work disappeared and I'm just a little concerned. That's all."

"What do you mean disappeared? Like kidnapped?"

I rolled my eyes. "You always assume the most dramatic scenario possible, don't you?"

She slipped off her stool and grabbed the wine from the refrigerator. "Well, if it's got you all somber and mopey with dark circles under your eyes, I'm assuming something really bad happened."

"I'm not somber and mopey," I snapped. "Harper resigned and I can't get ahold of her."

"Harper?" she asked.

I could tell from the tone in her voice and the smile she wore that I'd just let open the gates of Troy. Fuck. I should have kept my mouth shut.

"What's up?" Violet asked as she set her glass on the counter. "Are we eating soon? I'm famished."

"Harper resigned and Max can't get hold of her," Scarlett said, slowing her words, trying to convey meaning to Violet. She was an idiot if she didn't think I knew what she was doing.

"It's no big deal," I said. "Do you want a refill?" I asked Violet.

"Always. Where do you think she's gone?" Violet asked.

Her matter-of-fact tone flicked a switch. I was sick of keeping all this in.

I released the knife onto the chopping board. "I have no idea." I pushed the heels of my hands over my eyes. "I've called her a million times but she's just not answering. I can only hope she's mad and not, you know, hurting." I found it hard to even think she'd be in pain because of anything I'd done. What was worse was I couldn't do anything to make it right. That loss of power wasn't something I was used to or comfortable with. Since Amanda, I'd worked hard to be the guy who had a solution—to everything. It was part of the reason I was so focused at work—I knew money solved a lot of problems.

I ignored the glance that passed between my sisters. I was too frustrated to care. I hadn't met any of Harper's friends, didn't know any of her hangouts. We'd existed in a perfect bubble together, and I was happy with that. Or had been. Now I just wish I'd known her better. Partly because I might know where she was, and partly because I realized now there was so much more to get to know. And I hated myself for fucking things up and missing out on it all.

"What did you do?" Scarlett asked.

"I fucked everything up. That's what I did. I tossed her off a big pitch and she quit." I explained everything that had happened with JD Stanley and that Charles Jayne was Harper's father. I barely paused for breath—it felt good to get it out. How I hadn't taken Harper's feelings into account when I told her she was off the team. Whenever clients made team change requests, I'd never had to concern myself with the feelings of the person receiving the news. It was just business. But Charles Jayne's decision to cut Harper was personal. And I should have realized that. The fact I'd accepted his ultimatum so easily made me feel uneasy—a little dirty. I was sure I didn't want to do business with a man who made such cold decisions in relation to his daughter. To me, Amanda would come ahead of business, my pride. Everything. I'd never not put her first. Charles Jayne wasn't a man to be trusted.

"I feel like you're missing an important part of the story," Scarlett said. "I'm not sure, but you kicking an employee off the team and her quitting wouldn't normally get you this ruffled."

I didn't know what to say. I'd never discussed women with my sisters. Never talked about heartache or discussed a fight with a girlfriend—because I'd never experienced any of those things. I picked up the bottle of Pinot Noir Violet had left sitting on the counter and topped up my wine, impatient to get the glass as full as possible.

"You like her?" Violet asked.

I nodded.

"Finally," Scarlett said, almost to herself.

"And was it reciprocated?" Violet asked.

I took a deep breath. Was it? Things had been good between us, I thought. "How could I tell?"

Violet's smile lit up her face as if she'd been waiting for this conversation her whole life. "Well, does she maintain eye contact with you? Does she—"

"Jesus, Violet, do you know our brother at all? The man's not a monk; he knows when women want him. He's asking how does he know if she has feelings. Am I right?" Scarlett asked.

I nodded. "Yes." This was excruciating. I was rarely in a position where Scarlett had more of a handle on the conversation than I did.

"So you were sleeping together?" Violet asked.

Scarlett slapped her hand on the counter. "Try to keep up."

"What?" Violet shrieked. "No one told me he was sleeping with her. You knew?"

"I suspected."

"You did not," I said. "You say that now, but you knew nothing."

"I could tell when I met her in the elevator that there

was something between you two." Scarlett shrugged. "I have a sixth sense for these things. Anyway, let's get back to the fact that our brother has feelings for someone. I mean, this has never happened before. We need to stay focused. How long has the sex been going on?"

There was no point in suggesting I didn't want to talk about it now—that ship had sailed. And anyway, I did want to talk about it. I needed to know if there was anything I could do. I wanted a chance to tell Harper how I felt, that I wanted her back.

"It was casual; we didn't go out." Did she think it had been just sex? "I should have taken her on a date or something. I was planning to talk to her about what she wanted when she came up for Amanda's dance."

"What, so it was a series of booty calls?" Violet asked.

Is that what it had been? Not for me, but looking at it maybe that was all it had been for her. "I've never really done the dating thing," I admitted. "We live in the same building and I'm here so much of the time . . ." From the outside it did look like convenient sex. But for me, since she'd started at King & Associates, she'd had my attention like no other woman.

"Did you do things together? Cook? Hang out without the sex?" Violet asked.

I winced. "We got takeout, does that count?"

Apparently not, if my sisters' faces were anything to go by.

"We'd spend the evening together. Talk." Take a bath, although I wasn't admitting that to my sisters. I loved hearing her take on the world. She was ballsy mixed with a little bit of idealistic. It was a perfect combination.

"Well, that's good. And it was early days, right?"

"Yeah," I replied, but it had felt so good between us.

When we were together it was as if I didn't want to rush forward to the next part because the space we were in was so good and I wanted to squeeze out every last drop.

"And she quit because you kicked her off the team pitching to her father?" Violet asked.

"Yes. Her father called and said he didn't want her involved in the account because he wanted to keep business and personal separate."

"And you thought that was fine because it's how you like to operate too?" Scarlett asked.

"Yeah. I saw him as a potential client asking for a simple team change, rather than a father who was not putting his daughter first."

"Honestly," Violet said, "that doesn't sound like anything you can't come back from."

"I pulled out of the pitch," I said.

"You did?" Scarlett asked. "Wow. Does she know?"

I shook my head. "No, I did it after I saw how upset she was and I realized how he just hadn't given a shit about her. If he was prepared to do that to his daughter, what would he do to a business partner?" It wasn't the first time I'd turned down a client because I didn't like their approach to business. I just wished I could explain to her that I understood I'd made the wrong call. "Now she's gone, just disappeared."

"You must really love this girl." Scarlett grinned. "I've never seen you like this."

"Quit the dramatics. I'm not saying I love her, I . . ." I was lost. In new territory with no map. "But if she won't speak to me, won't answer the phone or the door, what do I do?"

Scarlett tilted her head to the side. "Amanda!" she yelled.

"Don't say anything to her," I whispered.

"Just trust me" she said.

Amanda wandered in, her stare fixed on her phone. How she didn't break bones on a regular basis I had no idea. She never looked where she was going. "Put your phone down while you're walking. One day you're going to step out in front of a bus because you're fixating over Snapchat."

Amanda rolled her eyes but slipped her phone into her jeans pocket. "Is dinner ready? I'm hungry."

"Are you looking forward to the dance tomorrow?" Scarlett asked. I wasn't sure what she was up to, but I could tell she had a plan.

Amanda's eyes lit up. "Yes, it's going to be perfect. Callum finally asked me yesterday. I told him I was going stag. I don't need a man."

The King women shared a chorus of good for yous, absolutelys, and high fives. I could only hope it was the first step in a lifetime of celibacy for my daughter.

"And your dress is all set?" Scarlett asked.

Amanda slipped onto the barstool facing me. "Yes, you saw it right? The one Harper helped me pick out."

"Harper's the girl your dad works with who you like to hang out with?" Violet asked. Christ, they were playing tag team.

Amanda nodded, her eyes flickering from me to her two aunts. "You met her, right, Scarlett? She's so cool and pretty. Isn't she, Dad?"

The sound of Harper's name sped up my pulse. I smiled sadly. "Yes, she's very pretty."

"You'll get to meet her too, Violet. You're coming to help me get ready for the dance, right?"

Shit, how could I break it to my daughter that Harper wasn't going to make it?

"Of course. Wouldn't miss it for the world." My daughter was the only person who could get my sisters to do anything.

"I need to talk to you about Harper, sweetheart," I said.

"What? She doesn't need a ride from the station because she's driving."

What? I'd never talked to Harper about how she was getting to Connecticut.

"I'm not sure if she's still going to make it, peanut. But you'll have your aunts. And we can put your mother on Skype the entire time you're getting ready."

Amanda looked at me, her lips pursed. "What are you talking about? Of course Harper's going to make it. She said this morning that she'd be here by four. She's bringing her makeup."

My heart started to pound. Had I heard her right? Had Amanda been talking to Harper? I gripped the counter, trying to make sense of what she was saying.

"You spoke to her?" Scarlett asked.

"Of course I did. She's my friend." Amanda looked around at the three of us. "What's the matter with you guys? You're all acting weird."

Harper was coming here. I would get a chance to explain, tell her she was important to me. More than important. I wouldn't let her go until she'd heard my arguments, understood I was sorry. I wouldn't let her push me away. I was used to getting what I wanted and Harper Jayne would be no exception.

———

"JUST BECAUSE SHE'S agreed to come and help Amanda doesn't mean she wants anything to do with me," I reminded my sister a little after three thirty in the afternoon. "You don't think this is a little bit much?" I looked around at the dining room, the table set with the china and glassware my mother had forced me to buy when I hit thirty and she decided I was finally an adult, despite having been a father for over a decade at that point.

"No, it's not too much," Scarlett said. "And anyway, what have you got to lose? Worst case scenario you're no worse off than you were before she walked in."

I had to keep reminding myself I knew how to go after what I wanted. I did it for a living. Winning Harper back had to be a possibility, didn't it?

"I polished all the silverware, just how Grandma King showed me," Amanda said, joining Scarlett and I at the table. She patted me on the back. "It looks good. She won't be able to resist your lasagna, Dad. It's the best."

I didn't have the heart to tell her I had no idea whether Harper would even hear me out.

I had to admit, the table looked nice, but something was missing. "We forgot the flowers," I said.

Amanda had helped me pick some from the garden that we could use as a centerpiece. I couldn't find a vase, so we'd improvised and used a water glass. Amanda disappeared to retrieve them

"So what, you guys are going to take Amanda and then I just turn around and ask Harper if she's hungry?" I asked Scarlett.

"Jesus, did you lose your balls somewhere along the line?" Scarlett asked. "You ask her if you can talk for a few minutes. Then you apologize and admit you're an idiot. See how she reacts—if you need to apologize again, do it and then tell her how you feel. Jesus, man, you run a multimillion-dollar company; it's not that hard."

This was much harder than anything I'd ever done, but she was right; I needed to find my balls. I'd tell Harper how I felt. Tell her we shouldn't let business get in the way.

It was going to be easy, right?

"You're not wearing that, are you?" Violet asked as she wandered in.

"Good point," Scarlett said. "Go put on your best jeans and a blue button down. The slogan T-shirt isn't working for you."

"Hey, this is vintage," I said.

"Go change," Violet said.

Did I have time for a shower? I looked at my watch and my stomach churned. Only twenty minutes until she'd be here. In my house. In the place I'd fantasied about fucking her. Harper was the only woman I'd ever wanted to bring here, into my home, into my life.

I bounded upstairs, taking the steps two at a time. I needed to run through what I wanted to say and I didn't want anyone disturbing me.

It was the most important pitch of my life and I hadn't rehearsed.

SEVENTEEN

Harper

"What did you make me do?" I yelled into the speaker of my phone as I pulled off the I-95. The GPS told me I was six minutes away. I hated driving, especially on routes I didn't know, and this was my first time in Connecticut. "This is a terrible idea."

"It's a great idea," Grace said. "And anyway, whatever happens, you've done the right thing by Amanda."

I'd promised Amanda I'd help her get ready for her dance and I wasn't about to let a fourteen-year-old girl down. I knew what it felt like to be disappointed by an adult, and I'd never knowingly inflict that feeling on someone else.

"What did you end up wearing?" Grace said. "Please tell me you put a skirt on. Men like skirts."

"I'm wearing shorts."

"That hot combination you do with the buttoned-up blouse and the casual, bordering on slutty shorts?"

I grinned, secretly pleased with the endorsement.

"They're not slutty. Just short." Okay, they were a *little* bit slutty.

Amanda was only part of the reason I'd borrowed Grace's new car to drive to Connecticut. I wanted to see Max. To figure out whether the ache in my bones would ease when I saw him. To work out whether it was love or just regret that tugged at my heart.

Men before Max had always been a stop on the way to something else. I'd always seen the way out, never had both feet in. With Max I wasn't constantly seeking the exit. I'd been happy to be in the moment with him, share things, talk, enjoy just being together. My feelings for him had snuck up from behind me and only screamed *boo* when Max had already gone.

"Okay, well, you won't need it, but good luck."

How could she say that? There was a real possibility Max would be furious with me. I'd walked out of my job without giving any notice. I'd screamed at him in his office, then turned off my phone and ignored every one of his messages.

Worst of all, Max hadn't really done anything wrong when he'd agreed to take me off the team. Maybe he'd been a little insensitive, but my relationship with my father wasn't Max's battle to fight. It wasn't as if the only reason King & Associates had landed the pitch was because I worked there.

My stomach churned at the thought of no longer being an employee at King & Associates. I'd worked so hard to get there. But I wouldn't have any regrets. I'd met Max and whatever happened between us, I'd always be grateful for that. It had forced me to deal with my father. I'd thought King & Associates would help build my career, but really it had helped patch up my soul.

As I pulled up in front of the gray clapboard, two-story house, my nerves took hold. I didn't know the man who lived here. The place looked so . . . domestic. There was a field to one side, and what looked like a barn on the other. I counted four cars in the gravel driveway. Wow. Were they having a party?

I reached into the backseat and pulled out the sparkling cider I'd brought along with my makeup.

"Hey, Harper."

I climbed out and saw Amanda waving at me from the doorway. I smiled, unable to wave back because I had my hands full.

"Hey, how are you?" I called, looking up over the roof of the car. "Are you nervous?"

"Not nervous at all," she said as I locked the car. "Especially not now that you're here."

Voices grew louder as Amanda and I crossed the slate-floored entry. The home had a completely different feel from Max's office. Photographs of Amanda dotted the walls. The doors, frames, and ceiling beams were stained a warm honey and the space was large and airy with open doors leading out onto a pool area. As we headed toward the kitchen, Max came into view.

My ache for him disappeared, my body sagging with relief as if it had been starved of water and had finally found an oasis.

Aware of everyone around us, I avoided eye contact. If he was angry with me, I wasn't sure how I'd react.

"Harper," he said. "Come in. You're kind to come all this way. I'm sure I don't know what Amanda did to deserve it." He didn't sound in the least bit angry, so I looked up to find him grinning at me. I tried to cover my delight, nodding as I glanced behind him at two women looking at us.

His sister Scarlett I'd met before. Who was the other one? I knew Amanda's mother couldn't make it back from Europe. Was I too late? Had Max moved on? No, it must be Violet. She looked like Max and Amanda.

"Come on upstairs. We don't have long," Amanda said.

"You have two hours, which is plenty long enough to introduce Harper to your aunts," Max said.

I was sure my relief showed in my sharp exhale. Yes, aunts. "Hi," I said, offering a half wave. They both slipped off their barstools to greet me.

"I'm Scarlett—we met in the elevator," the blonde said as she pulled me into a hug as if I'd known her my whole life.

"I'm Violet, the youngest." Violet's hug was slightly less effusive but a little more familiar than I'd expected.

I got the distinct impression I'd been the subject of a discussion between the two of them.

"Can I get you something to drink?" Max asked.

I held up the cider. "I brought something." I glanced between Max and his daughter.

"You should know what to do when someone brings you a gift," Max said.

Amanda covered her mouth with both hands, then said, "I'm so sorry. That's really kind of you and you didn't have to."

She was such a sweet girl. "It's my total pleasure," I replied.

"Why don't you get into the shower? Violet can bring you some cider when she comes to do your hair."

Amanda raced upstairs, leaving me in the kitchen with Max and his two sisters. I'd expected to have Amanda as a buffer while I was here. And I didn't know whether Max's friendly veil would drop once she'd left the room. I took a breath. I could do this. Max deserved the humble pie I was about to dish up.

"I have the grown-up alternative to sparkling cider if you're interested?" he asked.

"What's that?" I couldn't help but smile. Not seeing him for so long, I'd forgotten the pull. Forgotten how every time I was around him, I wanted to touch him. And now that I was here I wanted to talk to him, apologize, ask him if it was too late to go back to how things had been between us.

"Champagne," he said with a grin. He didn't seem mad, but I'd seen him at the lunch with my father; he was great at making people feel comfortable. Was he just putting on an act?

"Did someone drop you on your head?" Scarlett asked. "I'm always asking for a glass of champagne."

Max shrugged. "What can I say, I'm not wasting champagne on my sister." He shot me a glance as he pulled out three glasses and set them on the counter.

Was he trying to impress me? I rolled my lips together, trying to hold back a grin at just the thought he might be.

"It's so nice of you to come out all the way from the city," Violet said, leaving the sentence a little unfinished. Did I look ridiculous coming all this way for a fourteen-year-old girl I barely knew? Did she know that although I genuinely wanted to make tonight special for Amanda, I wanted to see Max? I needed to apologize.

I glanced around, wanting to tell Max I'd come for him as much as I had for his daughter. "Amanda's a lovely girl and . . ." I shrugged, unable to get the words out quite yet.

"Well, I know that my brother is pleased you came."

My heart squeezed. Was Max pleased I was here? Because of Amanda or because he wanted to see me?

Max handed me a glass and as I took it from him our fingers brushed. I glanced up at him and he grinned. Should I pull him to one side and apologize now?

"Violet, Harper," Amanda called from upstairs. "I need my glam squad. I'm out of the shower."

I giggled. "Glam squad? She's fourteen, right?"

Max rolled his eyes. "Going on twenty-seven."

"Coming," I yelled, bending to pick up my bag. I hated to see overly made up teenagers, and I knew Max didn't want his daughter to look like the twenty-seven-year-old she thought she was, so alongside some bits of my makeup, I'd brought a tinted moisturizer and a glittery lip gloss. Add in a bit of mascara and I didn't think she'd need much else.

"I'll follow with the drinks," Max said pulling out a tray as Violet and I made our way upstairs. As we passed a table on the landing, I bent to look more closely at a wedding picture.

"Beautiful," I said to myself. Amanda, dressed as a flower girl, stood alongside a bride and groom I didn't recognize.

"Pandora and Jason's wedding," Max said from behind me.

He had his ex's wedding photo up in his house? "Wow, that's . . ." I wanted to say weird because it was, but it was also sweet and open hearted and all the things I knew Max to be.

"Pandora's beautiful," I said, turning to look over my shoulder at Max. He nodded as if it were just a statement of fact.

Amanda's room was everything I'd expected of a normal fourteen-year-old girl. A Pitch Perfect poster over her bed, a blue-and-white-striped bedspread, and full bookshelves running across the length of one wall. Despite the house being large, it was all about family. There were no airs or graces.

"How about a face mask while Violet dries your hair?" I suggested.

Amanda grinned. "That would be awesome."

Max set the tray down.

"Thanks, Dad. Make sure you put the oven on for the lasagna." She took a champagne glass from her father, who obviously wanted to make her feel special. "You'll love it, Harper. My dad's a great chef and pasta is his specialty."

It was sweet that she thought I was staying for dinner. I didn't need to set her straight. I'd pull Max to the side before he left to take Amanda and then when he'd had a chance to consider what I had to say, maybe he'd call. Hopefully he'd forgive me.

"Thank you, peanut, but I think I can handle the stove." He continued to speak but held my gaze and I couldn't look away. "And anyway, Harper hasn't agreed to stay for dinner yet."

My heart fluttered, suddenly beating twice as fast. He *wanted* me to stay for dinner. But I hadn't apologized yet.

"But she will, won't you, Harper? Keep my dad company while I'm at the dance?"

"Amanda," Max warned.

"Dad, ask her. She can't say yes until you do. Tell him, Violet."

"It may sound like my daughter is strong-arming me into this, which is the last thing I want you to think." He sighed, shaking his head at his sister and daughter. "And I really appreciate getting the opportunity to ask you in front of the two most interfering women on this planet." Max turned to look at me. "But I'd really like you to stay to dinner so we can talk and hopefully set things straight between us." He pushed his hands through his hair.

I tried to hide my grin. I wasn't sure what set things straight meant. I hoped at the very least it would mean we wouldn't hate each other. But a huge part of me really wanted more, more than I deserved. I wanted Max. I had to believe I wasn't too late.

"Lasagna's my favorite," I replied.

"OH MY GOD, I remember when she was born," Violet said as we came down the stairs after primping Amanda for as long as we could stretch out. "It seems like yesterday. And now . . ."

Max slung his phone on the counter and raised his eyebrows, instantly in the moment with his family despite whatever corporate emergency was bound to be causing him stress. "Is she ready?" he asked. He'd left us to primp and prime his daughter, but was clearly as invested in the event as the rest of us were.

I nodded. "She's coming."

Violet had put some waves in Amanda's hair, so it looked very natural falling over her shoulders. And although I'd spent a lot of time on her makeup, it could have been done in two minutes—it was just a little mascara and a touch of lip gloss. Hopefully Max would approve.

I watched Max as he gazed at his daughter coming down the stairs in the blue and silver dress we'd picked out. His eyes went glassy and he tilted his head. "Peanut, you look completely beautiful."

My heart squeezed. I wanted to reach out for him.

He walked toward her and she stepped back, putting her hands up to stop him from coming closer.

"You can't touch me; you'll ruin my hair or smudge my makeup."

He chuckled, bent down, and kissed the top of her head. "You're getting so tall. Are you going to FaceTime your mom?"

She shook her head. "She'll just get emotional. We took some photos. I'll send them tomorrow."

She might only be fourteen but worrying about her mother's feelings in a situation that was really all about her showed a great deal about her character. A personality that had been shaped in part by the man I'd so foolishly let go.

I hung back as Scarlett and Violet gathered their things and ushered Amanda out the door. Max followed, then stopped to lean against the doorway.

Before she got in the car, Amanda turned and waved. "Bye, Dad. Bye, Harper. Enjoy your date."

I got the impression Amanda would be very happy to see our dinner become something more than apology and air clearing and that gave me some hope she knew something of Max's intentions.

We watched them drive off until their taillights had completely disappeared.

"She's beautiful, Max," I said.

"She is. Thank you for being here, for helping her. I wanted this to be special; she's been so excited."

"It's been a total pleasure. You didn't want to go with them?" I asked as Max closed the door.

"Amanda wouldn't let me. I think she was concerned I'd kick Callum Ryder's ass given half a chance. And anyway, we have things to talk about," he replied. He held my gaze and my breathing hitched.

I had things to apologize for. "Max, I don't know what to say. I'm so sorry. I've been an idiot and selfish and I lost all judgment when it came to JD Stanley. You did nothing wrong . . ." My words were running together; I wanted to get them all out before he had a chance to say anything that would make it harder to get them out, wanted to make him see how I understood he'd done nothing wrong. I covered my face with my hands.

"I'm the one who's sorry." He removed my hands from my face and threaded his fingers through mine. "We were involved and I didn't think through the consequences of accepting your father's ultimatum. I have no experience mixing the personal and the professional, so I didn't think about you or your feelings. I should have."

"It wasn't as if we were serious, but if we had been . . ."

He squeezed my hands and heat travelled up my body. "Maybe I gave you the impression that it was just sex, but I'm not sure it was ever that for me. I want to take you out on dates, to have you here with me and Amanda. I want to talk and laugh and wake up together." He sighed and shook his head. "I thought we had time. I missed the bit where I told you how important you were to me. I told you I've had zero practice at this stuff."

My stomach twisted. "I *was* important?" Did that mean he'd moved on?

"Was and *are*," he said. "I'm just so sorry I screwed it up."

How was he making this so easy for me? I'd expected to have to try to convince him, talk him round.

It wasn't too late. I closed my eyes, trying to compose myself. "You didn't. We'd made no promises to each other, and my issues with my father aren't your battles to fight."

"I want your battles to be my battles," he replied.

The corners of my lips twitched. "You do?"

He nodded. "And I'm ready to make any promises you want. I want to be the man who deserves you. The man who will do anything for the woman he loves."

I swallowed. "Loves?" I stepped toward him until our bodies were almost touching.

He shrugged. "Yeah. I love you and I need you to know. And I want you to give me a chance. I'm going to get this wrong. A lot. I haven't had much practice—I'll need you to stick with me."

"Max, I've never trusted a man. I don't know how to be that woman." I'd never expected a relationship to work before, never needed it to. "You're going to have to be patient with me, but I promise I will do my best if you give me another chance."

"You can have a lifetime of chances," he said. "I can't think of anything I wouldn't forgive you for." His eyes were soft and I reached out and stroked his jaw. He was still breathtakingly handsome but somehow the photographs I'd seen of him before I knew him had never done him justice. They'd not seen what a beautiful soul he had, what a wonderful father he was.

I tilted my head to one side. "You know someone told me about this thing Michael Jordan once said." I released his hands and smoothed my palms up his chest, staring up at him. "He said, 'I've missed more than nine-thousand shots in my career and I've lost almost three-hundred games.'"

Max lifted an eyebrow.

I continued. "He said, 'I've failed over and over and over again in my life. And that is why I succeed.'"

I lifted my shoulder in a half shrug as he slid his hands around my waist. "Some guy I'm in love with told me about it. I think he'd say that we should keep trying until we win."

Max's grin made my stomach swoop. "Sounds like a smart guy." He paused, then said, "Sounds like a lucky guy." He pulled me closer and pressed his lips against mine. "I've missed you so much."

His tongue trailed along my lips before pushing in to find my tongue. I'd forgotten how urgent his mouth was, how passionate his kisses could be. With every second, my knees got weaker, my breaths got shorter, but I wanted more.

We separated, panting, our foreheads resting against each other. "I've missed you, too." I slid my arms around his neck. As he lifted me, I wrapped my legs around his waist.

"Lasagna will have to wait," he said as he carried me toward the stairs. "I've fantasized about having you in this house a million times. I've dreamt about bending you over on the kitchen counter and fucking you from behind, thought about laying you out on the dining table and making your pussy quiver with my tongue. But right now I'm going to make love to you in my bed."

When we got to the bedroom, I unwrapped myself from Max's body and pulled his shirt from his jeans, undoing the buttons keeping his skin from mine. I wanted time to take in where I was, to get to know more about Max, to hear stories of the black-and-white photographs that lined his bedroom walls and to understand why he'd chosen the huge mahogany four-poster bed. But his touch temporarily wiped all my questions from my head.

"These have been driving me crazy," he said, reaching under my shorts and cupping my ass.

"They had the desired effect then," I replied.

"Harper, you could turn up in a trash bag and it would work magic on me."

"I know that feeling," I said.

When we were both naked, we stood, staring into each other's eyes, Max cupping my face. "It's so good to have you here," he whispered. "I've missed your beautiful, soft skin." He smoothed his hands over my breasts, around my waist, and across my ass, "Your perfectly wet pussy." He dipped his hand between my legs and groaned. "I've missed this. Your sounds, your wetness."

My skin tightened and I shivered.

"I've got to be inside you. I'll take my time with you later, but I need to feel you around me. I need to be close."

It was what I needed, too.

He spun us around, then pushed me against the wall. Lifting my leg, he rubbed his tip along the length of my sex.

"Max, condom," I said, breathless and desperate.

He shook his head. "I just had my annual checks. I'm all good."

Oh. I hadn't slept with anyone but him since I'd last been tested. "Me too, and I'm on the pill."

I moaned as he pushed into me and stilled. "Good," he said.

"Max." I tightened my fingers around his arms. I needed him to wait a few seconds for me to adjust to him. After not having him for so long, in this position, he seemed to fill me more than usual.

He increased his rhythm. "I'm not going to be able to last long, and after I'm done, I'm going to have you on the bed, then in the shower. I'm going to be inside you for *hours*."

The thought of the relentless drive of his dick in and out of me chased my breath from my lungs.

"Once is never enough with you. I need you all the time, forever."

I felt as if I were cycling toward the top of a mountain, panting and moaning, desperate to get to the top. As Max thrust into me again, his dick reaching deep inside me, I found myself at the summit. I arched my back as I began to freewheel down the other side.

"I love you," I whispered into the wind.

Max was right behind me, grunting my name in my ear as he jabbed his hips into me so sharply it would have hurt if it weren't for the insulating effect of my orgasm. "I love you," he shouted out.

His skin was hot and sticky with exertion when I put my arms around him, pressing my breasts to his chest, hoping I could attach myself to him permanently. He lifted my ass and I wrapped my legs around him as he walked us toward the bed, still joined, him still inside me. He sat on the edge of the bed, my knees coming to rest on either side of him.

"Lie back," I said. His eyes looked dazed as he did what I said. "I wasn't too late," I mumbled as I began to move my hips, just slightly, enjoying the feel of him still inside me.

He reached toward my breasts, rubbing my nipples with his thumbs as he looked up. His touch melted me around my edges. I contracted my muscles, trying to stem the wetness his touch released.

He groaned, and slipped one hand down to my clit. "Too late?"

I wasn't sure I could get the words out to clarify. Already I wanted him again, wanted to make the climb up the mountain, even though I was still out of breath from my first trip.

"I was worried you'd be . . ." I gasped as he increased the

pressure on my clit. "I was . . ." I couldn't speak or move while ribbons of pleasure unraveled over and through me. My brain didn't have capacity.

As if he understood, Max lifted his hips off the bed and I stilled, happy to sit on him, to be taken by him.

"Tell me what you were worried about," Max said, the muscles in his neck straining.

I pressed my palms against his chest. "That it was too late for us," I said.

He grabbed my hips and rolled me to my back. "Never," he said as he pushed into me. "Not ever."

It was just what I needed to hear. I reached up and traced my fingers over his eyebrows. "I love you." I couldn't stop repeating those words. I'd never said them to any man before. No one before Max had ever deserved them.

My orgasm crept up on me, pushing through my body like a tremor: silent, intense, and powerful.

"Oh God, your face when you come." Max growled and thrust again, erupting into me.

He rolled off me, then pulled me toward him.

"When I get my breath back I'm going to kiss every inch of your skin, then make you come with my tongue."

"We may run out of time." I fingered his hair. "I have to make my way back to the city."

He squeezed me tighter. "Stay. Don't ever leave."

I chuckled. "You're ridiculous."

"Maybe."

"Things feel a little different," I said. Perhaps because we were away from the city. Perhaps because I knew how painful losing him had been and knew I'd work hard never to make that mistake again. "I don't know why, I just—"

"I think it feels like the beginning of forever," he replied simply.

EPILOGUE

Three months later

Max

"Come in," I barked without looking away from my laptop. I thought I was the last one in the office. I was keen to get this piece of work finished and get back to the apartment and get my girl naked, and I didn't really want any interruptions.

"I'm looking for the King of Wall Street," Harper said as she opened my door.

I pushed my chair back from my desk. "Hey, I thought I was meeting you back at the apartment."

She walked toward me, rounding my desk, trailing her hands over the papers stacked up on it. "I couldn't wait," she replied, placing her purse on the table by the window.

I swiveled my chair so I was facing her. "How was dinner with your father?" Harper and her dad had seen each other a couple of times in the last few months.

"It was good." At times I wondered whether or not it

was worth the tears that often followed one of their meetings, but she assured me she was crying over their history not their future. If she wanted to try to build a relationship with her father, I was happy to support her in anything she did. "Nice actually. We're getting to know each other a bit better now." She leaned forward and unknotted my tie. "And I thought I'd come back here and make sure you were keeping focused." Gently, she pulled my tie from my neck and sat on my desk. "I remember how you used to tell me how you *weren't* so focused when I worked here," she said, pulling up her skirt a little, revealing more of her long, brown thighs.

"Yeah," I said, a little dazed by the woman in front of me. "It's better for the bottom line that you don't work here anymore."

"I agree," she said, pushing my chair around with her foot so I was facing her.

"I like your shoes," I said. They were the first pair I'd bought her from Jimmy Choo. I was becoming quite the regular customer. I'd never seen her wear them outside of the bedroom and they seemed a little much for dinner with her father.

She began unbuttoning her blouse. "I remember you saying you used to think about me . . ." She opened the cream silk, revealing her high, tight breasts. ". . . here." She leaned back. "On your desk."

Jesus. Blood rushed to my cock. I'd thought about little else while Harper worked at King & Associates. And despite us being together as a couple, I couldn't persuade Harper to come back to work for me. Perhaps it was better all round.

"Tell me what you used to think about." Her back arched and she slid her feet over my thighs.

I grabbed her legs and pushed them apart, her skirt riding up around her waist. Yes, this was just how I'd imagined her.

"Christ, Harper, you're not wearing underwear."

She tilted her head. "Is that what you imagined?"

I lifted her legs, putting them over my shoulders, and dipped my head. "Yeah, you making my desk all wet." I breathed over her pussy. She moaned, her pitch getting higher as I licked over her slit before slipping a thumb into her entrance. "I fantasized about making you come on this desk." I circled her clit with my tongue and she slid down onto her back as if admitting defeat, her fingers snaking through my hair. She'd come to get fucked in the office and she was about to get her wish.

Her moans got louder and louder as her pussy got wetter and wetter. For a brief moment I worried we'd be overheard, but fuck it, I was the boss and I could do what I wanted with the woman who I was going to be with for the rest of my life.

I fumbled with my fly, my erection straining almost painfully against my zipper. It sprung free and I fisted it in my hand. Eating her out here, making her crazy with my tongue, the lights of the city behind me, the wealth of Manhattan around us, made me feel like a king.

"I have to fuck you," I said, peeling her legs from around my neck and standing. I dropped my pants and plunged into her. Jesus, she was always so fucking tight. Her hands reached behind her for the edge of the desk as she tried to resist my thrusts pushing her off the other side. She was perfect. I circled my hands around her waist and pulled her onto me harder as she began to twist her hips. She was too close, too soon.

"I think you fantasized about this too," I said, slamming into her again and again.

She cried out. "Max." Her calling my name was always the starting pistol for my orgasm. I thrust harder and she screamed louder, "Max, Max, oh Jesus."

Just before I came I pulled out of her and pulled her up. "Lean over, I want to see that beautiful ass bent over my desk." If she wanted to give me my fantasy, I wanted the whole thing.

She grinned and spun around, her heels thrusting her firm, tight ass in the air. Her arms spread across the desk, my papers flying off the edges. "You want me like this?" she asked.

I responded by parting her legs slightly and thrusting into her again. My force pushed her further onto the desk and she curled her fingers around the edge as if hanging on for her life.

"Yes," I groaned. "This is how I wanted you, that first day you stepped into my office." She shuddered underneath me, the start of her orgasm stirring across her skin. "And how I've thought about you every day since."

"Max," she whimpered, lifting up her head with what energy she had left. "Please, God, Max." And she tightened and stilled and I allowed myself a final thrust before pouring into her and collapsing over her back.

We stayed there for a minute or so, panting, our clothes half hanging off us, sweaty and rumpled.

"Well, that was a nice surprise," I said as I stood up, fastening my pants.

Harper was still wobbly on her feet as she got up from the desk and I reached out to steady her. "I thought it was weird we'd never fucked here, given this was where it all began," she said and glanced around my office while doing up her blouse.

Bending forward, I gave her a kiss on the lips. "It doesn't have to be a one-time deal," I said. "I'm all for working late if this is the reward I get." I didn't work late in the office very often. I still only spent two nights a week in Manhattan and both those nights were always spent with Harper.

"You get plenty of rewards, my friend," she said, smoothing her hand over my chest.

I grabbed her wrist. "I want more."

She opened her mouth slightly and I could tell she had some sarcastic comeback and then changed her mind about sharing it with me. "More?" she asked.

I nodded. "For us, for you and me. I want us to be fucking on my desk when we're ninety and have been married sixty years and have four kids."

Harper took a step back. "What are you talking about?" She shook her head. "I'm not going anywhere."

"Do you promise?" I asked.

"Do I promise to fuck you on your desk when you're ninety?" she asked, laughing.

"Marry me, Harper." This wasn't what I had planned. I assumed we'd be together forever and I'd thought about proposing but I hadn't expected those words would leave my lips today.

My eyes flickered between hers and I circled my hands around her waist. "Marry me," I said again. "I can do the big proposal thing, another time, with a ring and a string quartet but just tell me now you'll say yes. I don't want to go another day without knowing you're going to be my wife."

She tilted her head and gave me a small smile. "Okay, but I get two proposals, right? This one and one with a ring?"

"Jesus, always so demanding."

She shrugged. "I'm just confirming what the offer was."

"Yeah, two proposals. And you agree to be my wife, have ten kids with me, and fuck me on my desk when I'm ninety."

"Sounds like a deal," she said and she wound her hand around my neck, pulling my mouth down to meet hers.

One Year Later

Harper

"Holy crap," I shouted from the downstairs bathroom.

"I told you," Max yelled back.

I wandered back into the kitchen, clutching the pregnancy test. "We're going to need a bigger boat," I said.

Max grinned. He'd gotten me pregnant with Amy just over a year ago, the night we'd first fucked on his desk. It had happened several times since then. Pregnancy had made me hornier than usual.

"What are you talking about?" Amanda said as she lifted her little sister out of her bouncer and put her on her hip. "We don't have a boat."

As I reached Max, he put his arm around my neck and pulled me toward him, kissing me on the head. "Congratulations."

"What did you do to me?" I asked, shaking my head.

"What I do best," he said. "No doubt it's another girl, because I don't have enough women in my life."

"What are you talking about?" Amanda repeated, her eyes narrowed as she glanced between us.

"Harper's pregnant," Max announced.

"Again?" Amanda asked.

I grinned. "Again."

Amanda handed me Amy and hugged us both. "This is amazing. I wanted a sister for so long and now I'm going to lose count."

"You're going to *have* to marry me now," Max said.

"I don't see why. I told you there's no rush, and anyway, if you were serious, you'd propose properly. Like on one knee, with a ring. That was the deal. Remember, effort gets rewarded, Mr. King." I stood with my hands on my hips.

"Do you ever do as you're told?" he asked, rolling his eyes.

"Apparently, I get pregnant on demand. Does that count?"

"I do all the hard work as far as that's concerned." He grinned at me.

I rolled my eyes. "Oh really?"

"Now's the time, Harper."

"Max, I'm pregnant. Did you miss that? I'm not walking down the aisle knocked up."

"I really want to be bridesmaid," Amanda said. "In fact, I might just buy a dress and wear it around the house if you two don't get your act together."

"Mr. King." One of the guys from the catering company came from the pool area into the dining room. Thank God we had help today. We lived in a state of perpetual chaos on the best of days. Today we'd added to the fray, throwing a welcome home barbeque for Pandora and Jason. "We're set up and ready for whenever your guests arrive. I'm just going to start pouring some drinks."

I turned to Max. "Holy crap. That's another eighteen months without booze."

"Well, you'll be in good company," Max said, hugging me close, Amy grabbing at his hair.

Pandora and Jason were pregnant as well. It was the reason they were coming back to America. That and they missed Amanda.

"I'm not sure everyone at this party's going to fit," I mumbled. The party was just a family occasion but that list was growing by the day. Along with my mom, we were expecting Max's parents, Pandora's parents, Scarlett and her new boyfriend, Violet, Grace, and Jason's brother.

"I spoke to an architect last week," Max said, taking Amy. Max King was never short of female attention of any kind, so of course Amy was a daddy's girl.

"An architect?" I asked, opening the refrigerator. Now I had an explanation for that cheese craving; I was going to give in to it.

"You're right; we need a bigger space. I thought maybe we'd add a pool house, too, because we need live-in help." Max wandered out of the kitchen mid-conversation before I could tell him I was sure we could manage without anyone living in.

It was as if life was set to fast forward—Max and I living together, Amy, a second baby.

"Girls," Max called from the study.

I knocked the fridge door shut with my hip "What does he want?" I asked Amanda.

"I don't know, but let's go," she replied, bundling me toward the study.

"Do you smell that?" I asked. "And where's that music coming from?"

I opened the door to the study to find the room empty but the doors leading out onto the patio open, the white curtains lifting in the breeze.

"What's going on, Amanda?" I asked. She shrugged, nudging me toward the patio doors. As I stepped outside I saw Max right in front of me, on one knee, surrounded by every colored rose ever to exist. I glanced around. Flowers covered the ground and huge vases were scattered across the lawn, adding color wherever I looked. To my left was a cello player, and I instantly recognized the music as Bach's cello suites, the same piece Max had turned up to full volume the night we'd first slept together.

Amy was on her mat next to Max, looking up at me, grinning, her eyes a beautiful green, just like her father.

"What are you doing?" I asked. "How . . . when—" I turned to Amanda, whose grin told me she was clearly in on the whole setup.

"Well, where effort's required, there's no excuse not to make things perfect," he said. "And I thought, the four of us here, together and now with number five on the way . . ." He took a deep breath. "I can't imagine anything more perfect than that."

He opened the red box he held, revealing a huge princess-cut diamond. "Harper, I've loved you from the very moment I laid eyes on you. You are already my heart, my soul, my family—and now I want the world to know. As the King of Wall Street, I need you to be my queen. Marry me."

I smiled. How could a girl say no to a proposal like that?

Have you read
Park Avenue Prince- Sam & Grace's story
Duke of Manhattan - Ryder & Scarlett's story
The British Knight - Alexander & Violet's story

The Earl of London - Logan & Darcy's story

HAVE YOU READ **MR. MAYFAIR**? Stella is shocked when she receives an invitation to the wedding of her newly ex-boyfriend and her best friend. There's no way she'll go, will she?

BOOKS BY LOUISE BAY

The Mister Series

Mr. Mayfair

Mr. Knightsbridge

Mr. Smithfield

Mr. Park Lane

Mr. Bloomsbury

Mr. Notting Hill

The Christmas Collection

The 14 Days of Christmas

This Christmas

The Player Series

International Player

Private Player

Dr. Off Limits

Standalones

Hollywood Scandal

Love Unexpected

Hopeful

The Empire State Series

Sign up to the Louise Bay mailing list at
www.louisebay/mailinglist

Read more at www.louisebay.com

KEEP IN TOUCH!

Sign up for my mailing list to get the latest news and gossip
www.louisebay.com/newsletter

Or find me on

www.twitter.com/louiseSbay
www.facebook.com/authorlouisebay
www.instagram.com/louiseSbay
www.pinterest.com/louisebay
www.goodreads.com/author/show/8056592.Louise_Bay

ACKNOWLEDGMENTS

Acknowledgments

Thank you so much for reading King of Wall Street. It's been a crazy year for me and I know some of you wanted something from me before now. Thank you for waiting patiently. Hopefully you won't have to wait so long for the next one. I love hearing from you on social media—you never let me feel lonely! (I'm about to go exclamation mark-tastic)

I still wake up every day unable to believe I'm able to share my stories with you and that you'll read them! Thank you. I love you!

Elizabeth—You're the best. Thank you for your patience and wisdom on this journey.

Nina – My sister wife. What would I do without you? Who would I speak to while I do my breast exams? Who would I melt down all over? You make me howl. You're amazing. PS, thank Charlie for his cover advice.

Jessica Hawkins. What is BFF? Ha! I love you. I love your writing. I love your attitude and drive. Looking forward to moving to the dessert just so you can drive me around.

Karen Booth—I'm so lucky to have you in my virtual life! How you've taken over the world in 2016 is awesome! Long may it continue. It's bound to given your magical powers with blurbs.

To all the incredible authors that constantly give me help and support—I love this community and I'm so proud to be a member.

Najla Qamber – thanks for awesome cover and for coming to my rescue. You're so talented.

Letitia Hasser – That font's so good I want to eat it. Thank you.

Jules Rapley Collins—Thank you for being such a great support babycakes. Megan Fields you're a doll. Thanks for telling me the truth, always.

Thanks to Jacquie Jax Denison, Lucy May, Lauren Hutton, Kingston Westmoreland, Lauren Luman, Mimi Perez Sanchez, Ashton Williams Shone, Tina Haynes Marshall, Susan Ann Whitaker, Vicky Marsh and Sally Ann Cole.

Twirly, your input is invaluable as always. Did you find out what twat sits on a gold chair? The classical reference is for you, obvs.

Printed in Great Britain
by Amazon